WET PAINT

WET PAINT

CHLOË ASHBY

First published in Great Britain in 2022 by Trapeze
an imprint of The Orion Publishing Group Ltd
Carmelite House, 50 Victoria Embankment
London EC4Y 0DZ

An Hachette UK Company

1 3 5 7 9 10 8 6 4 2

A CIP catalogue record for this book is
available from the British Library.

ISBN (Hardback) 978 1 3987 0298 1
ISBN (Export Trade Paperback) 978 1 3987 0299 8
ISBN (eBook) 978 1 3987 0301 8
ISBN (Audio) 978 1 3987 0302 5

Typeset by Born Group
Printed and bound in Great Britain by Clays Ltd, Elcograf S.p.A.

MIX
Paper from
responsible sources
FSC
www.fsc.org   FSC® C104740

www.orionbooks.co.uk

For Ollie, and for Rose

Édouard Manet, *A Bar at the Folies-Bergères* (1882)

'In the figure, look for the main light and the main shadow, the rest will come of itself: often, it amounts to very little.'

– *Édouard Manet*

After

'I can tell this is one of those days when you're not going to say a word and I do all the talking. Which is fine – really. And anyway, if it wasn't fine, would that make any difference?

'It is harder when you go quiet, though, when it's me doing all the work. Do you remember the day we both sat in total silence? That was terrible. I actually feel a bit sick. It's hot in here, hotter than usual. Mind if I open a window? Thanks. That's better, a breeze.

'I've been thinking about what you said – that fear-of-abandonment thing. At first, I found it funny. I know, *defence mechanism* (I'm getting good at this). It just hadn't occurred to me that I might be afraid of something I grew up with. Sort of like being an only child or missing a limb.

'If I'm honest, yes, I suppose I have been a bit . . . what was the word you used? Compulsive. I know it sounded like stealing, but really it was just borrowing. The sex – that came earlier – probably *was* escapism. The drinking . . . Oh for fuck's sake, sorry, can I have a tissue? I can't blame Dad for everything, but I can blame him for the drinking.

'Anyway, I'm doing it again – back to the timeline. That's what you want, isn't it? I can't seem to focus on the hours, days or weeks before. I just keep rushing forward to that moment. It was morning. We were going to catch a train. I wanted – gah, sorry, I'm picking at your chair again. I know, it's better than pulling at my cuticles. But still, I'd rather not leave your armrests looking like one of those cats – you know the ones I mean, with not enough hair and too much skin. Is it OK if I stand?

'When we got to the station something snapped inside me – here, just under my ribs. In my head it sounded like cracking knuckles, the finger joints popping. I was tired and worried about what I'd done, worried I wouldn't be allowed to see her again. I remember wondering if there was an alternate universe where all the people who stepped out of my life hang out together – I know, I know, abandonment – and if she'd end up there too.

'People were getting off a train on the platform opposite. I remember taking a step towards the tracks and peering down at my feet. There was that yellow line. And then the nubby bit. Some grooves. A faded white stripe at the very edge. The edge of the abyss. God, that's a bit dramatic, isn't it? It's funny how some things stay with you, though. Like these! How long have you had them? I'm pretty sure they had to wipe "mansize" from the box a couple of years ago. Because women blow their noses too. Sorry – tangent. Maybe if I sit down again.

'When I looked up, the train was gone. There was another coming, this time on our side of the tracks. A speaker announced that it wouldn't be stopping.

'I know what you're thinking: what was I doing there in the first place? I probably told you I hadn't been back since university. The truth is, I can't remember making any decisions, I just felt I had no choice. I had to go back because that's where it started so that's where it had to end. But I never meant for the ending to look like that: me standing on a platform, toes sticking out over the tracks.

'Honestly I don't know why I'm smiling – obviously there's nothing to smile about. Not a thing. It's just, if you'd told me a year ago that I'd be sitting here, I'd have laughed.'

One

My alarm shrieks in my ear, an awful, garish sound. *Beepity-beep, beepity-beep, beepity-beep, beeeeeeeeeeeeep.* I bury my face in my pillow, which smells musty. I can't remember when I last washed my sheets.

'Eve? Are you in there?'

I walk my fingertips across my bedside table, feeling at various inanimate objects – including an open tin of Vaseline – before reaching the alarm clock and switching it off. 'Yes? And yes.'

'What's wrong with your voice?'

'Nothing.'

'It sounds funny.'

'It's in my pillow.'

'What?'

I give up, flipping front to back like a fried egg in a pan of foaming butter. Must be hungry because I hate eggs. 'I said, it's in my pillow.' And before he asks why it sounds different again, 'It's not anymore.'

'Oh right.'

'You were saying?'

'Are you working today? It's past eleven.'

No, Mum. (Mum left me when I was four, the first screw to come loose.) 'Not today, Bill.'

Bill works for a shiny tech start-up that lets its bright-bulb employees work from home – a show of trust, he says. I say they're blurring the boundaries, lulling them into a false sense of freedom where they're forever on hand, where home is work and work is home. They're brainwashing you, I tell him. He's a hard worker, though he has a lazy eye. He says I need to learn to trust people.

Anyway, that's why he's still here. *Shuffle, shuffle*. Sounds like he's wearing his felt slippers – blue with orange crabs.

I starfish, naked, eyes closed and fingers and toes reaching for the columns of a four-poster bed. In fact, mine's a single. Imagine being tied up, rope lassoed between the polished wood and your wrists and ankles. Yanking, jerking, clawing. I close my eyes and curl up in a protective ball.

Karina and Bill are kind to everyone except each other. They take people, 'like you', they told me, nodding and smiling encouragingly, under their wing. We've been through a couple of fine but forgettable fourth flatmates since I moved in. First up was Rick, a tight-T-shirt-wearing gym obsessive who worked in construction, was scared of ladybirds and ate his Cheerios with a fork. Next came Sadie, a delirious (in reality: coke, MDMA, tons of weed) philosophy student who took herself too seriously and the bills not seriously enough – not that I can talk. Anyway, now it's just us three. Them and me.

I heave myself up and out of my body-shaped hole in the squashy mattress, like an ice cube out of one of those rubbery trays. Shower. I grab my greying towel from the back of the chair – a chair for clothes, not for sitting – and wrap it around my body, beginning to shiver. Winter's come early this year. I wonder when Karina will let us switch on the heating. She's Norwegian and impressively thick-skinned despite being stick-thin.

'As you were, Bill.' I tiptoe past him, his spine curved, finger pads tapping away at his keyboard.

'Eve, would you mind focusing on the kitchen today?' He likes to start conversations when I'm wrapped in a towel. 'It could do with some love.'

I stifle a sigh. It's part of the deal: cheap rent in exchange for a day's cleaning a week. Their way of 'doing good'. It's also better than sexual favours. I glance over at him – heavily hair-gelled, lazy eye in full swing. 'Whatever you say.'

I close the bathroom door behind me and, ignoring the hook, sling my towel over the laundry basket, which is overflowing with his and Karina's clothes. One polka-dot sock is making a run for it. Too slow: I snatch it by the thinning heel.

'Probably be gone by the time you're out,' calls Bill as I sit on the loo. 'Got to go and meet a client.'

I nod silently. Well, thank goodness you told me, I'd have been sick with worry. I start to wee. 'Enjoy.' *Tinkle, tinkle. Shuffle, shuffle.*

I flush, and twist the shower dial, adjusting the temperature – Karina always turns it down, but I prefer it piping hot. By the time I'm done brushing my teeth the water is warm enough to stand under. I squeeze a swirl of shampoo into my palm and, after jiggling it around like a collapsed crème brûlée (happens all the time to the new pastry chef at the restaurant, poor guy), knead it into my hair. Karina has a thing with toiletries and enjoys rotating the flavours.

Last month lime, this month coconut. I'm about to tip my head back to rinse when I hear the front door slam. I pause, straining to hear through the crackle of soapy suds whispering in and around my ears.

I decide to skip her 'smooth and creamy coconut' conditioner and hop back onto dry land. The mirror's all steam so I crack the window, ushering in a waft of curry that makes my belly flop. As I head back to my bedroom, my skin breaks out in goosebumps. I look down at my arm – a chicken wing newly plucked. Smoothing down the raised hairs, I can see little white scars caused by little picking nails. I was an anxious child. It could have been worse.

It's been four years since I moved into Prince's Court – nothing regal about it. Before that I was back at Dad's, our 'family home' in Finsbury Park, the shabby flat where he's slowly disintegrating. I haven't visited since the summer, when I finally stopped trying to reason with him and forced myself to walk away. I said I won't see him again until he gets help; of course, I've tried this before and failed. Swinging like a shoddy hypnotist's pendulum between ultimatums and acceptance. I can picture him now, slouched in his favourite armchair with the TV on loud, but not loud enough for me not to hear his sad stories. Sipping from the branded mug his team at British Gas gave him at the start of his so-called sabbatical, chipped in three places – maybe four by now. I don't know why he doesn't just use a glass. We're both familiar with the contents: whisky at the start of the month; super-strength cider straight from the can when he's low on funds. The three little words I associated with him most as a child were: 'Top me up.'

The sad stories are mainly about Mum. She left when I was six days short of my fifth birthday. I don't remember her saying goodbye or holding me extra close that morning as she kissed my squidgy cheeks and nuzzled her nose against mine – our Eskimo game. That evening, sitting on the pebble-coloured carpet by her side of the bed, Dad told me in a strange voice (shaky, harsh, hoarse) that she'd disappeared. I wasn't worried and wondered why he was. I pulled on my slip-on shoes and told him we'd find her if we looked hard enough.

It's a boxy building, Prince's Court, ex-council, cut off from the road by chocolate-finger railings that make it look like a prison. Our flat's number three and nice enough. I say our – it's Karina and Bill's. They got a good deal because it had been badly infested with moths, one species that chomps expensive clothes and another that breeds in dry food. They paid for two treatments – had the dusty carpet ripped up and every nook doused – but I still find fresh holes gnawed in my one and only cashmere jumper, my one and only stitch of Mum.

The flat's a bit of a mess; it has been since I moved in and found Rick the gym rat's muddy boots bathing in a puddle of equally muddy water in the sink. I've done nothing to fix it up. There are five rooms – bedroom, bedroom, bathroom, kitchen and 'communal area' (or third bedroom) – and I have decent taste. The problem is I have no money or incentive: the place doesn't belong to me, and Karina and Bill aren't exactly the sort to invite people round.

Hence the dried strands of spaghetti stuck to the medium-sized saucepan this morning and the glass jar of pesto standing on the kitchen table without its lid. The fridge is always near empty – it doesn't help that Karina's never here and, when she is, doesn't eat. This morning's inventory: half a pint of milk; one leek, browning at the end, its little white hairs extra curly; a crumb-infested knob of butter; three mature tomatoes, two with crooked stalks and one oozing yellow-red fluid as if fighting infection; a slab of Cheddar marked with the grooves of a serrated knife; half a wrinkled lime; and a sticky-rimmed jar of chutney.

I wriggle my fingers into the rubber gloves suspended, lifeless, over the tap and curl my lip. On Wednesdays, when they know I'm cleaning, they leave their cereal bowls on the side – Bill's a pool of milk swimming with soggy Weetabix scraps, Karina's smeared with creamy yoghurt, occasionally stained blood-red from berries. I let the hot tap run in a steady stream, not quite burning through the rubber, and squirt some Fairy Liquid onto the matted sponge (I'm also supposed to keep an eye on the under-sink supplies). In quiet moments I like to suggest they invest in a dishwasher – think of the value of the flat – and pretend each time that it has just occurred to me.

By the time I'm done with the dishes, the plug has a piece of spaghetti poking through one hole and a streak of yoghurt around the rim. I twist the tap again and watch as the torrent dislodges the clingers-on. I give the counter a quick once-over – even lift up the salt and pepper shakers to wipe away the loose grains – and chuck any perishables back in the fridge. Ten minutes' hard graft. Gloves off.

Karina and Bill have a bad habit of leaving their bedroom door open. It's like they're inviting me in – or, better yet, daring me. When they're out, I mean. We're not that kind of three.

9

In the beginning I just looked. Looked at their things: Bill's primary-coloured self-betterment books; Karina's curling iron, its lead never not knotted; their dressing gowns, one silky, the other the texture of a towel with tissues sticking out of one pocket. After a while I touched. I rootled through her jewellery box – nothing fancy save for the gold ring that could have been inherited from a dead relative. Flicked through the files on the chest of drawers (mainly letters from Thames Water) and found some porn stashed away in the wardrobe. I sat in the lumpy armchair by the window to compare their view out the back with my own. The windowsill's home to an ashtray littered with carcasses – Karina's a big fan of the *sigaretter*.

It's quite tidy today, for them. The duvet may be lolling off one side of the mattress, but at least the bed's made. There's only one pair of pants on the floor, inside out, marking the spot where she stepped out of them. The full-length mirror is pretty smudge-free. I walk towards it and lift the necklace – a string of big green beads like boiled garden peas – over and off its frame. I sit on the end of the bed and let my eyes lose focus, working the beads through my fingers. What would a Catholic say? Hail Mary, full of grace. *Grace.* I unhook the clasp and loop it around my neck, feeling my shoulders drop as the relief bleeds through me. Sometimes, recently, when I come into their bedroom, I borrow things.

After swallowing a mug of instant coffee – no milk, two sugars – I pull the front door shut behind me. My day off always works like this: cleaning, then gallery. I saunter out of the cell block in broad daylight and turn left onto South Lambeth Road, a peculiar Portuguese stretch running between Vauxhall and Stockwell. It's lined with red-and-green cafés and restaurants churning out grilled sardines, salt cod, cinnamon-sprinkled custard tarts. Popular with families.

The sun's shining, providing a smidge of warmth, but the air's biting, gnashing like a small dog at my face and fingers. I stuff my hands into my pockets, bury my chin into my bunched scarf and power on, wondering – as I do each week when I walk to the gallery around midday on a Wednesday – what reason everyone else has to be away from their office (or building site, studio, classroom). I tend to pass plenty of people, but today, as I cut across the main road in front of Vauxhall Station, the pedestrians are a fraction of their usual number, like there's some public holiday I haven't been told about.

That happened twice when I was little. Dad deposited me on the bus to school and, when I arrived at the tall iron gates, they were chained and padlocked, and no one was there to greet me. I didn't have a phone so I couldn't call him, and the first time I didn't even have enough change to ride the bus home. Eventually, after a long walk that retraced the wiggly bus route I luckily had lodged in my mind, I ended up back at the flat. I buzzed and he let me in, a familiar musky smell wafting through the air. Neither of us mentioned the fact that I was home earlier than usual. Just like, after a while, neither of us mentioned the fact that Mum wasn't coming back.

'The monkey isn't real.'

Excuse me?

I've caught up with a bow-legged man and, I assume, his young daughter. Every wide-kneed step he takes, she takes two or three. As I get closer, I realise he's trying to persuade her that the golden monkey illustrated on her backpack isn't helping her carry it.

'See?' he says, poking one of its googly eyes with his finger. 'You're carrying it all by yourself.'

'Well, I can feel him helping,' she replies adamantly, hopping daintily from one foot to the other to demonstrate the lightness of her load.

Her daddy smacks his forehead with his palm. I smack mine. No imagination. Dad never believed me when I told him I'd seen Mum on the street.

I overtake the little girl with her little legs and, when I turn back, downer dad's on the phone. I give her an encouraging smile: just keep doing what you're doing.

She scowls.

Across Waterloo Bridge, I follow the road around to the right, east along the Strand. As I arrive at the grand entrance of Somerset House, a couple stroll past me and head through the automatic glass doors to the gallery. She, in an ankle-length grey coat and a pair of leather work boots, is laughing at something he's said. He looks like a writer – small round glasses, beaten-up satchel, slipping into cliché – and has his arm draped around her neck, a human scarf. I imagine him describing a fumbling sex scene in the manuscript he's just submitted to his editor, leaning in to whisper intimate details in her ear, breaking away to ask earnest questions about his protagonist. Even if the Courtauld weren't at the heart of my weekly ritual, I'd be tempted to follow.

They've bought their tickets and are winding their way up the spiral staircase, hand in hand, by the time I've untoggled my duffle coat. I approach Marjorie – that's what I call the woman who mans the desk – the woman who *womans* the desk – who's sitting very upright, her legs concealed. Maybe she's wearing patent shoes today, doing a jig from the waist down, though I doubt it. Her face is as frosty as ever and fails to soften as I approach; permanent frown lines score her forehead. Standing above her, I get a good view of the white roots twisting into her crow-black hair.

'How much is a ticket?' I ask, bending down to try to see her eyes. Green really does go nicely with black.

'Seven pounds,' she replies, tone jaded, eyes downcast.

We have a mutual agreement, I think. We pretend not to know each other even though I've been visiting every Wednesday, more or less, for the past four years. I probably should have become a member to save money, but I'm not a joiner – can't commit. I pause, as always, debating whether it's worth it and after a few seconds, as always, I rummage through my bag. Today's contents: stickerless apple, couple of dozen coffee stirrers, battered paperback. Eventually I find my purse and count out the correct change.

Without looking up, Marjorie holds out her hand. She could be quite pretty, I think, if she smiled once in a while. God, I shake my head sharply. I sound like a builder, mentally catcalling women as they walk by.

I know exactly where to go. I hiss at the pair of self-satisfied stone centaurs keeping watch over the foyer – pointed hooves, puffed-up chests – and skip the drawings on the first floor. Having climbed up one more notch, I glide through the first, second and third rooms. Today I pause in the fourth – there's a gallery assistant lurking by the entrance and I don't want him to think I can't appreciate good art when I see it. Really, though, I couldn't care less about Degas's troupe of twirling ballerinas, graceful in their gleaming pastels. After a couple of minutes I give them a cursory clap and continue. Straight to room six.

I hear the laugh of the girl with the grey coat as I cross the threshold. Are they here to see her too? No, they're standing in front of a piddly landscape in the corner of the room, him squinting through his glasses at the brushstrokes. She's carrying her coat now and has rolled up the sleeves of her sheer white shirt. Hint of a black bra.

As she turns around I step to the right, avert my eyes and end up staring – as if by chance – at the big canvas on the opposite side of the room. My old friend, Manet's barmaid. I mouth a hello, hear a bit of sound escape by accident. Glancing behind me, I see the girl giving me a funny look.

I edge closer until I'm standing directly in front of the painting, the largest in the room, and lower my bag to the floor. Still staring, I unbundle my scarf – must be wool because it's moth-nibbled too. I slide Karina's necklace around so the clasp is at the back. Eyes gliding across the canvas, I fiddle with the beads again, slipping one into my mouth. Hail Mary.

Our routine never varies. First, I size her up as if we've never met: her fitted blue jacket trimmed with lace around the upturned collar, square neckline and cuffs; that reddish-green flower pinned between her breasts, a locket on a black ribbon hanging around her neck, small studs piercing her lobes. Then, knowing how shallow it is to judge someone on their appearance, I force myself to admire the lush still life on the marble counter instead: bottles of Bass Pale Ale and champagne topped with golden foil, glossy clementines in a crystal bowl and a couple of roses plonked in a half-filled glass of water. It never lasts long. Finally, I allow myself to concentrate on what bothers me: what's she thinking? I give up on the peripherals and stare long and hard at her face.

It's only when my phone vibrates in my pocket that I realise how much time has passed. This happens a lot. I blink and wonder whether I was blinking before.

I turn to the corner where the couple had been standing by the landscape but they're nowhere to be seen. Probably long gone, hand in hand again, strolling along the Strand. Back to my barmaid and this time my eyes drift to the shady reflection of a man in the upper right-hand corner of the mirror. He has a neat goatee and a full moustache. He's wearing a top hat and holding a cane. I know him well. Lurking there, so sinister, he reminds me of someone.

Another vibration. I pull my phone out of my pocket. Karina: *Have you seen my new gloves? The ones Bill gave me for my birthday.*

Oops. I type out a quick reply: *nope, sorry*

As my fingers begin to itch, I pick up my bag and walk away through the next room. Gauguin's vulnerable Tahitian beauty, apprehension in her eyes. Monet's dappled Paris in autumn, part Seine, part sky. I wave hello and goodbye to Van Gogh in his green coat and blue hat – no point in saying it, the guy's obviously hard of hearing.

By the time I'm down the stairs and back on the Strand the sun has melted away, any little warmth it offered now vanished. I feel a sliver of cold air slip between the waist of my jeans and the bottom of my jumper, hoiked up from winding my scarf around my neck.

There's been a shower. Out on the pavement, puddles gleam, metallic bands of colour appearing in the tiny oil spills on their surface. Pedestrians are doing their best to avoid them as they march along, heads down. It's getting late; time to go home to families and flatmates. I slow down.

I feel uneasy – I always do when I leave her. My mind catches on those heavy eyes, that jagged fringe. Marooned behind the bar. Not in pain or sad, but not happy either. Lonely maybe. I blink, pulling down the tight skin below my temples with my thumb and middle finger. I wonder, if work is shitty, if she at least has a stellar home life. If she dreams of doing more. Is she at a pivotal point in her life but unable to pivot – life on pause, numb mind, sticky feet? I think of the little buffering wheel spinning on my laptop.

Two

Two days later there's no sign of Martins, the tetchy maître d', when I arrive at the restaurant so I take the opportunity to catch up on some reading. Typically, just as things are getting interesting—

'Eve?'

I jump, my paperback tumbling to the floor with a dull thud and closing up like a clam. I know I'm more than halfway: this morning I turned down the corner of a page almost slap bang in the middle. When I was reading, I traced my finger across the spine and it reminded me of an arched back, its hundreds of pages bony ribs. I slip off the wooden stool and reach out my hand but, before I have time to retrieve the book, Martins swipes it.

'I need you out front,' he says, raising his bushy eyebrows.

I've always found it hard to take him seriously, my eyes straying to the wiry hairs springing out of place like loose pieces of thread. Still, I can see where he's coming from: service is about to start ramping up. I just don't have the energy, especially not to serve a certain regular, sadly our biggest spender. I call him BS. He's at table three.

'I'm sorry,' I say, shaking the wandering thought about accidental spillages from my head. I stand up straight and rearrange my unironed shirt. 'You know what he's like.'

'What who's like? Actually, never mind.' His hand moves to the small of my back as he urges me through the door. 'I need you to take the order at table three.'

I pull the bent notepad out of my back pocket, quickly tearing off the first page before he sees it – must stop doodling. I sneak a glacé cherry from the colourful assortment of cocktail garnishes on the bar, then cut across the busy restaurant to the soundtrack of clinking glasses, scraping cutlery and senseless chatter. Martins would make a lousy conductor.

'What can I get for you?' I ask, candied cherry swallowed, chewed biro poised, as I arrive at the round table centre stage.

Nothing. As usual, he's too caught up in his own conversation to hear me. Or, more likely, he's waiting for me to put on a smile. He's mid-story, *the* story – the one he recites to every prospective client he wines and dines. Today's catch: three men, one old, two young. A father and his budding sons maybe. There's a certain resemblance between them: squared-off shoulders, thick necks, milk-chocolate-coloured hair (the father's sprinkled with icing). All lean eagerly towards BS as he reels off a list of the men he's made. Mouths open, gobbling up each word with glee, they look like fish waiting to be hooked. I want to warn them but it's too late – the net's descending.

'Sir?' I ask, a little louder, grinning through my teeth.

'Ah, Eve, I was wondering where you had got to,' he says, smirking rather than smiling. 'Gentlemen, direct your attention to God's first woman. And what a woman she is!'

I don't rise to it – I'm used to this – and, managing to ignore the leer that materialises on the creased face of the older man opposite, I make it through the order. I walk away and enter the dishes into the system, the prickly feeling on my skin subsiding as I tap on the screen.

There are parts of this job – one in a long line of jobs I toppled into, after life turned septic – that drive me insane. The incessant 'banter' of the creamy whites in the kitchen. Mr Laurence Martins, who's boringly devoted to his job. And these men I have to smile at sweetly, day after day. I wonder if showering in aftershave is a prerequisite in their line of work.

But the money's fine and most of the waiting staff perfectly nice – easy-going and up for a laugh after hours. Occasionally you get a good customer too. There: at a table by the golden entrance to the loos (unfortunate) is a frail woman dressed in watery shades of blue and green. She's lunching with her suited son. I recognise his baby face – probably works at one of the nearby banks or consultancies, as do they all – but I haven't seen him like this before. He's hunched over, leaning forward in an effort to grasp every word of her wispy voice before it gets carried away with the flick of a napkin or the swoosh of a passing waiter. I chew my pen, wondering where his father is. Divorce? No, I decide, he died. And now she comes to London once in a while to meet their son, their only child.

'Eve!' Martins again, this time clapping his hands together. 'You're not with it today – or any day for that matter!' He pauses, waiting for a reaction, then mutters bitterly about women and headcases under his too-minty breath.

'I'm sorry,' I say, though my apology must sound lukewarm because his eyebrows are raised higher than I've ever seen them.

Ding, ding.

The plates of hot food piling up on the pass save me.

'Better get those,' I say, nipping past him and picking up two dishes.

'Table five,' instructs Chef, a pale, skinny man who never leaves the kitchen. His hands shake as he fingers the long row of order tickets.

'We're not done here, Eve,' says Martins.

'I know.' I walk away with one 'deconstructed' fish and chips (fucking London) and one leafy salad strewn with sliced beetroot and crumbled goat's cheese.

It took me a while to memorise the table numbers, but now I think I could locate each one with my eyes closed. Squeezing through the gap between one and two, shimmying around the indoor silver birch tree by three. Maybe I could get a job at that gimmicky restaurant where people pay to dine in the dark, though someone told me all the staff there are blind, not blindfolded. I test myself by keeping my eyes on the floor, lifting my gaze only as I arrive. Ta-da!

'Eve?'

What? No. My breath snags and I say nothing, brain playing catch-up.

'Gosh, what a lovely surprise.'

I open my mouth but there's no sound.

'How are you, dear?'

I inhale, exhale and say, in a voice that belongs to a stranger, 'Fine, thank you.' I try my hardest to smile, to be normal. 'And you?'

'Oh, we're fine too,' she says, nodding her head. She looks older than I remember, or maybe thinner, the skin around her arms a little loose, like sleeves that need to be rolled up. She looks like her. The same green eyes, blinking behind a simple pair of glasses. Matching chestnut hair, though hers is coarser and threaded with grey, held in place with a large tortoiseshell clip. Even her mannerisms. The way she turns her head to say: 'Aren't we, William?'

'Yes, fine.' He's the shade of his napkin, the colour drained from his face. It was the same at the funeral, I remember, which was the last time I saw them. His chalky-white face moon-like at the front of the church as he read from a page of printed notes, using that word, more than once: 'misadventure'. He shifts awkwardly in his chair and says, 'So you're a waitress now.'

They don't know I didn't graduate – that I couldn't do it without Grace. That I sat in a dank cubicle in the overused, undercleaned bathroom until the sound of metal chair legs scraping against wooden floorboards had stopped and the invigilator's voice was soothingly muffled. Looking down at my ill-fitting gown – sleeveless, bum-length. Testing my skin with one of three sharpened pencils. I realise I'm still holding their lunch and unload my arms, too quickly, the stack of chips tumbling down. 'Oh, I'm sorry.'

He smiles, waves his hand in front of his plate, saying without saying that it's OK. I picture him stepping down from the lectern and pausing, for just a moment, with his hand on the polished wooden coffin. Frowning to stop himself from crying. Bowing his head.

'You know Grace's birthday is coming up?' She smiles at me, hopeful, eyes searching my face, looking for an ally in her remembering. As her cheeks rise, curly lines multiply at the corners of her eyes. Eyelash extensions.

Eve, stop blinking.

You take a step back, leaving me perched on the foot of your bed.

I'm sorry, I say, pulling you towards me so your knees knock against mine. I just feel like you're going to scratch my eyeball.

I told you I'm not good at this, you say, waving the mascara wand in front of my face. And I definitely can't do it if you keep fidgeting. In fact, if you keep fidgeting, I probably will scratch your eyeball.

I open my eyes wide. Can you see my wrinkles up close? Should I consider Botox?

You know how I feel about wrinkles, Eve. Stop fishing.

I pause, threatening the tears in my eyes with physical violence if they fall. 'Yes.' It comes out as a croak.

'She would have been twenty-six this year,' says her mum, still smiling, though just with her mouth now. She was composed at the funeral, from start to end. Poker-faced. Though the crumpled tissue in her hand, clutched so tightly her knuckles gleamed white, gave her away. 'Well, we don't want to keep you.'

'Yes, of course.' I go to give her a hug, then decide against it, clasping my hands in front of my chest. 'Bye.' I walk away with panic billowing inside me. Some guilty part of my brain knows I'm picking at my cuticles. I must have imagined this day, bumping into Grace's parents, a thousand times.

I make a dash for the loos, but Martins calls my name and points towards the pass. Table three is up. I take a deep breath and curl my fingers into my palms, nails stabbing skin in a bid to release the pressure building inside me. I reload my arms.

'OK,' I say, still concentrating on my breathing, 'who's having the pâté?'

Once again BS seems engrossed in conversation, this time to my relief. So after serving the food – including six glutinous oysters, lounging in their shells like fleshy bodies in sunken deckchairs – I turn, planning a more leisurely retreat. Too leisurely. As I place one foot in front of the other, he runs his hand up and down the inside of my thigh, his palm rough and raging against my already irritated skin. I imagine a hole burning in my tights, the material fraying, smoking slightly. The smell of scorched nylon. My skin blistering. The burning feeling rips through my body, from that patch up my spine and down to my fingertips.

'You bitch!'

That's him, not me – I've slapped him across the face. My palm's stinging and I can feel the heat rising to my cheeks. I whip my head around and see Grace's parents staring, her mum's mouth open wide, a forkful of salad hovering in front of it.

'Sir, I'm so very sorry.' Martins, who must have witnessed the action unfold, is by my side in seconds.

Not a word from BS, just a flaring of his nostrils, which are stretched into alarmingly large gateways.

'Lunch is on us, naturally.'

I part my lips to protest but, before my tongue has time to flick out the words, find myself being escorted to the back of the building. This time Martins isn't gently guiding me. He's holding my forearm as he pushes me away from the table.

'What the hell do you think you're doing?' he barks as soon as we're out of earshot.

'He fucking groped me.' I mean to shout this at him, but it comes out as a whisper. 'Don't pretend you didn't see,' I add, almost inaudibly, testing that patch of skin with my fingers.

'I don't know what you think happened, but it doesn't give you the right to assault him. You just have to be careful when you know what these guys are like. Come on, Eve, he's a paying customer.'

'Is that what he's paying for?'

He's got nothing, looks away embarrassed.

That's it, I'm done. I tell him so. Ignoring the sting in my eyes, I undo my apron, struggling with the double bow at the back before dramatically screwing the whole thing up and dumping it at his feet. I pick up my book, pissed off now about the lost page number, and shove it in my bag.

Martins is staring, a look of disbelief on his face, eyebrows raised so high I imagine them shooting up above his head.

Grabbing my coat and scarf, I storm out into the street by the service entrance, flinging my notepad behind me via the closing door. I don't know whether it's made it or it's sitting sadly outside the building – I won't look back. I've done this before.

I used to think I had a knack for not dwelling on things I didn't want to dwell on, especially the no-hopers. That I could bury my memories like we did Grace, five years ago on a Wednesday morning in June that I'm fairly sure was dry and sunny but, in my mind, looks wet and grey. Both the good memories and the bad. The way she whispered to herself when she was reading over her essays. Her little toes, which she could shift to the side, indicating left and right. Her unique ability to hide behind her fringe. How she sounded like a sultry film star when she spoke French. Her sneezes, which only ever came in threes. Her love of litera-ture: she wanted to read *all* the books. Her laugh, as catching as a cold. The way she used to worry about work. Her sad spells, which would dampen the day before disappearing as if they never existed. The weight of her head on my stomach; no wonder that's where everything hits me. The phone calls with her mum, which she'd always try to cut short: 'Well . . . anyway . . . right . . . so . . . I'd better go . . .' The look in her eye when she told me what he'd done. The last thing she said to me.

I tilt my head back and wait for the waterworks to dry up, only to feel a raindrop land on the tip of my nose. I duck into a sardine-tin coffee shop around the corner, but I can't sit still. All I can think about is Grace's parents, Martins' eyebrows. A hand on my thigh. My apron balled up on the floor. I let myself imagine slapping her dad's face instead, his pale cheek turning red. I remember the cold fury I felt towards him on the day of the funeral as he tried to round the edges of her death, make it more palatable for the gathered mourners. Like that was what mattered. I lean against the wall and look out of the window, raindrops wriggling down the panes. Grace is the only person I know (knew) who enjoyed being out in the rain.

I decide to walk home, to try to clear my head. I peel myself away from the wall, slowly, one limb at a time. The door dings merrily as I open it and pull it shut behind me. Windows are steamed up like people are inside having hot and sticky sex. Across the road, summer holidays on bill-boards are suddenly drenched.

We did everything together: studying, flirting, sleeping, drinking, dancing, dressing, undressing, studying, studying, studying. At least until she met him. It's a special form of torture to imagine everything you'd do differently, if you'd known what was coming.

I pull the well-loved umbrella out of my bag, ignore Bank Station and head west to Fleet Street.

By the time I reach the Royal Courts of Justice it's pouring. I keep moving, quickly crossing the road, and dive under the first bit of shelter I find. What a coincidence: Somerset House. I walk on, walk back, walk on again. I loop around and stand beside one of the free-standing columns supporting the grand arches.

I'm not supposed to be here today. It's not a Wednesday. I made a pact with myself that I wouldn't visit more than once a week. Too expensive. Too needy. Besides, that's what they recommend, isn't it? Weekly sessions. Regular enough to build trust without creating an unhealthy dependency. Then again, maybe it wouldn't hurt to see her. An emergency appointment. Or maybe today I'll have a proper browse. I consider for the first time why anyone would choose to paint a barmaid. How vanilla.

My patience begins to wane in room one. Of course, a painting of Adam and Eve. I close my eyes, BS's slurred voice, laced with wine, ringing in my ears.

Painted Eve has plucked a shiny red apple from a tree and is passing it to a puzzled Adam, who's scratching his head. I cast my eyes over the coils of the snake and follow the fruit-laden branch to Eve's fingertips, along her willowy arm and down her bare body to her toes. I wriggle my own, suddenly aware of how soggy they are in my cheap nylon tights (right big toe poking through a hole) and waterlogged pumps. All around are animals: greedy lion, grazing lamb. In the corner a young deer is slurping from a puddle bearing its reflection.

I pass by some more religious scenes – I can only take a few of these at a time. Too many bloody crucifixes, writing bodies, floating haloes, flying doves. Onwards to a series of portraits, more my type of thing. I weave my way from piece to piece, droplets of water falling from my sopping umbrella. I dip my head apologetically at *Portrait of Mrs Gainsborough*.

There are two women in room six – based on the similarity of their flat profiles, which are almost devoid of noses, they're sisters. They're absorbed with a piece of furniture encased in glass across the room. I lay my coat on the floor like a picnic rug, collapse inelegantly on top of it, legs crossed, and crane my neck to look at the familiar face of my barmaid. Our barmaid. Her name is Suzon.

Suzon? Ha. Are you sure?
  You look again, then click another link to double-check, ever conscientious. Yes, it says so here too.
  Suzon as in Macron? I start my own Google search.
  Your eyes roll but your lips curl. Suzon as in Suzon.
  Another search. Macaron?
  You glance at my screen, plastered with pastel-coloured sweet treats, and, giving in, offer a courtly bow. Why, thank you.

It was Grace's favourite painting and her fascination with it was infectious. At university Suzon stared out at us from grimy laptop screens more times than I can remember. We'd gawk at her for hours, trying to read her mind. Now, I fix my eyes on hers. How do you do it? Stand here all day. Look at that immaculate posture. Don't you ever get angry?
  Hurried footsteps behind me.
  We were supposed to discuss her appearance, the trappings of nineteenth-century Parisian life. But Grace found

27

her ghostly expression – or lack of it – deeply distracting. And soon so did I. I came across some old notes when I was moving my things from Dad's to Karina and Bill's, and there she was again. Our Suzon. When I first saw her in the flesh, maybe a year after Grace's funeral, I felt lighter somehow, my body flooded with relief. I've been visiting her, in this room, every week, ever since. I hug my knees into my chest.

Standing behind the bar, it's like she's poised on the edge of a platform, feet planted in dust and old chewing gum, eyes half-closed, watching a sea of indiscriminate faces wash past her with every chock-a-block tube or high-speed train. Everyone around her is a blur, no more than fleshy smudges of paint. I work my way across the crowd: dark top hat, ruffled white shirt, orange gloves – silk, I suppose – classy fur shawl.

A knock at the door.

Eve? Grace? Are you guys coming?

We're curled up on your bed, laptop balanced precariously in front of us, passing a can of beer back and forth. You wince, shooting a grin my way, press the space bar to pause the film. You whisper, Did you lock it?

I nod, stuffing some duvet into my mouth to stifle the laughter rising up my throat.

A huff and then a pissy voice saying, I knew they wouldn't come, they never do.

Heels click on wooden floorboards. A couple of other doors slam. A moment later we're alone again.

I love this bit, you say, leaning forward to restart it, gnawing at your lower lip, sticky with cherry-scented Carmex.

Me too. I rest my head on your shoulder and close my eyes.

It's just me and you.

'Excuse me, miss?'

I freeze. Her voice is gruffer than I expected. I look up and search her face for some change.

There she goes again, giving me that blank look, pretending she can't hear me.

'Miss?' enquires the voice again, a little louder. 'Just to let you know, the gallery's closing in five minutes.'

Oh, I recognise that voice now – it belongs to the badger-faced gallery assistant (all black-and-white hair and pointy nose) who works Wednesday afternoons. I give him a fleeting glance. He's standing with both hands behind his back, bent forward slightly as he beckons me. The room around us is silent. He reminds me of those nodding dogs whose noses nearly touch the floor when you tap their stubby tails. I used to imagine having one on my desk in my cubicle on my office floor in my work building – back when I imagined pursuing a job that entailed any of the above.

'Sorry about this,' I whisper to the barmaid through cupped palms.

Badger clears his throat.

I try and fail to stand up with no hands before giving in, pushing the floor away. 'I was leaving anyway,' I tell him.

He's not my friend. For all he knows, I have somewhere to get to.

There's a group haemorrhaging at the exit, so I stop and peruse the notice board – not the typical cork kind with red, yellow and blue pins, but a glass-fronted display case.

'Art History short courses, lectures and tours'
'Summer School'

29

'Artist residency in a historic seafront house in Brighton'
'Life-drawing models wanted'

Grace and I always said we'd try modelling for a life-drawing class, that we'd pose as a pair. At university we used to attend a weekly evening session and the model was almost always the same – a suitably flabby woman called Sandra. She was great to draw, with a stomach full of rolls, saggy breasts, chunky legs with purple veins squirming up her calves, a furrowed face, corkscrew hair. But our attention did begin to flag after drawing her week in, week out for nearly two years. Clearly no one else was brave enough to get naked.

I rootle around in my bag for my phone and snap a photo. How hard can it be? Sitting or standing naked – sorry, *nude* – in front of a small crowd for a couple of hours. It sounds like easy money and presumably there's no interview, unless they want to check I have the right kind of body. Maybe I don't. They're probably not used to seeing such dry, anaemic-looking limbs. Like parsnips. They might take one look and turn me away.

Back outside I start to see her everywhere. Hear her laugh. Smell her. Feel her in my hair, on my skin. Grace. It was like this for weeks, months after she died. The memories never entirely faded, but after a while I managed to mute them – at least most of the time. Suddenly they're louder, more threatening than ever.

I pick up a few cans of gin and tonic for the bus journey home. Drowning it out worked pretty well before. And besides, it's OK because if I were still at the restaurant we'd drink this after closing and then some. Plus there's a deal: three for two.

When I open the door to the flat, I'm greeted by the smell of pre-prepared chilli. Bill's wearing a pair of grey tracksuit bottoms and, tucked into them, a T-shirt that pulls tight across his back as he bends forward to stare at the microwave, glowing an artificial yellow. He taps his hands on the counter as he waits.

'Where's Karina?' He only ever eats ready-meals when she's out.

'Oh, Eve, I didn't see you there.' He glances briefly in my direction before returning to his dinner.

I find myself wondering if he'd be more attentive if I were wearing my towel and realise I'm drunk. 'She's working late?'

'Mm, yes. An opening.'

She works in food and drink PR so gets invited to tons of restaurant and bar launches.

All of a sudden, he springs into action. 'Glass of wine? I bought red.'

'Probably shouldn't.'

He eyes me warily as I walk towards the microwave like a cuckoo commandeering a momentarily abandoned nest. Before he informs me, regretfully, that it's a meal for one, I tell him I'm not hungry.

'Well, wine then.' He hands me a glass and I accept.

Half an hour later, I've got the giggles and I can't stop. Little things set me off. The corners of Bill's mouth, which are tinged reddish orange. The way he occasionally tightens his lips and swallows down a burp. What it might feel like to be a ready-meal and spend your days sloshing around in a shallow plastic tub.

'So, Eve,' he says, laughing along, 'how was your day?'

'Ah . . .' I melodramatically cover my eyes with my hands. 'My day didn't go so well.'

'What do you mean?' He's smiling and frowning at once.

'I may have lost my job.' I say it quickly, then clamp my mouth shut.

'Eve, what happened?'

'It's fine, everything is fine,' I say, now holding my hands up in front of his face. 'I have a plan.'

'Which is?'

I go to pour myself some more wine, but he takes the bottle from me.

'Bill!'

'I'll open another.'

'Oh.' More laughter. 'To tell you the truth, I'm not sure you'd approve.'

He pauses, picking up a corkscrew, then putting it down again. Screw top. 'You don't mean . . .' He gestures with his fingers.

'Eww, no!'

His cheeks redden as he refills our glasses. 'Sorry, just checking.' I expect him to ask another question but instead he returns to his final couple of mouthfuls, then runs his finger around the plastic, mopping up the dregs.

'Do you want to know?'

He licks his finger. 'Do you want to tell me?'

'Yes.'

'Well?'

I knock back some more wine. 'I'm going to be a life model.'

He doesn't say anything for a few seconds, then he furrows his brow. 'A model?'

'Ha, no need to act so surprised, Bill.' I poke him in the ribs and nearly fall off my chair.

'Oh no, I didn't mean that. I just, I don't know. A model, really?'

I'm laughing and his cheeks are red again. Before he says anything else, I ask if he knows what a life model is.

'Of course.' He stands up, plonks the plastic container in the sink.

'So, what is it?'

'Hm?'

'A life model.'

'Oh, that.' He returns to the table. 'You know, photo-shoots, that sort of thing.'

'Well, I'm very flattered that you think I could be a model, Bill, but life-modelling is a slightly different sort of thing.'

He tops up both our glasses again even though there's still plenty in them. 'Different, how?'

'Well, first of all, life models model naked.'

His eyes widen like a cartoon character's. 'Naked?'

'Naked.'

He lets out a whistle.

'I'm going to model for art students,' I say, manoeuvring myself on the chair. 'I'll pose, they'll draw me.' I cross my legs and, once I feel semi-stable, twist my arms overhead. 'Like this.' I lose my balance and topple forward.

Bill guffaws and holds out his arms to catch me. I feel another wave of hysteria descend and he's laughing too, pulling me upright with his hands on my waist, tickling me.

'No, stop it, I might wee!' I try to catch my breath.

'Gross, don't do that!'

The next thing I know, our lips are locked, fumbling. I start to laugh again, because the situation is so ridiculous. Eve and Bill? Bill and Eve? Ridiculous! His hands pull at my hair and I cling onto his. When he tugs at the buttons of my shirt, I yank his T-shirt up and over his head. His hands are on my bare skin now, grasping, grappling. His mouth tastes of chilli.

Seconds later, his phone dings. We spring apart and he has a look of horror in his eyes that surely matches mine, both suddenly sober. Neither of us speaks. For a brief moment, neither of us moves. Then I reach for my shirt and return to my room, feeling numb, like cold anaesthetic is coursing through me.

Three

For a split second, when I wake, I think I have somewhere to get to – memory can be such a tease – and for a few seconds more I revel in the idea. Right, must get up, showered, dried, dressed, on my way. I open my eyes one at a time and that's when the bullets hit. Grace's parents. The restaurant. And the killer blow: Bill.

I don't know what I was thinking – if I was thinking, which clearly I wasn't. And neither was he. He and Karina are the closest thing I have to family. They've been nothing but nice to me. I sit up. I need to talk to him, make sure he doesn't say anything. It was a mistake, something that needs deleting.

If only my stomach didn't feel like raw cake mixture. I move onto my front to try to quell the feeling, as I do when my womb aches once a month. A hangover, though, like guilt, is harder to suppress.

I've always been afraid that in hard times I might reach for a bottle: everybody knows it can run in the family. But although I'm not shy when it comes to drinking, I'm not an alcoholic. She told me so, the college nurse with the slanted eyes and ski-slope nose. Said I was 'just depressed' and would get over it.

I've never been good at handling my alcohol anyway. There was that botched house party one Friday night after school – I must have been sixteen, wearing my favourite sequin triangle top and frayed jeans – where the punch tasted so fruity-sweet I forgot it had any rum in it. The party ended with me projectile-vomiting in my friend's parents' pristine en suite; fluffy white towels, velvety cream carpets. I can still smell the honeysuckle hand cream, which I'd smeared along my wrists and arms moments before the burning fluid erupted.

By the time I reached university I assumed I'd grown out of it. I'd experienced a few forgotten nights since that not-so-sweet sixteen but thankfully had very little sick to show for it. But on the first night out with people from college I slipped up again. We were all drinking more than we should, partly to numb the nerves but mainly to prove that we could. Turns out I couldn't. More vomiting, this time on the cobbled street for all my new 'friends' to see. Grace, who'd sensibly stopped after her third vodka lemonade, was the one who took care of me.

Wow, this isn't your natural habitat, is it?

As you say it, you move my hair to one side, your fingers cool against my clammy skin.

More vomit. I'm about to come out of my crumpled bow when I feel your hand gently rubbing my back.

You mean with Sebastian and Ophelia and Arabella? No, I say, it's not. And not just because my name only has one syllable.

Well, it will get easier, you say, smoothing my hair. And in the meantime you've got me. I also have a syllable deficiency.

36

Do you think we should be taking supplements? I ask, wiping the corners of my mouth with my fingers before standing upright. You laugh. In the evening light, your skin looks dewy.

I pull my duvet up and over my head. When I was little, and bad things happened, I'd blink – hard and fast – to try to undo them. Maybe if I manage to stay under here long enough . . . The sound of the TV snaps me out of my self-absorbed spiral. Slowly, I slip out of bed, pull on Mum's jumper and open my door.

'Eve.'

Karina. I freeze.

'We need to talk.'

I can't look her in the eye. Instead, I stare at her mouth, her teeth pearly white and straight as a rod, her lips rosy. She's sitting on the sofa next to Bill, who's munching cereal, watching Louis Theroux wangle his way into some sex cult in small-town America.

When I sit down to join them she mutes it and – like Mum might have done, should have done – says she's disappointed in me. 'Bill told me.'

I glance at him. Told her what, exactly?

'Eve, he told me about the restaurant. What now?'

My mouth twitches.

'Why are you smiling? You can't just bum around, you know, you need to do something.'

I give a quick shake of the head, still smiling. 'I know, I'm sorry.' I think of the life-modelling advert, how Grace would laugh. 'I have a plan.'

'Which is?'

'Nothing's settled yet. In fact, I have to make a phone call.'

'Well, keep us posted.'

'Will do.' I mean it. The last thing I want is for Karina to add my name to her to-do list:

Call Mamma
Book dentist
Buy fat-free yoghurt, berries, face wipes, batteries
Gym
Post office (Bill)
EVE

Me doing well at work means Karina's happy and Bill and I get to enact our morning routine: him tapping away at his keyboard as I run the living room gauntlet. When I'm ready for our friendship to return to normal, that is.

'Bill, anything to add?' She swats him with the back of her hand.

'You'll be all right, Eve, you can get Theroux this.' He says it through a gummy smile.

I press my lips tight together and say nothing. Must preserve the ecosystem.

So apparently prospective life models *are* required to interview. When I called the number on the notice board, a softly spoken man – Hello, Paul speaking – answered after two rings and asked if I could 'pop in' this afternoon. I resisted pointing out that he sounded a bit desperate and agreed. My interview is at half past three at an address in South Kensington, presumably the studio.

I asked Paul whether I'd have to undress in the interview and, after letting out a brief bark of a laugh, he told me, That won't be necessary. Fortunate: with Karina at home, it would make borrowing her moisturiser difficult. My legs are dry and scaly and my forearms – when I rub them hard, like I'm trying to erase the freckles – shed flecks of white. I also need to borrow her bikini-line trimmer – or do I? I'm not sure what artists prefer: hair or no hair. It might be nice to have a little bit of coverage. Maybe one for question time at the end.

I try to ignore the prickly feeling flowering in my stomach and, after a cup of coffee, I shower and dress: red corduroy skirt, beige jumper over white shirt. For the first time in months, I take the time to blow-dry my hair, twisting it round my index finger and into a clip at the nape of my neck. The skin around my nails is red raw after a night of picking, but that can't be helped.

It's a sunny day – a pastel-blue sky and, by the looks of the unmoving trees, not too much wind. After a final check in the mirror, I set out walking. By the time I'm on Vauxhall Bridge the prickles have multiplied, tunnelling through my intestines.

My phone vibrates in my pocket.

Max: *Coffee?*

In an instant, my stomach starts to settle. I check the time and reply: *south ken? could be there in twenty?*

Three dots as he types. *South Ken? Someone's moving up in the world.*

ha. the pret by the station?

On my way.

Max is the assistant manager of a bar in the City. Also my oldest London friend (as in my London friend I've known the longest). We grew up a couple of streets apart, not far from the station in Finsbury Park. His dad and my dad used to meet at the local pub to watch football and drink beer, until my dad decided he preferred to drink whisky while staring at a blank screen from the comfort of his own armchair. We even had a brief fling in sixth form, Max and I, sparked by one drunken New Year's Eve. And a few other things. He was good with Dad, helping him to bed when his legs were wobbly with whisky. Talking to him as he stared mutely at the TV and never getting frustrated when all he would do in response was blink. He would walk me home from school, kiss me goodbye, send me texts telling me to sleep well. Then I went to Oxford and he stayed in London; I slowly stopped replying and like most long-distance relationships we fizzled. Max is kind and charismatic and funny, and always surrounded by people, and I arrived home assuming I'd sacrificed my place in his life a long time ago, but he made room.

I order two black coffees and a blueberry muffin from the guy behind the counter, who's chewing his already-stubby fingernails, then grab a seat at the window beside a teenage girl. She's studying, I suppose, jotting things down on a pad of lined A4 paper, reaching every now and then for one of a rainbow of coloured pens. I smile, remembering when I too thought highlighting was revising. Her long dark hair falls forward in front of her alabaster ears as she bends over her notes. Maybe she's waiting for her parents, which is why she's actually studying and not watching *Friends* reruns on her phone. Or maybe she's just here for some peace and quiet, time out from home. Books don't drink, don't yell about needing more loo roll, don't get dressed one morning and decide to walk out. She flicks her hair back, notices me watching, returns to her pens.

Eve?

You're hunched over your desk, squinting at a textbook fringed with mini Post-it notes. Your fingernail traces a line as you read.

I shift on your bed, hotching from stomach to side, and pause our Spotify playlist mid-song. Yes?

You know I love you, but you have to stop distracting me.

You mean the music?

The music and the nattering. I have about four hours to commit all of this to memory.

I close my laptop, mime zipping up my lips.

You blow me a kiss.

I catch it and plant it on my mouth.

I'm done with my coffee and halfway through Max's by the time he arrives, helmet in hand. He cycles in London, which never fails to impress me. I don't have the concentration.

'Eve!'

'Max!' I leap out of my chair – careful not to kick over my bag, crammed with long and skinny sachets of brown and white sugar – and throw my arms around him. It's been a few weeks.

'I see you've eaten,' he says, his already-high cheekbones rising as he smiles. He brushes remnants of blueberry muffin off my jumper.

'Ah yes, sorry, we were supposed to share that.'

'No worries, I'll just go and grab something.' He rakes his fingers through his auburn hair, thick and free from gunky products. 'More coffee?'

'I've already drunk mine and yours so I'm probably good.'

He laughs and I press my hands together, praying for forgiveness.

I watch as he picks something out from the fridge and joins the queue. While he waits, he slips off his jacket. His freckly skin, inherited from his Irish mam, is coppery from the sun. I catch a glimpse of the dog-leg scar puckered across his elbow – a memento from the time he tripped and fell down the stairs as a child. Against his reddish-brown skin, it looks salty white.

I scoot my chair in closer to the table as he takes a seat opposite. 'Good holiday?'

'I'm not sure I'd call it that,' he says, eyes crinkling, irises as brown as coffee beans, 'but yeah, it was great.'

'Remind me where you were?'

He removes the lid from his frothy cappuccino. 'We started in Barcelona and ended in Rome. The cycling was hard, but the scenery was beautiful.' He unwraps his bacon sandwich, steaming in its plastic wrapper. 'Great food.'

'Well, you look very healthy and happy.'

'Thanks.' He smiles. 'Anyway, how are you? How's work, the flat, etcetera?'

Only happy people ask you those kinds of questions.

He starts tucking in, eyes skipping between me and his sandwich. His questions – his genuine curiosity about people – are usually one of my favourite things about him. Today they make me uncomfortable. (The one question we never ask is: are you seeing anyone?)

'I'm good, thanks,' I reply, a little overenthusiastically. 'The flat's great. In fact, Karina asked after you the other day. Must get you over soon, for dinner or something.' I sound weird, I can hear it. He knows how terrible I am at cooking – I've tried and failed to bake him a birthday cake more than once – and I have no idea what I mean by 'or something'.

'Pleased to hear it. And yeah, sure, it would be good to catch up with Bill too.'

It would? I cringe at the thought of them sitting together, talking.

'And the restaurant?' He takes a big bite, squirting some ketchup onto the table. A silent splat.

'What?' I heard him.

He holds up a finger. 'One sec.' A groove reveals itself on his left cheek as he chews, always so polite. A gulp later: 'I asked how the restaurant was.'

I flick away the remaining morsels of muffin. One's now drowning in red sauce. Every woman for herself. 'The restaurant isn't so good.'

He takes a sip of cappuccino, all the while looking at me over the top of the cup. I want to wipe away the foam on his upper lip but stop myself. He brushes it with the back of his hand (I must have been staring) and asks, in a rather grown-up voice, if it's in financial trouble.

'Oh no, it's fine, doing well, in fact – or, at least, I assume it is. It's me, it just wasn't the right fit. You know how it is.' I'm sure he doesn't.

He takes another sip, still looking, waiting, his head just slightly cocked to one side. Like a strangely sexy therapist. He's unwilling to fill in the blanks for me or give me any guidance.

Two can play at this game. I clamp my lips together, uncross and recross my legs under the table, accidentally bumping against his in the process.

'Don't try to distract me, Eve.'

My face reddens, I can feel it.

Still he's looking, waiting.

'I quit yesterday.' I stop talking and try to gauge his reaction. Again, he says nothing. 'They were going to fire me anyway.'

Surprise, outrage, pity. I see flickers of all three – but mainly the third. This is becoming a pattern.

'Eve, I'm sorry.'

He says it like someone has died. I remember it well – hearing 'I'm sorry' a handful of times and thinking it was an odd thing to say. I had to stop myself from replying, 'Not your fault.' I knew who to blame.

'What happened?'

I should be an expert at knowing how to respond. 'Oh, you know, the usual. I just can't deal with that crowd. I can't do it. And I won't – or rather, I didn't.'

'Oh, Eve.' He puts a hand on mine. There we go again. The soft pat of the hand, the earnest look in the eyes, the slightly patronising nod of the head.

'It's fine,' I say, patting his hand in return, then moving both of mine under the table and onto my lap. I consider telling him about my interview but decide against it, in case it's a dud.

'Are you feeling OK?'

He knows me too well, can sense my toes creeping dangerously close to the edge. 'I'm fine,' I say, rearranging my face into a smile the way Karina refolds her clothes after I iron them. 'Please, just tell me more about your trip.'

He smiles back, accepting the diversion. 'There was a circus in one of the villages we cycled through in France,' he says. 'Acrobats, knife-throwers, tightrope-walkers. A ringmaster with a moustache the length of my arm.'

'Did you consider joining?' That was our plan when we were kids – to run away and become fire-eaters. Max suggested it one day at school after I'd had a particularly shitty night with Dad, trying and failing to stop him drinking with a game of Simon Says.

'They only had openings for pairs.'

'Shame. They don't know what they're missing.'

'Yeah, well,' he says, leaning back in his chair, 'I couldn't have done it without you.'

By the time I reach the address I plugged into my phone, it's twenty past three. I'm early – Karina would be proud. It's a rarity for me, though, and I hesitate at the door, wondering what to do with myself. Walk around the block, maybe, or wait outside for a few minutes? I start to feel the cold and give in, ringing the bell.

The building's quite beautiful. It must have been a private house at some point. It's part of a red-brick terrace, with cream-coloured stone framing the doors and the windows and running beneath the gutter – a kind of cornice or frieze, like you see on Ancient Greek temples. Stone steps lead to a gooseberry-green front door, which is set back behind a curved archway, bordered by the same creamy stone. Above it is a vast arched window. Lots of natural light. Must be the studio.

After a few seconds the buzzer sounds and the door springs open. I step inside and come head-to-head with a group of people spilling down the stairs. Some are holding hardback sketchbooks, while others have scrolls of paper tucked under their arms like rolled-up swimming towels. Class is over.

I'm busy wondering who the model is (potentially the middle-aged man with the paunch), when an older woman wearing too much floral perfume asks me to move away from the door, please.

45

I step aside and cough involuntarily.

After hooking their coats and scarves off a row of pegs that remind me of primary school, they disappear through the door. I rest my bag on the floor and untoggle my coat.

'Are you here for an interview?'

I turn around and find a woman walking towards me in a pair of black loafers that clip smartly on the stairs. She has honey-blonde hair that falls a couple of inches below her shoulders, and she's either hot or her cheeks are powdered with blusher.

'How could you tell?' I ask, stuffing my coat into a cubby as she pulls something the colour of porridge off a peg.

'Ah, easy,' she says, squinting as she smiles. 'The skittish eyes, the biting of the lip.'

I laugh. 'And you?'

She doesn't look like an artistic type, especially now that she's swaddled in her suede coat and a matching off-white shawl.

'Third-rate drawer,' she says, holding out her hand, gold bangles jangling. 'I'm Annie.'

'Eve.' I offer her my chilly-fingered hand and we shake, surprisingly firm from her, and she smiles again.

'Well, good luck, Eve.' She gives my hand a squeeze and walks towards the door. 'Up the stairs and round to the right.'

'Thank you,' I say, watching as she disappears from view.

The stairs creak as I climb them, three at a time because they're so tiny. When I reach the landing a man appears. He's tall and thin – though in a muscular way, I think – and wearing a leather jacket with padded shoulders and elbows. Underneath, a white T-shirt tucked into black jeans, secured

46

in place with a belt. His feet are clad in black boots. Not what I expected.

'You must be Eve.'

'I am. Paul?'

'Yes. Thank you for coming.'

'Thank you for having me.' I can't help but think this all sounds a bit sexual.

Maybe he thinks so too because he smiles, lines springing up around his mouth and eyes. He's handsome, with wavy hair – a muddle of dark brown and grey – and sticking-out ears that make him look like a puckish schoolboy. He has clear-rimmed glasses that he pushes up his nose with his index finger, twice in the space of ten seconds. Whether it's a tic or they're fantastically ill-fitting is hard to tell.

He gestures into the room from which he emerged and asks whether I'd like a glass of water. 'Or would you prefer coffee or tea?'

'Coffee would be great, thanks.'

The room's set up for a class. A dozen or so folding chairs, each paired with a spindly wooden easel, face towards a slightly raised wooden stage by the whopping arched window – almost a theatre in the round. In the centre of the stage is a non-folding chair and to the right stands a screen, a panelled room divider, one corner draped with floral fabric. To the left a leafy plant is growing too tall for its terracotta pot, which sits on a plate. I look up at the ceiling: in the centre is a skylight, a square of blue. The smell of white spirit lingers in the air.

The back wall of the room is lined with a kitchen counter, one compartment home to a squat fridge and another a small sink. Paul's bending down, retrieving an extra mug from a cupboard; the yellow one by the kettle must be his. A rattle as the water begins to boil – the drum roll – then a whistle.

'So, Eve, what do you do?' He hoiks the gurgling kettle off its cradle.

'I'm a waitress.' I was a waitress.

'Wonderful, so you're used to being on your feet.'

'I am.' I was.

'And have you done any life-modelling before?' he asks, handing me a mug with an upside-down rainbow on it.

I didn't ask for milk. 'No, but I have attended classes.' I lay the mug down on the floor, straddling the gap between two wooden floorboards.

'Oh, lovely, so you have an artistic background?' he asks, hopping up. He takes three long strides towards the counter and returns with a coaster, which he slips beneath my mug.

'Not especially, I just studied art history.'

'Oh, splendid. Where was that?'

'Oxford.'

'Very impressive.'

'If you say so.'

A brief pause as he takes a sip of his own milky coffee, grey-blue eyes clocking me over the rim. All of a sudden I'm curious to know about him – what he does (other than run life-drawing classes). Whether he has a family, girlfriend or boyfriend, wife or husband, kids. I can't see a ring and the leather jacket screams some kind of mid-life crisis.

'So, Eve. Just a few routine questions to make sure you know what you're letting yourself in for.'

There's something disarming about him too. Something in his brittle smile – a little crooked, like his two front teeth. As he talks, I find myself leaning towards him. The way he's

48

holding my gaze, unwavering. I wonder if he could do the same if I were sitting in front of him naked. 'Fire away.'

He takes off his glasses and balances them on his knee, rubs his eyes, then picks them up and puts them back on. 'Do you think you would be comfortable standing, without any clothes on, in front of a group of people who are fully clothed?'

I picture them drawing me, all those eyes on my body, turning it into lines on a page, paper and charcoal dedicated to pinning down the shape of me. I feel myself blush.

'Most of our models come from a dramatic background – acting or dancing – so they're comfortable performing for a crowd, at ease in their own skin.'

'I'm at ease,' I say, slouching a bit on my chair to prove it, though it's not a particularly comfy chair on which to slouch. I think cold thoughts to cool myself down. Will it snow this year? Did Bill finish that strawberry ice cream? The year our central heating conked out and Dad neglected to fix it for two long icy weeks.

'Great. And you would be happy having the students scrutinise your body? There are times when we not only look at the human form, but also discuss what we see – imperfections, blemishes, irregularities.'

'Fine by me.'

'Are you reasonably fit?'

I stifle a laugh.

'It takes stamina – and patience, of course – to hold a pose. It can be physically demanding.'

'I can do it.'

'Right, OK then.' He leans forward, elbows on knees, hands clasped. Eyes still glued to mine. 'Let's talk specifics.'

He tells me that each two-hour class will follow roughly the same format. I'll be expected to work through a series of short, sharp dynamic poses in the first hour – some thirty seconds long, others up to ten minutes. Sounds similar to yoga, I think. After a brief tea break, the second part of the class will be devoted to one posture, which I'll have to hold for forty-five minutes. He tells me how important it is that I go home and practise some stances, that I get to know my own limitations. I should be daring with the quick bursts – have fun, try something a tad dramatic. He recommends something more neutral – but not so neutral that it sends his students to sleep – for the longer poses.

'Would you mind working with another model?'

'I don't see why not.'

'Of the opposite sex?'

'I've seen men naked before.'

He laughs. Was that a wink or a blink?

Um, that's not Sandra, you say, nodding towards an old man with skin like Play-Doh, ambling towards the podium in a Hawaiian dressing gown.

Who would have thought it, I reply, a real-live man.

As he turns to the back wall and removes his robe, saggy bum on show, you hunch down behind your easel.

Come on, Grace, you don't want to miss this.

Your shoulders begin to shake.

One . . .

You cover your face with your charcoaly hands.

Two . . .

OK, you say, I can do this. I'm not a child.

I cock an eyebrow. Three.

*Just as he turns round, you pop up and catch his eye. Choking
back a giggle, you duck back down.*

'So, Eve,' he says, standing up and reaching for his notebook
– more black leather. 'How about we start you off with two
classes a week?'

That's it?

'If you would rather, we can start with one and see how
it goes?'

'Oh no, two classes a week would be great – thanks. And
I can definitely take on more if you need.'

'Glad to hear that,' he says, jotting down my name here
and there as he leafs through the pages.

I rock forward onto the balls of my feet as I try to see
what or who else fills his days. His handwriting is very small,
like it's trying to be neat. No crossings out, probably because
it's all in pencil.

'You might want to bring your own cushion and a robe –
when you arrive you'll undress behind the screen, but most
models prefer to sling something over them until the class
begins.'

'Right. And pay?'

'Ah, of course. We pay thirty pounds a class, cash in hand.
Does that work for you?'

Fifteen pounds an hour to sit or stand still? 'Deal.'

After pausing outside the front door and making a note of
the times and dates – six until eight on Tuesdays, ten until
twelve on Sundays – I head back to the station, light on my
feet. When Karina said I needed to find another job I bet
she didn't think I'd find one this quickly. I'll be scraping rent

51

together in no time. And Bill and I will just forget that last night ever happened.

The broad boulevard of Exhibition Road is buzzing with tourists ticking off the Natural History Museum, the V&A, the Science Museum. Look at me, I think, getting my kit off in the name of art, a stone's throw from these first-rate cultural institutions.

As I round the bend, I inhale the floral notes of bouquets propped up in black buckets at a roadside florist, a soothing whiff of the countryside for commuters leaking out of the Underground.

Another vibration in my pocket, this time one long, continuous buzz.

Max again. Actually, My Max (that's what he changed his name to in my contacts when he noticed there were two).

I press the green button. 'Oh, hey there.'

'I have a plan.'

'Wonderful. Which is?'

'There's an opening at the bar.'

Ah. 'Max, that's great – and thank you – but I'm actually not sure I want to rush into anything.' Especially a bar back in the City.

'Don't be daft, this is perfect,' he says assuredly. 'The pay's good, the people working here are great. We'd get to see a bit more of each other. And besides, you need a job, don't you?'

OK, so maybe two life-modelling shifts a week won't quite sustain me.

'At least let me introduce you to the manager. How about Monday?'

I turn to the station entrance, following the trail of people heading in against the flow, salmon swimming upstream.

Maybe it's not the worst idea in the world. I picture us working together, sneaking handfuls of nuts between customers, staying on after closing for late-night drinks. With other staff or just us? The lights low. Music fading. Vision a bit blurry.

'Come on, Eve. What do you have to lose?'

'OK,' I reply, eyes widening. 'I'll come and meet the manager. But I'm telling you now, Max, I can't promise anything.'

'Well, neither can I,' he replies, laughing. 'Nina can be a total bitch when she wants to be.'

Four

Suzon. As soon as I set foot in the bar, brightly lit before it opens to thirsty post-work punters, she comes tumbling into my head. Just like in the painting, there's a glossy marble-topped counter, a glass bowl of oranges (what is it about having fruit on a bar?), golden-topped champagne bottles. I squint as I try to picture her face, then change tack and imagine her naked.

'Eve?'

Shit.

'I'd like to introduce you to Nina,' says Max. 'Nina, this is Eve.'

I make a conscious effort to unfurrow my lost-in-thought eyebrows and in the process must end up raising them to the point of surprise.

'Expecting someone else?'

Nina looks like the kind of girl I both fantasise about being and fear being around. Self-confidence oozes from every inch of her petite body. Her hazel eyes are shaded by long lashes coated in a thick layer of mascara and her lips are painted a fresh-looking peach, offsetting her ivory skin.

She opens her mouth to say something else (is that a silver stud glinting against her tongue?) but I beat her to it.

'Nina, of course,' I say, stretching my clammy hand towards her. 'It's great to meet you.'

'How do you know? You haven't met me yet.'

That's a first. Paul was much easier to please. I glance at her silver hair (has to be dyed) and wonder how old she is. Chopped into a severe bob, it skirts around her pixie ears, well paired with her pointy nose. A tiny figure of eight on a delicate chain dangles, nearly out of sight, below her neckline.

'Well, Eve, what can I do for you?'

I look at Max. I know he spoke to her at the weekend, but I don't know exactly what he said about my sad situation. Is she aware that I essentially got fired? If not, should I tell her? If she calls the restaurant for a reference, she'll know soon enough. I can picture Martins glowing with delight as he details my many failings.

'OK, let's continue this conversation of sorts in my office,' she says, not exactly impatiently but with an edge. 'Max, the deliveries came early today so can you make a start on the unpacking?'

'On it,' he replies, heading towards the bar without so much as a glance in my direction.

I narrow my eyes at his desertion, then widen them – again, too much – when they lock with Nina's. Her irises are so hazel, almost yellow like a black cat's, that I find myself peering at her to see if I can detect contacts.

'This way, Eve.'

Her office is a blank canvas, the white walls devoid of decoration except for a year-long rota stamped from Monday through to Saturday with upper-case names in red ink. There are no photographs of family or friends and, apart from a black velvet coat slung over the back of a swivel chair, very few signs of Nina herself. A floor-to-ceiling bookshelf extends across the length of the wall behind her desk but, other than the odd fruity spine, that too is monochrome. Crossing the threshold, I imagine the apple-green dye of my (Karina's) new socks running as if in a washing machine for the first time.

'Please,' she says, sitting down and gesturing to the folding metal chair opposite.

I eye her ergonomic padded seat enviously. 'Thanks.' I get the feeling she's not going to be making me a coffee, milky or otherwise.

'So, I'll ask you again now your boyfriend isn't listening in. What can I do for you?'

'Oh no, Max isn't my boyfriend,' I say, stumbling over the word, wondering how it would feel to claim him as my own. 'We're just friends. In fact, I hadn't seen him for a few weeks before—'

'Not important,' she says, eyes flickering down to her laptop and fingers typing, quickly but quietly.

This isn't going well.

'Eve, why are you here?' she asks, fingers still plugging away.

'Max mentioned you had an opening?'

'You want a job?'

Now it's her turn to raise her rather more well-tended eyebrows. A caricaturist would probably sketch her in shrunken form on the page, an even more petite and perfect version of herself, with big Disney eyes, long curled lashes, a peach-tinted pout and elfin ears.

'Do you have experience?' Still typing. I resist the urge to peer round at the screen.

'Absolutely,' I say eagerly, straightening up in my chair. 'Until a few days ago I worked at a smart restaurant ten minutes down the road. I've been waitressing on and off for five years now.' No need to mention the bar work in Oxford.

So I thought you lot weren't allowed to have jobs during term time? Niall, the manager, is interviewing us both but, judging by his eye contact, directing this question at you. We're sitting at a square table, us on one side, him opposite. I notice your cheeks change colour and when he starts to smile I assume he's noticed too.

You meet his gaze, then look down at the table, your fringe falling forward over your eyes. The thing is, you begin, fiddling with a paper coaster . . .

You tap your toe against mine.

The thing is, I continue, not every student at Oxford has a savings account.

This makes you blush more, because actually you do have a savings account. I hook my foot around your ankle, thanking you, silently, for doing this with me.

Niall nods, laughs a little, a rusty laugh that tells me he smokes, which together with his stubble adds an edge to his boyish good looks. He glances down at our CVs, then back up at you.

You let out a little laugh of your own that sounds more like a mew. You're not used to this.

Also, I add, it's only weekend work.

When neither of you responds I wonder if I said it out loud.

Fine, he says, come back tomorrow for a trial shift. Five o'clock.

We watch him walk away and resume his position behind the bar.

As soon as he's out of earshot I whisper, I think you have an admirer.

I do not, you smile.

I smile too and turn away, but when I glance back in your direction a moment later, you're still watching him.

My heart beats fast inside my chest. I puff out my cheeks, rub my hands surreptitiously on my jeans. (Thankfully Nina's oblivious, cat eyes squinting at her screen.) As my heart rate returns to normal, I continue. 'I can work the till, the coffee machine, make drinks, pull pints, whatever you need.' Pull pints? I hope she doesn't test me – I never was good at that.

'So why did you leave?'

'Excuse me?'

'You left your previous job – the one at the "smart" restaurant.' The audible speech marks drip with disdain.

I feel my body temperature rise like I'm sitting in a sauna, the air soupy with steam.

'Eve?'

'I quit.' Confess. 'Before they had a chance to fire me.' I pause to gauge the effect of my words, but her peaceful face, as if she's hit pause on herself, is giving nothing away. I press on. 'A customer was being inappropriate.'

'And?' she asks, hitting one last key with feeling and leaning back in her chair, an impish smile tugging at the corners of her mouth.

I frown, see that impassive sneer on Martins' face again, feel that same swelling frustration. I don't need this. 'And I thought it was degrading so I slapped him,' I say, standing up and turning to leave.

'Brilliant.'

I turn back and find her running a silver fingernail along her lower lip.

'When can you start?'

By the time I'm heading for the exit the bar is piled high with blue plastic crates and cardboard boxes – a recyclable fortress. I scan the scene but there's no sign of Max, who must still be unpacking. I'm a little disappointed. It would have been nice to celebrate the new job together. Still, we'll see each other soon enough. I start on Friday.

Back outside, I make a conscious effort to saunter and soak everything up: this is a good day. I pass a girl (woman?) – must be about my age (girl) – in a shaggy grey coat. It's unzipped, revealing a small baby in a bobble hat bundled up and strapped to her chest. I feel the weight against my own body for a moment, like carrying around a hot-water bottle that wriggles and wails. Maybe that's why Mum left, because I made too much noise. Maybe if I'd learned to keep quiet Grace would still be here too. I dig my nails into my palms: a good day. I glance over my shoulder and spy leggings and trainers peeping out beneath her coat. I wonder if she's heading to a mum-and-baby yoga class and make a mental note to go and see Youla, my local yoga teacher, this evening; somehow she hasn't clocked that I keep booking the six-week trial offer. I try to picture making my way home with a baby, nobody to help me or show me what to do, and feel a slight tightening in my throat. I know how *not* to be a mother at least. Maybe that's enough.

At the end of the block, three men in high-vis jackets and low-slung jeans are drilling down into the concrete pavement. Behind them, a handful of clean-shaven, suited men are shaking hands outside the entrance to a glass office tower, their corporate-logo backpacks making them look like overgrown schoolkids.

'You know, Eve, I almost didn't recognise you.'

Fuck. Well, I recognise that drawl. I spin around and there he is, BS, standing uncomfortably close and, as usual, reeking of aftershave. No hint of wine on his smirking lips, though, nor any droplets on his starched shirt. He hasn't had lunch yet.

'See anything you like?' he asks, gesturing to the suits who have stopped nattering and are slowly filtering into the building.

Two by two.

'Not my type – you know that.' I turn to walk away but he grasps hold of my forearm, a smile spreading across his face. I yank it free and cross my arms tightly in front of my chest.

'Such a sad business, you losing your job,' he says, looking me up and down. 'Always so uptight.'

'Actually I've already found two new jobs – better pay, better hours – so you did me a favour really.' That was rash. The last thing I want is for him to have any idea where I work. It's also a lie: the pay is worse.

'Oh, is that so? Which desperate establishments have been generous enough to take you on?'

'That's none of your business.' I turn to walk away again, only to see Max emerging from the bar and heading towards me. 'Max!' Never have I been so happy to see him. He raises a hand in greeting and I wave him over energetically. As he approaches I beg him silently not to let anything slip.

'Eve, congratulations. You got the job!' He's hugging me and I'm pinching him, trying to say, without saying, that we should leave.

'Excuse me, we were in the middle of a conversation.'

Max's eyes flash towards BS and widen slightly. 'Oh, I'm sorry,' he says, sounding genuine, extending his hand. 'Max.'

'My boyfriend,' I add, without skipping a beat.

Max is frozen for a split second before catching on. When he does, he moves quickly into character and even kisses me for dramatic effect. A good kiss, a proper kiss, his hand curled around the back of my neck. A kiss that takes me wholly by surprise, on several levels. I have to cling onto his arms to stop myself from stumbling, and when I do I feel the muscles tensing beneath his shirt. I can't remember the last time someone kissed me in broad daylight.

I recover just in time to tell BS we have somewhere we need to be. While he's busy readjusting his face, I turn to Max. 'Ready?'

'Ready.' As he says it, he puts his arm around me and, together, we continue the way I was heading.

Still walking, I sneak a glance at Max, who's staring right back at me, a smile playing on his lips. 'Who was that, Eve?'

'That was one of the reasons I no longer work at the restaurant,' I say, grimacing.

Max nods. 'And he was always part of the plan?' The smile's still there.

'The plan?'

We round a corner and he stops, turns to me. 'I'm just saying, you didn't need to come up with such an elaborate ruse. I was always going to say yes.'

I laugh and so does he, then I clap my hands together. 'Well, good to know – and thank you for playing along so gallantly.'

'That's what I'm here for,' he says. 'Is this going to be a regular occurrence now that we work together?'

'Ha, I guess we'll find out soon enough.'

He looks up at the sky and closes his eyes, biting his lower lip. 'Yes!'

I laugh.

We say goodbye (hug only) and I turn to head home. It's only now, as I clock my reflection in a shop window, that I notice the grin stretching wide across my face.

I roll onto Embankment by Blackfriars Bridge (not nearly as lovely to walk across as Waterloo) and park myself on an iron bench encrusted with black paint. I reach into my bag for a clementine – it's not stealing if you're an employee.

My knuckles sting as the juice of the orange seeps between them, my pink skin bleached chalky-white. They're dry and cracked from the cold, and probably from cleaning products. Of course, the scratching doesn't help. Karina always says I should take better care of myself, pushing her many moisturisers into my hands. I rest the clementine in my lap and stretch out my fingers – skin loose and wrinkled – then curl them inwards, imagining blood trickling out as the skin parts, stretched taut. I do enjoy sampling that posh Aesop stuff, always regrettably nailed to the shopfront.

I try to sit still, paying attention to my body, imagining my first life-modelling session tomorrow. I zone out my thoughts and focus on the background noise: car engines, conversations, the odd seagull. A siren rises in volume as it gets closer and closer, drowning out the lot. Grace. I press my hands over my ears and let my eyes flit over strangers, cataloguing.

A bird-like face, tiny within a mammoth, fur-trimmed hood – not clear if it's faux or real. Gauzy tights crumple around ankles. Tattoo on the left: I ♥ Jack. Who do I ♥?

A mop of pigeon-grey hair that I itch to run my fingers through. Unkempt eyebrows the same shade, crinkled brow (makes me think of those dogs – what are they? Shar Pei), long Roman nose, emerald-green eyes.

Grace.

A ponytail swings to and fro like a pendulum in an old-fashioned clock. A high-waisted pencil skirt and fitted jacket showcase curves. Red nails. I stop biting my own, which taste of orange.

Your toes – long and slim like fingers – with nails painted poppy red.

I sit for an hour or so watching the sunlight on the dappled water, a thousand flashing cameras. The river looks sparkling clean in the middle but, by the time the gentle waves reach the pebbly shore, it's murky brown, swimming with litter.

My phone vibrates, but I ignore it. I'm struggling to ignore the backs of my thighs, though, which are slowly assuming an imprint of the bench's metal slats. I shift in my seat.

Squawk.

Seagull.

I throw a curl of peel at its head.

My phone keeps vibrating, one unbroken buzz, like the fat fly that's been circling above my bed for the past few nights. I give in, rootling around in my bag to find it among the sugar sachets and three more clementines, one attached to a stalk with waxy green leaves.

Max. I imagine a grainy CCTV recording the orange theft frame by frame. 'Hello?'

'Eve, hey.'

'What's up, Max?' I gather the evidence onto my lap and get ready to toss it into the Thames.

'Do you want to grab a quick drink tonight?'

'Well, actually—'

'Don't worry, Eve, it's not a date.'

I smile. 'Ha, no, it's not that. I was planning on going to yoga.'

'How about Thursday then? Before your first shift.'

'OK, but it's on me, Max. I owe you.'

'Fine by me.'

'Maybe one of the bars by the river?'

'Perfect. I'll text you. Namaste.'

I arrive home to an empty flat. Karina and Bill are away until the morning. Part of me is relieved – I haven't managed to entirely shake the feeling of guilt about Bill's hands, my tits, our lips – but then, good news doesn't feel so good when there's no one to share it with.

They don't go abroad very often but they do spend lots of time out of London, bickering in various cold and damp towns around the UK. (She felt ill when they took the train yesterday, bidding me farewell while squirting something eucalyptus-scented into her nostrils, so I expect this trip will have been particularly challenging for Bill.) Some highlights from their previous excursions: Bath, where the weather was so grisly they spent most of their time in a tiny cinema that played only old films; Cambridge, where Bill fell in the River Cam as he tried to punt them past colleges (arrived back in London still soggy); and Norwich, which feels like it ought to be on the seashore but, it transpired, isn't. They're also often travelling for weddings. All their friends seem to be getting promoted or getting married or getting pregnant. Pivoting into the next stages of their perfectly plotted lives. I'm not sure how Karina would cope with the baby weight.

I dump my coat and, one by one, empty the brown and white sugar sachets into the near-empty pot by the kettle, stirring up the grains until they're roughly one shade. I'm the only one who takes sugar, so who cares? A couple of months ago, Karina asked me if I thought they'd enjoy Oxford. I told her I wouldn't know. She said I must have an opinion because I went to university there. I haven't been back since, I told her, swallowing a surge of panic.

I can't go back.

I unpeel another clementine.

Five

I wake up sore all over after my long-awaited yoga class. Youla didn't go easy on me. It turns out the number of people attending dips in winter, so it was just me and one other (very keen, very bendy, dressed from head to toe in Lululemon) at last night's session. This may sound good in theory – a private lesson for a smidge of the price – but in reality it means nowhere to hide.

'Eve, why don't you come forward?' suggested Youla, just as I'd started to feel comfortable, lying face down on my rubbery mat at the far end of the low-lit studio, where the makes-me-sneeze musk of incense doesn't hit you quite so hard.

I reluctantly rolled onto my back and came to standing, not 'one vertebra at a time' but like a malcoordinated jack-in-the-box. I dragged my mat to the front of the room with exaggerated effort, flashing my eyes at Lulu – now sporting nothing on her upper half except for a flamingo-pink sports bra. By the time I was sitting cross-legged, facing forward, Youla's eyes were shut, her Medusa tendrils twisted back into a carefree bun.

'OK, let's begin this practice with three oms,' she said, in her characteristically husky (sleep-inducing) voice.

I hate om-ing.

We began chanting, me barely audible beside Lulu, who was emitting the low-pitched sounds from deep within her sculpted belly for the entire complex to hear. Next came a whole lot of breathing exercises, which I always expect to nail (because I know how to breathe), but they turn out to be incredibly tricky. To make matters worse, I'm suffering from what I assume is the start of a winter cold, so emitting rapid breaths from one nostril while covering the other is a risk for everyone around me. Cue Lulu subtly hotching her mat towards the wall.

Anyway, the class proceeded to be very intense, with too much 'flow' for my liking and not nearly enough shavasana (nap time) at the end. One awkward pigeon pose too many must be responsible for the pain still shooting down my thighs. I'm also experiencing a strange sort of muscle spasm in my lower back; probably the result of lying flat on my mat and then extending upwards through my belly button, pushing off with my hands and feet, as I tried to transition from a soon-to-buckle human bridge into a wonky wheel. Hopefully life-modelling doesn't involve much moving. Today's the day.

I'm ready, at least physically. And I'm hoping the distraction to come will dispel the residual anxiety swirling around inside me. An ant-like feeling that creeps and crawls along my limbs. The kind that kicks in when you remember something you left behind – something you forgot about, if only for a moment. A small child in a deep bath, maybe.

After yoga, I spent the majority of last night preening. I knew Karina was into hair products, but I didn't realise

67

quite how many washes and creams she lathers onto her lean body: exfoliators in every consistency and colour; a medley of moisturisers; many masks; four razors; two boxes of DIY wax strips. I promptly returned the latter to the wicker basket below her bedside table before carrying the rest of the spoils to the bathroom; the night before my first life-modelling class wasn't the time to trial my waxing capabilities.

I took a long shower, exfoliating and then shaving my long-neglected legs, underarms and bikini line (decided to leave a decent amount of coverage). I washed my hair – shampoo and conditioner – and even combed it through before rinsing, as Karina does.

I applied too much moisturiser and had to waft around the flat naked for about ten minutes before the surplus liquid soaked into my pink pores. Good practice. I even tried out a couple of poses on one of the kitchen chairs before self-consciousness overwhelmed me: one with legs and arms outstretched, another with my feet on the chair and my upper body huddled over my knees, protruding like mountain peaks. I returned Karina's things in exchange for her silky dressing gown and I also borrowed one of the softer cushions off the sofa. Hopefully they won't notice.

I arrive at quarter to six, as Paul suggested. No need to ring the bell: Annie, the woman I bumped into before my interview, is heading through the door so I follow, ignoring the small sign that reads 'No Tailgaters'. I go to say hello, but another woman gets there first with some trivial comment about the weather. Annie sheds her coat. Underneath she's wearing a long cardigan over a frilly shirt buttoned up to her neck and encircled by three rows of silver beads. Classic blue jeans, those black loafers. I think about tapping her on the shoulder as I follow her up the stairs but decide it's a bit over-familiar and hold onto the banister instead.

'Darling.' Paul's standing at the top of the stairs with his notebook. 'Looking lovely as always.'

He's not wrong. Her silky hair is loose, framing her face in soft waves. Her skin is smooth and blemish-free.

'Oh, Paul, you are a charmer.' She smiles and playfully pats his lingering hand.

'Eve, welcome. I didn't see you there.'

No offence taken.

Annie turns around and flashes me a smile. 'You got the job. Congratulations.'

'Thanks,' I say, feeling my cheeks flush. 'I'm only slightly terrified,' I add as Paul turns away to talk to someone else.

'You'll be fine,' she says, reaching out and giving my hand a squeeze like she did last time. 'Just pretend we're the naked ones.'

Paul turns back to us. 'Eve, why don't you head on in and change?'

I nod and sidle past them, wondering why he doesn't just say undress. As I walk away I hear him whispering that it's my first time.

There are a couple of people already sitting at easels. I smile at a middle-aged man with a neatly trimmed beard when I catch his eye but he swiftly looks away, as if he's not supposed to fraternise with the subject. I hop up onto the stage – looks confident – and duck behind the screen, crouching for a few seconds and breathing deeply in a bid to slow my racing heart rate. By my toes are some props – a box, a pole, some rope (am I in the right place?) – presumably for extending my very limited range of poses.

69

I stand up and realise the screen is only shoulder-height. I hunch my back and bend my legs a little, like I'm struggling out of my clothes beneath a sheet before slinking into bed with someone for the first time. I can do this. I untoggle my coat, which I should have left downstairs, and slip off my Converse without untying the laces. I roll down my jeans, examining the seam marks on my skin and making a mental note to wear something softer next time. Goosebumps prick up on my arms and legs, despite the electric heater on full blast beside me. I reach my fingers towards the giant window behind the stage: single-glazed. My neck begins to ache so, after pulling off my pants, I stand up straight, aware that now I must look like a floating head.

I wrap my stripped body in Karina's robe and notice my heart rate return to normal, just as it would when I was a child and I'd crawl into Mum's wardrobe after a recurring nightmare about being force-fed boiled eggs by a bad man. I'd bury my face in the clothes she'd left behind, the fabrics soft and infused with a woody scent. Bill's dressing gown might have been cosier – the hooded towelling kind, the kind loving parents bundle their shivering children in after a swim in the sea – but Karina's will do. Now what?

'How are you getting on, Eve?'

I turn around and find Paul onstage. A complete stranger, eyes on mine with only the screen between us. My breasts harden like a suit of armour. I squeeze my pelvic-floor muscles up inside me. 'I think I'm ready.' Coaxing my feet forward one at a time, I walk out from behind the screen and see that the room has filled up since I disappeared behind it. A room full of people I might pass on the pavement on any given day. On the wall to my left is a round clock with

70

a white face. A short black hand denotes the hour and a long red hand tracks the minutes: one minute to six.

'So, Eve, we're going to start with a series of thirty-second poses, what we call "gestures".' He pokes at his glasses with his index finger. I still can't tell whether they're ill-fitting or it's just a tic. 'In later classes I might ask you to count these in your head but today I'll lend you a hand.'

I feel my eyebrows raise infinitesimally and order them back down.

'Every time I say the word "change", you adopt a new pose.' And my safe word? 'OK.'

He steps off the stage and skulks to the corner by the door, out of reach of the natural sunlight filtering in through the glass shaft above our heads. He gives me a nod and, after willing my trembling fingers into motion, I clumsily undo the tie fixing my robe in place. The cutting of the red ribbon. The big reveal. Karina's robe slides off my body, too easily, and crumples into a pile by my feet. My entire body tenses.

There are no gasps, no giggles. No one recoils, storms out, asks for a refund. No applause either. Just Paul nudging his head to one side as if he has a twitch or some water in his ear. I toss the robe away with my toes – which, like the rest of my body, feel electric, too real, high-definition. I sense my hairs stand on end, leaping to attention – my only protection.

'OK, Eve, over to you in five.'

I imagine this little show beaming out live on air and shiver. I step towards the chair, brain struggling to decide what it is my body should do. I glance at the clock and take a seat, ankles crossed, legs locked, hands instinctively clasped together on my knee. I feel a throbbing between my legs – not exactly turned on but definitely something. Damn, I left my cushion behind the screen. I try not to think about how many bare cheeks have been on this seat: old and wrinkly, young and taut, hopefully not hairy.

Before I know it, the room's whirring with the gentle scratching of charcoal. Makes me want to itch deep within my ear. Heads don't move but each pair of eyes flutters up and down between my bare body and their blank sheet of paper – the way Bill's flit back and forth between his laptop screen and keyboard. There must be twenty people in the room, more women than men, some –

'Change.'

My right leg juts out as if I'm experiencing a spasm, heel to floor, foot flexed. I lean back in the chair and cling onto the seat. My heart's thumping so my chest must be moving. I breathe in, ribcage raised. I glance down and notice stringy violet veins visible beneath the surface of my tits, the skin tracing-paper thin. I imagine pencils sketching those lines, writhing, wriggling.

'Change.'

I go to extend my left leg to mirror my right, both at forty-five-degree angles, but quickly change my mind – we've only just met and none of you, as far as I'm aware, are qualified gynaecologists. Instead, I cross my legs and stretch my arms up overhead, backs of hands together, fingers interlaced. I'm less concerned with exposing my bobbly nipples and flat chest. After thirty seconds, I can feel the blood struggling to pump beyond my biceps.

Another five or six of these breakneck poses, then Paul asks me to assume a position that I can hold for two minutes. My stomach growls, loudly enough for the class to hear, but everyone is very polite – again, no laughter. I manage to stand but my feet are rooted to the floor, so I face the students straight on, my hands hanging awkwardly by my sides. Strange that such a natural pose feels forced. I curl my fingers into my palms, making two fists, then uncurl them. A sigh from the heavy woman at two o'clock. I try to rid my mind of all thoughts but all I can think is vagina, vagina, vagina. After what seems like an age, the first two minutes are up. I shift to the side and, once again, lift up my arms, knees bent, weight tipped forward but not so much that I fall onto my face. I call this The Diver.

As I move on to the five- and ten-minute poses, I take the time to look around the studio at the characters gathered before me. How strange that each and every one of these human beings is taking two hours out of their Tuesday evening to draw me. Me! To my right are two girls, sitting side by side, who must be in their early twenties, maybe still at university. One, with burnt-orange hair that licks at her freckled cheeks like flames, is squinting at me through a finger-made frame. The other is holding a piece of string up in front of her face, then transferring the measurement to the page. To their left is an older woman who seems to have a more natural approach. Her forearm is rotating around her elbow as she drags a piece of charcoal across the paper in swooping curves (wasn't aware I had any of those). She brushes a loose lock of hair away from her face with her sooty fingers, leaving a black smudge by one of her almost non-existent eyebrows.

'OK, everyone, let's take a ten-minute break.'

Phew. I expect instant chatter, but it's not like school – no springing out of chairs and racing towards the door when the bell goes. Most of the group keep bums on seats for a couple more minutes, tilting their heads and chewing the insides of their cheeks as they examine their quick-fire drawings. I reach for Karina's robe and shroud my body. When I look up again, I'm alone.

I could do with a coffee – more likely they're on tea and biscuits – but I'm not sure I can face small talk with a bunch of people who are familiar with the length and shade of my pubic hair. Instead, I tentatively step down from the stage, still feeling a little shaky, and weave my way between the easels to the sink at the back of the room. I snatch a plastic cup from the stack on the side, twist the tap and feel the cold water rise up against my clammy palm.

Most of the students have left their belongings by the door but a few handbags are propped up against easels, most gaping open with contents on show for all to see. Brass and silver house keys perch on easel ledges along with charcoal, pencils and rubbers. I tease a stick of gum from a pack – decide to make it two (one for later) – then move my attention to the drawings.

'What do you think?'

I jump, almost trampling on someone's sketches; most of the group have laid out their 'gestures' in piles on the floor. Paul's approaching me with what looks like a cup of very weak tea.

'Thanks,' I say as he hands over the mug, which is only about half full, as if he doesn't trust me not to spill it. Or maybe he doesn't want me taking on too much liquid in case I look bloated or, worse, need a wee. 'Haven't looked yet.'

'Well, enjoy,' he says, strangely sincere. 'We'll be back in a few minutes.'

I wait until he's left the room, then pour the tepid tea down the drain. Back to the drawings. The last pose I struck remains on most easels and it's not the most flattering. My back was beginning to ache from all the standing so by this point I was sitting down again on the chair, legs slightly spread, elbows on knees, head supported by my knuckles. The effect, apparently, is that my stomach rolls and my tits, small though they are, start to sag like an old lady's.

I flick through the sheets of paper nearest to me. I see myself in some of the drawings – wispy hair, scrawny elbows, lumpy spine, oddly strong hips, what Dad used to call my 'piano-player fingers' – but none of them feature my face. One student reckons my thighs are narrower than my calves. I look old in that one, all skin and bone, the flesh that is there hanging loose. And this person has given me a giant watermelon of a head.

I'm not sure I've got the proportions right on this one, you say, frowning at your drawing of a boy wrestling with an open-beaked duck, goose or swan.

I lean over to get a better look. As I suspected. Grace, it's perfect, I say.

You like to wander among the plaster replicas of Greek and Roman sculptures in the Ashmolean's Cast Gallery, sitting down and sketching when you see something you fancy. Some figures stand upright, hips popped, while others twist and turn like ribbons, lunge like knights, muscles rippling, backs arched.

Mine isn't bad either, I say, wouldn't you agree?

You squint in an effort to make sense of my scribbles.

It's abstract, I say, solemn.

A smile slowly emerges on your face, your irises extra green against the top you're wearing. Of course. It's beautiful.

The door opens. This time, Annie. 'Well done, you're a natural.'

She's making conversation, taking pity on the subject.

'Ah, I'm not sure about that. But thank you.'

'No, really, you are,' she says, bangles jangling as she points out drawings of the poses she thinks worked best. 'Anyway, I wanted to ask just quickly before we start up again, Paul mentioned you might be looking for extra work?'

He did?

'I know this is a bit of a strange request, since we've just met, but my husband's away quite a lot at the moment and I could do with some help with my daughter.'

I'm obviously staring at her blankly because after a few seconds she adds: 'Babysitting, Eve.'

Babysitting? When I was eight, I remember writing a letter to Mary Poppins asking her to come and look after me, as she does Jane and Michael. I tore it up into tiny pieces and tossed them into the bathroom bin because we didn't have a fireplace. The message must have got lost in transit. Or maybe it was never sent due to the lack of heat.

'Look, no pressure, and you don't have to give me an answer right away. I just thought I would ask on the off-chance.'

'I don't have any experience with children.'

She throws her head back, laughs, pats me on the back. 'Neither did I. She's an easy kid, you would be fine.'

I would? How can she be so sure?

The door opens again and the students file back in.

'Look, just think about it,' she says, reiterating that there's no pressure.

I return to the stage, curious, the soles of my feet blackened by the dusty layer of charcoal covering the studio floor.

We're missing someone.

'She's just nipped to the loo,' a gravelly voice informs Paul upon questioning.

See, he's thinking, that's the problem with giving these people tea, especially the doddery ones.

'OK, well, let's get into position and she can catch up. Eve, this pose is going to last for forty-five minutes so I suggest you adopt something fairly straightforward. Perhaps lying down, facing the group?'

I glance at the wooden planks.

'You can use the blanket,' he adds, gesturing towards the screen.

They lie you flat on the floor – no, they must put a blanket down first, or a stretcher. Yes, a stretcher.

Wait, can I go with her? She needs someone. She needs me.

Are you family?

No, but –

Sorry, miss.

They strap you in, though you aren't moving.

Please.

The rolling of wheels.

Please.

'Everything OK, Eve?'

'Yes, fine, sorry.' I remove the robe, this time slinging it over the screen in exchange for the floral blanket, which I straighten out on the floor, doubled over for extra padding. I lie on my right-hand side, propped up on my elbow, head heavy in my hand. My left arm flails around for a few seconds, like a butterfly that doesn't know where to land, except less elegant. Maybe a moth. I settle for my thigh and bend my legs.

'That's great, Eve.' Paul nods, eyes flickering from my face to my toes and back again. 'OK, everyone, when you're ready.'

Once again, silence is replaced with scratching – though this time it sounds harsher, sharper, because most students have chosen to work with a pencil rather than charcoal. Eyes squint, eyebrows furrow, teeth jab into lower lips like forks into fatty meat. I'm at their mercy for the next three-quarters of an hour. I watch them tearing apart my limbs and reimagining the arrangement of my bones and muscles.

Annie's sitting towards the rear of the room, her honey-blonde hair now scraped back off her face. We lock eyes and she smiles, a kind smile, apologetic almost: I'm sorry I'm staring at you while you're not wearing any clothes. I smile back: go ahead, get an eyeful.

'That's ten minutes down, everyone.'

Oh good, only another thirty-five to go. I'm already losing feeling in my right arm and my right nostril tickles.

I try to distract myself by looking around the room again. Paul's still lingering in the back corner, watching me, super-vising. He's wearing a lurid purple jumper, paired with faded black jeans and those boots with the thick soles. He's holding one arm across his chest and another upright, his hand in front of his mouth. As my eyes move upwards, I see that he's staring right back at me. I wobble.

'Pick a point on the wall opposite and stare at it, Eve, hard.'

I do as he says, honing my attention. By the time the class is over, I have the kitchen section of the studio burnt on my brain.

Six

I had my non-date with Max last night. I felt weirdly nervous beforehand – that kiss had thrown me, let my imagination run riot, picturing us together doing things we shouldn't. I brushed my teeth before I left the flat. Dipped into Karina's make-up bag for lip gloss. Lip gloss! Walked more quickly than normal. As soon as I saw him I relaxed, at least as much as I ever do around him. There's always been a tingly undercurrent.

We had a couple of drinks at one of the more casual bars by the river – him beer, me gin and tonic (extra lime, always) – and chatted about our weeks. A half-dozen men and women were slouched on black leather sofas at the back, focused on one lady, all dolled up in a red dress. Presumably it was her birthday: she was tearing at striped wrapping paper and had a small pile of unopened presents beside her.

'Do you remember what I gave you for your fifteenth?' asked Max, the corners of his lips curling upwards.

'Oh, isn't that lovely, thank you!' the birthday girl crowed, tossing her new scarf around her neck as she leaned across to plant a kiss on the cheek of the man opposite.

'How could I forget?' I said, taking a sip of my drink, glancing at Max with a grin. 'Did you really think I was capable of looking after a live animal?'

'Hey, the guy at Pets at Home told me hamsters were easy,' he said, hands up in defence. 'Parents give them to little kids. Like Tamagotchis.'

'Well, they should come with a warning: may have stroke, slump around for three days, then die.'

'Rest in peace, Nugget.'

We clinked glasses.

'So, heavy night?' I fished one wedge of lime from my glass and squeezed it into the clear liquid.

He tilted his head questioningly.

'The tinge of red in your eyes.'

'You know me too well,' he said, blinking. 'A friend's birthday dinner at a BYO Thai restaurant.' Apparently bowl-fuls of noodles were followed by drinking into the early hours.

'A-ha, so that explains it.' I licked my limey fingers.

'Busted.' As he said it, he pressed his wrists together and held them out to be cuffed. 'Anyway, what about you?'

'Did I have a heavy night?'

He laughed. 'That too, but more importantly, how are things going? Have you decided what you're going to do alongside the bar work?'

I opened my mouth to tell him about the life-modelling, then closed it again, glancing towards the group on the sofas, joking and jeering. I couldn't decide if he'd laugh some more and shake his head – surprised but unbothered – or look away like he had the sun in his eyes, blindsided.

'Sorry, I didn't mean to put pressure on you,' he said, nudging my arm with his. 'You'll find something.'

'Course, I'm not worried.' I dispensed with my straw and gulped some gin and tonic. 'But thanks for caring.'

We locked eyes for what felt like a few seconds longer than usual.

At some point he took a swig of beer.

'So, anything I need to know before I start?'

Over another drink he talked me through the staff – mostly part-timers like me.

'Nina's hot,' I offered.

'I guess.'

The lady in red was still opening presents. I tried to remember the last time I had a birthday party.

At about ten o'clock, Max stifled a yawn.

'We should head home.'

'We should,' he said, drawing his arms overhead and stretching them left and right. 'I'll walk you.'

'That's OK, I know the way.'

He laughed even though I hadn't meant it as a joke.

We both flinched when his upper back cracked between his shoulder blades.

When I started strolling he fell into step beside me, wheeling his bike along the pavement, helmet hooked onto the handlebars, chatting about a mutual friend from school who I no longer see. I haven't kept up with anyone from Oxford: some stuck around to do more studying; others leap-frogged into specialist positions in the art world; all were insanely privileged with heaps of high-flying contacts. They were appalled by my willingness to throw it all away. My connections, despite all the promises, were non-existent.

But there's a light sprinkling of our school lot in London. It's not a long list and Max is the only one I'm close with. In fact, I haven't seen Rishi for a few months, partly because he works nights in A&E. The same with Em. She got married at twenty-three to a high-earning, privately educated friend of her older brother, who enjoys things like shooting and fishing (deep-pocketed parents who live in the country). Giulia is God knows where – Vienna, Budapest or maybe Berlin, last I heard. A whistle-stop tour of Europe, temping and partying.

'Anyway, let's hope she doesn't get arrested at airport security this time,' Max said, laughing.

By the time we reached the flat I sort of wished we'd walked more slowly. Out of nowhere, and uncontrollably, I began to bombard him with questions about cycling etiquette.

He humoured me, gave highly detailed answers. When I'd obviously run out of material, he smiled and said, 'OK then, night, Eve.'

While I contemplated what to do next, he kissed me on the cheek. When he pulled away I had to stop myself – physically, holding tight onto the door frame – from leaning in to kiss him again, harder, and pulling him inside with me. He isn't like the others. It's Max. And honestly, what would happen if I screwed this up? I have to squash these urges like bugs with my bare hands. When I closed the door, though, I realised that same wide smile had stretched itself across my face again and I had to make a conscious effort to compose myself before I bumped into Karina.

She was up and wanted to hear all my 'news'. I told her about one of my jobs – not the naked modelling – and she said she was happy for me and proud of the way I've turned things around so quickly since that 'unfortunate incident' at the restaurant. Thirty seconds later she asked what other job

I intended to get, told me three evenings a week doing bar work clearly won't cut it. (She and Bill may be kind but they're not a registered charity and I'm not up for extra cleaning – or anything else for that matter.) I know, I said, I'm on it, and swiftly changed the subject: tell me more about Margate. She said it was fun, except for the fact that it rained non-stop and *Bill* – said with force – forgot to pack their waterproofs.

The good thing about working in a bar is that you pretty much have the day to yourself. Although Max mentioned he sometimes has to head in early to help with deliveries, my shifts don't start until four o'clock.

I contemplate lying in a while longer but decide against it. I finally washed my only set of sheets and have yet to put them back on (bed-making's never a one-woman job). My naked duvet's scratchy, my bare pillows bobbled with age. I slide out of bed, pull on a slouchy jumper and a woolly pair of socks, and draw back my flesh-coloured curtains; there's too much material so they're replete with rolls. A flabby stomach on its side. A Jenny Saville painting, mighty, meaty and flawed. I smile at the neighbour's tabby cat, splayed out in a patch of sun on the pavement, and wander into the kitchen to make coffee. I wonder if Max is up yet.

The ashtray on the counter contains the cold carcasses of three skinny rollies. Karina's long gone. No sign of Bill. I fill the kettle up to the rim – means you're less in danger of swallowing the limescale, which looks like the flakes of dried coconut Karina sometimes lets herself eat.

Their bedroom door is pulled to today. She's the one who closes it (maybe she's onto me) so he must have had an unusually early start. After flicking the switch of the kettle,

I tiptoe across the living room and slowly twist the door handle. A moan. I leap backwards, shaking my hand as if it's been shocked. Latest booby trap: the handle has electric volts running through it. Another moan. Are they really at home having sex mid-morning on a Friday? I'm impressed. Louder and louder until – nothing. Heavy breathing. Bedsprings. Why am I still standing here? Door handle. Oh God. I leap back and pretend to be attending to the large indoor rubber plant just as the door swings open.

'Oh, morning, Eve.' Bill sidles past me and walks to the bathroom wrapped in a towel. Hand full of tissues.

I wave enthusiastically over my shoulder, still fiddling with a leaf.

I guess we know whose porn it is.

The morning's flown by – that's what immersing yourself in a weird and wonderful novel about a teenage girl and a Renaissance painter to forget about your flatmate wanking will do to you – and now I'm running the risk of being late. I'd planned to borrow Karina's hairdryer, perhaps even do something with my hair if I could get to grips with her curling iron, but I'm not ready to return to the crime scene. It'll have to air en route, as usual, lifeless except for the few resident kinks.

I decide to catch the bus.

'Spare some change, please.'

Fred, the homeless man who spends his days trundling between the entrances to Vauxhall tube and train stations, is slumped against the low brick wall that shelters the main flight of steps to the tube. From the chest down, his wiry body is cocooned in a frayed sleeping bag. Reminds me of when I used to squirm into one leg of a pair of tights and hop around the living room pretending to be a kangaroo, peering around to see if Dad had noticed.

'I'll bring you something later, Fred,' I call, continuing towards Albert Embankment. 'Or tomorrow, if I'm too late.'

'Bless you.'

He never remembers my name, but he does remember that, now and then, I buy him a coffee or a packet of chocolate digestives.

I hop on the 344 to Fenchurch Street by the robotic MI6 building – always thought I'd make a good spy – and hurry upstairs, holding onto the rails in case there's a sudden jolt and happily finding three out of four front seats free. This is where I like to sit, driving the bus, in control. Plus, there's something thrilling about the lurch around corners. Leaning into disaster.

I rest my feet on the curved ledge in front and imagine what would happen if I flexed my toes and kicked at the glass above it with my heels. Surely it's sturdy enough to withstand a swift shock? I glance across at my one neighbour, elasticky strands of cheese clinging between a flaky croissant and his mouth, then crane my neck and see five more faces behind me: three looking down at phones or books, one gazing out of the window, one staring back at me. I slowly slide my feet to the floor, littered with sticky sweet wrappers and a leaky juice carton. Probably best not to test it.

By the time I arrive at the bar Max is polishing shapely wine glasses, holding each one up to the light to check that it's free of rosy lipstick stains and oily fingerprints.

'Eve, welcome,' says Nina, appearing from nowhere.

She's dressed all in black, except for a pair of leopard-print loafers with foamy platforms, and carrying a silver iPad. I look down at my own outfit – white shirt, black jeans, cheap pumps – and feel inadequate. She caresses the screen with her right index finger, her pupils dilating and contracting as she reads and flicks, reads and flicks. Her elfin ears are studded with three tiny silver hoops on one side, two on the other. Oops, still haven't said anything.

'Nina, hi, thank you, happy to be here.' I'm not sure why I sound so serious. 'How are you? Did you have a good week?'

She raises her eyes to mine without moving her head and then looks back down at the screen, pale eyelids fringed with those thick black lashes. Her eyeliner is perfectly streamlined. Ticking up at the outer corners of her eye, making her look feline.

I'm about to excuse myself and retreat to the loo when she says, 'So, Eve, you'll be manning the bar with Max this evening.'

I wonder if this counts as a second non-date.

'Is something wrong?'

Did my face change? Maybe I wouldn't have made a good spy after all. 'No, no, all good. Great, even!' I just gave my new and very cool boss a thumbs-up.

'Great.'

A pause, which I fail to fill. I glance at Max, who can hardly contain himself.

'Well, you know where the bar is,' she says, statement rather than question.

'Yes! Lovely.'

Five minutes into my first shift and she already thinks I'm crazy.

*

'Three vodka tonics – one with fresh lemon, one with fresh lime, one with lime cordial, all slimline – and a white wine spritzer, please. Oh, and do you have any of those salted pistachios?'

The main difference between here and the restaurant: the women. Lunches are dominated by suited men, schmoozing clients and expensing fancy three-course meals and big-dick bottles of Dom. Then again, I'm not sure female suits would be much better, with their silky locks, fake nails and meticulous make-up. I've never been a girly girl. I've also never been good at dealing with difficult customers. Visible twitches of impatience from a too-tanned blonde at twelve o'clock.

'Right, yes. Let me check.'

Sigh. Hair flick. Cherry-red claws drum clutch bag.

'Max?' I call.

He's down the other end of the bar serving a couple of debonair banker types, but somehow manages to hear me above the jazzy music and jabbering crowd. It's like we're on a slightly different plane to everyone else. We can hear each other even when we can't hear orders. I *think* this might be a parallel dimension.

'Salted pistachios live beside the olives.'

See? I test it by lowering my voice to a whisper: 'And the olives?'

'By the rums.'

Ha!

'Max, darling, I didn't see you over there.'

Suddenly the impatient blonde is more animated. She's stretching an arm down the bar towards Max, making eyes at him.

87

My insides do something strange, constricting like a vice.

'Rachel,' he says, giving her an awkward nod.

I raise my eyebrows – part surprised, part amused – as his eyes flicker towards mine and then shift back to his orders.

'Excuse me?'

I'm starting to feel dizzy. 'Yes?'

'You're just standing there. Pistachios. Plus, one vodka tonic with—'

'Got it.' I slide the glass jar off the shelf and decant a smattering of the salty, shell-on nuts into a small ceramic bowl. Next: three vodka tonics. I hesitate as I try to remember what she said about the garnishes. I hope when I ask for extra lime with my gin it's not this annoying. I know she said slimline so let's start with that. I measure out the shots of vodka, tumble in a ton of ice and top up the tall glasses with individual bottles of tonic.

'Remind me: one with fresh lemon—'

'For goodness' sake. One with fresh lemon, one with fresh lime and one with lime cordial. And don't forget the spritzer. You do know how to make one of those, don't you?'

There you have it. Just as patronising as the men.

I anxiously glance left and right, feigning panic, then look her in the eye. 'I'll give it a try.'

Max was kind to me tonight. I admitted my inability to pull a good pint before the shift began; he told me not to worry and that he'd take care of it – and he did. He talked me through the difference between the various gins, vodkas, rums and whiskies and showed me which brand of each spirit to choose when a buyer doesn't specify (neither the most expensive nor the cheapest). I listened intently and nodded along, even though I knew most of what he was telling me already. I didn't come close to mixing a cocktail – one thing he does very well, shaking it over his broad shoulders as groups of women watch with delight, nudging each other. All in good time. For now, I'm just glad to have made it through the night.

'Which way are you heading, Eve?' He's dimmed the lights and is zipping up his parka behind me.

It's late, I should probably hop on a bus. But then I think of the bridge, extra striking in the moonlight. 'I think I'm going to walk to Waterloo.'

'Mind if I join you?'

Max lives in Kilburn, and has his bike, so this makes zero sense. Still. 'Course not. You ready?'

As predicted, the bridge is a beauty, a solid stone walkway rising above the slow liquid of the river below. It's quiet. There's no traffic except for the odd red bus and black cab effortlessly gliding past us like the boats on the water. A couple are standing in the middle of the bridge, staring towards Vauxhall and beyond, past the regal Houses of Parliament on one side, and on the other the glittering Southbank. From where we are I've got a good view of Somerset House. I wonder what being in the gallery, alone and in the dark, would be like at this hour. I think of Suzon, staring out across an empty room, shadows and silence. Does she mind?

As we walk across the Parks sharing a Fanta, ignoring giant rugby players in weensy shorts, I ask when you're heading home for Easter. I try to keep my tone steady – flat, even. I take a gulp and pass you the bottle, slightly sticky.

When we're heading home, you mean. You take a significantly more ladylike sip, hand the bottle straight back. Mum and Dad are expecting us this weekend.

I wrap my arms around your waist and interlace my fingers. You laugh.

I cling on and we keep walking, even though our collective walk resembles a camel's.

You know, I say, trying to keep a hold, you don't always have to invite me.

Well, that's lucky, because I'm not inviting you. An invitation would imply it wasn't mandatory.

I squeeze tighter around your tummy.

He doesn't give me much warning. We're taking in the city-scape, the multicoloured lights flashing in the dark, his arm hanging by his side, just brushing against mine. He says my name, I look up and he kisses me, full of confidence but not in a desperate lurch sort of way – softer, somehow. His lips move against mine and a ripple of anxiety courses through me, telling me it's a mistake – a misadventure – and that I should pull away. Max and I are friends. I ignore it. His lips linger for long enough that I know it isn't an impulsive accident. He means it.

Somehow, though I hadn't seen it coming, I manage not to screw it up by biting down or clashing teeth or toppling straight over the bridge into the Thames. It helps that Max has wrapped his arms around me like a lifejacket.

Seven

My Wednesdays usually arrive like slow trains, chugging into the week at a sluggish pace after pausing for too long at too many stations. Not this time. All of a sudden it's an express, careering across the British countryside and stopping for nothing, no one. Passengers sound the alarm, rabbits with twitching noses and wild eyes leap to the safety of the nearest ditch. The driver's powerless: the train is steering itself. I sit up in bed, fiddling with a lighter I borrowed from the bar. I hover my little finger above the tip of the licking flame, the pad turning black with soot. Today is Grace's birthday. Yes, I told her mum, I know. I remember.

I remember the first time I saw her. She'd wedged open the door to her room while she was unpacking – something her mum had advised her to do as a way to make friends. She'd also advised her to go out and buy some snacks to share around. When I'd left London, Dad had given me a box of his favourite cider – cheap to buy, quick to get you wasted.

Do you want some blueberries? you ask as I wave awkwardly (elbow stuck to my waist) on my way to our shared bathroom.

You're kneeling on your chair, your skinny legs folded in two, arranging some books alphabetically on the narrow shelf above your desk. As you reach up, I catch a glimpse of parchment-white skin above your jeans. Your hair is long, the tips down by your waist. You wear it loose, tucked behind your ears.

Oh, better not, I say, I'm allergic.

Really? You scramble off the chair and stand, hands dangling by your sides, on the teal rug you've brought from home.

No, not really.

You laugh, wrinkle your nose. That was a weird joke.

It was, sorry. I shake my head. I'm Eve.

Nice to meet you, Eve. You laugh again, offering me the bowl of berries. I'm Grace.

She grew up in a big house with a big garden in the countryside. There were sixteen houses in the village, a pub that served decent tapas and a post office that also sold groceries. The Internet was iffy. She woke up to the sound of grumbling tractors in the next-door field and, on the road, clip-clopping horses. I thought about our flat on a busy road in Finsbury Park and decided it sounded idyllic.

The flat had become more and more ragged since Mum left, but I didn't recognise quite how bad it was until I came back from my first term at university: worn floral carpets, flowers rotten; peeling paint exposing the nakedness of walls; tired curtains, yellowing at the edges; damp prowling across the bathroom ceiling, black and menacing. I suggested we change things up, start again. Dad refused, his voice breaking slightly as he mumbled something about Mum having done the decoration.

Grace's parents had been married for twenty-four years by the time she started university. William was a deputy head at the private school she and her brother attended and Lucy was a special educational needs coordinator. They did look older, when I bumped into them in the restaurant. Softer too, their hard edges worn away. Maybe that's what grief does to a parent.

Grace told me they quarrelled, mainly about her or her brother – he was a few years older, worked on a local farm, married a local girl. He and Grace weren't very close; they didn't have much in common. When she was at Oxford, the family member she missed most was her dog, Mackerel.

We had nothing in common either, at least on paper, but Grace was my best friend from the beginning. She could work for seven hours straight, but she also loved to dance, to sing along to cheesy songs (even if she didn't know the words and needed some persuading at first), to drink rum and Coke from plastic cups on my bedroom floor. To hunt for salty chips and ketchup on the way home from a night out and, the next morning, climb hung-over into my bed and watch David Attenborough, our pounding headaches soothed by his grandfatherly voice. To bag free passes to stupidly expensive exercise classes – but you *look* like a ballerina, one teacher told her as she flailed about. To distract me after a crappy visit with my dad or save me from having to visit him altogether. To make me laugh when the happy ending of a film made me cry.

In our final year, everything changed. I flick the lighter, once, twice.

I close my eyes and make a wish as I blow out the little flame, the same wish I make on this day every year. I'll never forget her. How could I? I see her face everywhere, hear her voice whispering in my ear. She's a part of me. We're not done. Happy Birthday, Grace.

*

'Eve, I haven't seen you to congratulate you on your new job – your new jobs!' calls Bill, jumping up from the kitchen table and striding across the room, arms outstretched.

Yes, I'm in my towel, so old and rigid it feels more like a carpet, halfway between the bathroom and the haven of my bedroom.

'Thanks, Bill,' I say, holding the towel firmly in place as he wraps me in an awkward hug. I'm pleased we've silently agreed to pretend our drunken kiss didn't happen, but I'm not quite ready to resume our usual camaraderie.

'Very brave, if you ask me, standing up there in front of all those people.'

'I think they're the brave ones,' I say. 'I wouldn't want to draw me naked.'

He nods and smiles absently, saying nothing. Grabs his left elbow with his right hand, as if his left hand might reach out instinctively and yank at the towel.

No, that's not fair; he's all right. No more at fault for what happened than me. 'So, Bill, you're working from home today?'

He glances at his watch. 'No, actually, must be off. Can't keep those clients waiting.' He beetles back to the table and starts straightening out his papers – holding them together and knocking them against the tabletop, portrait, then landscape. He deposits them in his rucksack along with his laptop. One final smile and a head tilt, like he's trying to tip something off his crown. 'Right, see you later!'

I feel a flare of panic as the door closes behind him. It would have been nice to spend today with someone. Anyone.

This is the first time I've entered their bedroom since his morning episode and, thankfully, everything is as it should be. Karina's feather pillow is squashed up against the headboard – the result of her pushing off and away from it as she shuffles downstream in her sleep. Bill's double-height, fibre-filled pile (allergies) is firmly in place, sandwiching what I hope are just snotty tissues. I plump all three and smooth out the duvet before opening the curtains. Like mine, they're a foot too long, with surplus material bunched up at the bottom. I feel a smile tug at the corners of my mouth as I remember the time Grace grew out her fringe.

I told Karina about the life-modelling. I had to: after my second session on Sunday I walked into the flat carrying the cushion from the sofa and was too tired to think of an excuse. (Didn't confess about her dressing gown, screwed up in a ball in my bag, along with an assortment of other people's pencils and charcoal.)

'Wow,' she replied, mouth continuing to open and close, searching for the right words. She did that thing where she says nothing but slowly nods her head and looks up and a little to the left, as if she's picturing what I'm describing (in this case, me naked), talking herself round. After about a minute had passed, she asked me, 'How was it?'

It's exhausting, physically and mentally – no easier the second time than the first. Turns out sitting or standing still for two hours, every so often swinging between positions, is quite taxing. I've already learned that it's best to stick to symmetrical poses because at least they throb equally on both sides. I've also discovered that I shouldn't cock a leg unless required (neither flattering nor comfy) or raise my arms over-head for any length of time. It's true that staring at a spot on

95

the wall helps with balance. But with all those people lined up in front of me, how can I not spend my time watching them? Watching you, watching me. Sadly, what I've gathered from their facial expressions is that the poses they prefer are more distorted, contorted, crunching. They get a kick out of me trying to bend my body in ways it shouldn't, binding and extending my limbs to the point of pain. Animals.

I got my period just before Sunday's class, which made posing interesting. I hoped I could get away with wearing a tampon, even considered asking Annie if she'd ever spotted a little loop of white string dangling down between a model's legs, but I wimped out. Behind the screen, I tucked the string up inside me and prayed I could find it later. When I emerged, no one looked at me any differently, even though I felt bloated. No one pointed or pinched their nose. I chalked that up as a success.

So, aches aside, I enjoy it. It's exhilarating. I feel the thrill of exposure shoot up from my tapping toes (shouldn't do that, got a glare) to my goosebumpy neck. At times I forget I'm naked. I forget I'm posing in front of a room full of people I don't know. It's just me, in a kind of meditative state. That's how yoga should be, I suppose. Utterly still in a pose but with tingling skin, charged like a battery, body hair zinging with electricity.

At the end of both classes, Paul handed me a slim envelope of cash, stuck down with his saliva, and told me I did a good job. As he said it the second time, on Sunday, his hand rested on my shoulder. I might have imagined it, but it felt like he was teasing the silky robe between his fingers.

I hook Karina's bra off the corner of the radiator and free the armchair from the mass of clothes slung on top. I add them to the washing basket and tumble the whole lot into the machine. Spotting a checked shirt that's still folded in the centre of the pile, I pull it out, sleeve first, pre-capsule. A quick sniff confirms it's clean. Bill won't mind, I think, as I shrug it on. And I'll look like one of those girls who wears her boyfriend's jumpers (not just those of her estranged mum). Hey, look: someone loves me.

I'm the other side of Waterloo Bridge before I decide that going to the gallery is a bad idea, even if it is a Wednesday. Actually, my feet decide for me, turning left on the Strand instead of right, moving independently. It's too much today. Too quiet. I need to be somewhere loud, but also dark, surrounded by people without having to make eye contact or conversation. I picture Suzon staring at me, waiting for me to speak. She never makes the first move. No, I'm not going to the gallery today. Today I'm going to the cinema.

London's been transformed overnight into Santa's grotto. Grace hated that her birthday was so close to Christmas: absent friends, combination presents. Twinkling lights are strung across the Strand from building to building, rousing the dull day. I speed up, trying to escape the festive cheer.

Round the bend I feel my feet moving faster still, away from the towering Christmas tree in Trafalgar Square. Strange, Karina and Bill usually have one by now. Making Bill give it a fireman's lift home in a bulging white net is her favourite Christmas ritual. That and the unpacking of ornaments, each mummified in kitchen roll and laid top to toe in shoeboxes. Every year, as a child, I'd ask Dad if we could get a tree. Every year he'd tell me trees live outdoors for a reason.

The only matinee screening is a romcom, no doubt with a soppy storyline and starring Bill Nighy. It doesn't start for another twenty minutes so I linger over the pick 'n' mix. Just looking at the cherry cola bottles makes me salivate. I narrow my eyes sceptically at the foam bananas – enlarged edible maggots – and the foam shrimps, which could just about pass for sexual organs. I try each sweet before I make my selection, shovelling the tangiest into a paper bag.

By the time I reach the counter my tongue tingles, so much so that when the over-eager boy behind the till comments on the Christmas lights, I have trouble replying. I don't quite catch how much I owe for both the ticket and the sweets, so I hand him a crisp twenty-pound note, which Paul must have got hot and fresh from a hole-in-the-wall.

Still going on about lights shaped like snowflakes, the boy hands me a single pound change, and when I laugh, for some reason he does too.

'And the rest?' I ask.

'Um, it came to nineteen pounds.'

'Um, that's extortionate.'

He laughs again.

I stare at him.

I have the cinema pretty much to myself, so I ignore my designated seat number and plonk myself in a leather chair with extra leg room. I'm busy beheading a jelly snake when two middle-aged to elderly women roll down the aisle. What's the word for someone in between? Someone who's older than a parent but younger than a grandparent? Anyway, that.

The adverts are running but the lights aren't down, not fully, so I sneak a look at them: one's clutching two takeaway cups (smells like hot chocolate) and the other is peering at two printed tickets through a great big pair of bug-like glasses. Both are ferrying a decent number of shopping bags.

Despite the acres of free seats, they shuffle this way and stop right beside me. Before they sit down, in unison they flick away popcorn crumbs, somebody else's debris.

'Anyway, where was I?'

The bug-eyed one has taken out her phone and is now reading aloud (annoying) from a scathing review, probably the *Guardian*.

'Like alcohol-free eggnog.'

'Eish, that's not good.'

'A substandard Richard Curtis, who must be wetting himself.'

'Oh, I wish you had read it before we bought our tickets!'

I close my eyes and resist giving them a look. Consider moving but decide against it.

'Like an undercooked Christmas pudding, every scene ends with a squelch.'

Enough. 'Excuse me, do you mind?'

Bug Eyes pauses. They both lean back in their seats, which make a squeak. I must be looking intimidating for once in my life.

'Sorry, dear, didn't mean to disturb,' she says, gently slipping her phone into her pocket.

Do I look like the thieving kind?

'It's fine,' I reply, sensing my cheeks flush. 'I'm just easily distracted.'

'Well, don't worry, you won't hear another peep from us.'

I smile meekly, chastened, and turn back to the screen. Surely at their age they wouldn't be making faces.

As the trailers end and the room dims, I glimpse a phone light out of the corner of my left eye and take a long, deep (and apparently audible) breath.

'Sorry, dear, just switching it off!'

Rustle rustle.

'Care for a Softmint?'

Whoever wrote that review was right, even if it was an old curmudgeon. The film was a mess. The dialogue giggly, the backdrop sickeningly sparkly. Still, the credits are running and I'm in tears, my eyes watering like I'm walking headlong into the wind.

'Is everything all right, dear?'

I jump, forgetting I have company. Slowly, I crane my neck and find my two neighbours observing me. 'Everything's fine,' I say, though apparently unconvincingly, because as I stand up and shimmy over to the aisle, they shimmy after me.

'Are you sure? Such a pretty girl like you, here by yourself.'

'I'm fine, really.' At this point, I'm not sure why I don't just walk away.

They glance awkwardly at one another before coming to some silent agreement. Nodding in unison like it settles the matter, they invite me to join them for a drink. 'Come on, we won't take no for an answer. It's nearly Christmas!' With that, they each take one of my arms and march me to a bar off Leicester Square.

I've been listening to them talking for more than an hour, drinking fruity cocktails they chose. I know all about Catherine's telecoms engineer husband, who's got a dodgy heart, and Jan's bunions. Eventually, and with caution, they steer the conversation back to me. 'What about you, dear?'

All I can say is: 'It's my best friend's birthday.'

'Oh, lovely, what are you doing to celebrate?'

This time when my eyes fill there's no stopping the tears. They try to comfort me and, when that doesn't work, they order me a second drink. Jan starts to chew her lip. Catherine asks if there's someone she can call.

'Is there someone you can go and see?'

'It's too late,' I say. 'It's too late for me to see her now.'

Silence, except for straws slurping fruity dregs.

Jan looks at her watch.

'Shall we have another?' I ask, sitting up straight, forcing a smile.

Their eyes ping-pong between each other and me.

'I'm sorry, dear, we have to catch our train,' says Jan. 'You're sure there isn't anything we can do?'

I shake my head, try to keep my lips curled.

They pay, make their apologies again and give me one more anxious glance before walking out the door.

I retrace my steps back along the Strand, kidding myself that it might not be too late after all, but when I reach the gallery the automatic glass doors don't budge. By the time I'm on Waterloo Bridge I can't bear it. I can't bear to be alone. I flick through my contacts, trying to stop myself occasionally picturing a truck swerving through the stone barriers and mowing me down. Max. I call him and he picks up after the fifth ring, just before I hang up.

'Hey you, what's up?'

I can hear thumping music in the background, and he sounds out of breath, as if he's been running. At the gym maybe.

'Hi,' I say, leaning my elbows on the stone wall and looking down at the river. The water must be freezing. I imagine plunging into its depths, my body hair standing on end in an attempt to keep me warm. Bubbles rising to the surface as I sink, the final dregs of oxygen seeping out of my nostrils. I press harder against the stone.

'Is everything OK, Eve?'

'Kind of.'

'What is it?'

'It's Grace's birthday.' A big dove-white boat appears from beneath the bridge, its interior illuminated with bright bulbs and peopled with dolled-up men and women sitting at a dozen round tables. I can see a band setting up in one corner – drums, amplifiers, a couple of guitars – and an open space in front of them. The dance floor. 'Are you there?' I ask, gripping onto the stone with my free hand. He knows what Grace meant to me then, what she means to me today. It complicates things.

'I'm here. Where are you?'

'Waterloo Bridge.'

'OK, what are you doing?'

'Coming to see you?'

Silence, except for the background beat.

'Max?'

'Sorry, I was just checking the route.'

I loosen my grip.

'Meet you at that spot by the river?'

'I'll be there in ten,' I say, standing up straight and continuing on my way. I glance back at the boat, now a dwindling white speck.

*

We sit by the water for I don't know how long, watching the lights in various apartment blocks flick on and off in the dark. It would be pitch-black if it weren't for those, and the street lamps and headlights, and faint yellow stars. It's chilly at first and I feel the tips of my fingers going numb. When he sees how white they're turning he gives me his too-big gloves. He looks away and I give them a sniff. The essence of Max?

He asks me how I'm feeling and I tell him the truth: I'm fine, though maybe my version of fine isn't always the same as other people's. Especially not today.

'Are you seeing someone?' he asks.

'Bit forward,' I smile, watching the seagulls patrolling the shadowy water for their fishy dinner and wondering what they're doing so far from the coast.

'Ha, you know what I mean. Are you talking to someone?'

I do. 'I am,' I say, thinking of her standing behind the bar, staring back at me. Always listening. 'I have been for a while. Once a week.'

'And it's helping?' I can almost hear the thoughts whizzing through his mind, thoughts about how I'm getting my shit together, turning that proverbial corner.

'It's helping,' I say, drawing with a gloved finger my own invisible landscape on the bench. It really is. 'Though today's never easy.' Sun, sand, sea. 'And I bumped into her parents last month.'

'That must have been difficult.'

'They witnessed my last hurrah at the restaurant.'

He smiles and I add a hammock strung up between two palm trees. A bunch of coconuts.

'You never did tell me what happened there.'

'It was a bit dramatic. I may have slapped someone.'

Max guffaws and I add a stick figure on a surfboard.

'You know,' he says, sounding more serious, 'it will get better. Easier, at least.'

I pop some fins in the sea, then he takes hold of my hands. I look up, and he leans in slowly to kiss me.

Eight

Karina and Bill are going away for Christmas – that's why we don't have a tree. She claims that they told me weeks ago, but I have no memory of it. They're visiting her mum and stepdad in snowy Norway. What am I supposed to do now? I asked them, my cheeks reddening. We never said we'd be hanging out together. They suggested I spend the day with my dad, that it's been long enough, it's time to reach out. I can't, I told them, I can't spend another Christmas Day cleaning up after him in that flat. Stroking his thinning hair as he folds forward over the loo. Patting his sweaty back. Telling him everything will be OK. Too many times to count.

I take a deep, unsteady breath. He knows to call me when he's ready to get sober.

My phone buzzes on the kitchen table and I almost knock over my cup of coffee. The screen is face down, so I can't see who or what it is, but I know Dad wouldn't text. I take a sip and chase it with a spoon of Bran Flakes. The cellophane wrapper inside the cardboard box was almost empty so it's mostly bitty pieces and powder.

Karina says I've lost weight. I say she's projecting. It's always the same with girls like her. She'd probably call herself a woman – she is thirty-four – but still. She took me to a restaurant opening once, the soft launch of a bright and shiny space – Asian fusion, I think it was – on a quiet street in west London. They brought hand-thrown plate after plate for us to try. She had a mouthful of each, thirty-four chews per mouthful, before neatly lining up her knife and fork and clutching her hands in her lap. This is how it's done, Eve, she told me, when I asked whether she was embarrassed to let so much go to waste. She compared herself to a connoisseur who rarely swallows when tasting wine but told me I needn't worry – I was here to have fun so I should eat as much as I want. I did, mainly to try to calm the fretty waitress hovering beside us. I ate as much as I could and, between bites, I mopped up both my own wine and Karina's. When we got home, I locked myself in the bathroom and was violently sick.

Another buzz from my phone. This time I turn it over. Max. We've been talking every day this week, Grace's birthday week. I unlock the screen. *Knock knock.*

A joke. Unless, wait, is he outside? Presumably not. Still, I stop chewing and listen out for the tinkle of his bicycle bell. He's probably just trying to make me laugh. Or flirting. I smile and spoon some more sandy powder into my mouth, tapping out a reply as I start chewing again, the grains lodging themselves in the cracks between my teeth. *who's there?*

No reply. I give it a few minutes, then a few more, until I've finished my breakfast. Nothing. I wonder if he's trying some sort of bad advice column tactic to get my attention.

I flip my phone over, and then over again to double-check I have signal.

I guess it's working.

I arrive at the studio with five minutes to spare. By the time I'm scrambling out of my clothes, the room's three-quarters full.

'Eve?'

I jump as Paul pokes his head around the screen. It's now normal for him to see me naked onstage – I've taken to omitting the 'the', like I'm an actress in a Broadway show – but somehow him catching me undressing, before the action begins, feels uninvited. 'Yes?' With not enough time to find the arms, I wrap Karina's robe around my body as I would a towel, then bend forward to remove one sock and then the other. Of course I left those until last. Like a bad sex scene.

'Just to let you know it's an Open Studio day, meaning we welcome in the public – and hopefully prospective students – so they can get a feel for what we do.'

Wonderful, so perverts who have no interest in art are going to be wandering in off the street and gawking at me starkers.

'Are you OK with that?' he asks, taking one, two steps towards me so that his body is almost concealed behind the screen too.

Two floating heads in conversation. Talking Heads. Dad used to play the CD into the early hours on a school night. *Don't you want to make him stay up late.*

'You know, if there's ever anything you're not comfortable with, I want you to say.'

It's not clear if he's being genuine, but his proximity and lowered voice make my downy hairs stand on end – I can't tell whether it's in a good or bad way. I root myself to the spot, worried I'll waver if I move, trying to figure out if I'm nervous or turned on or both.

'I'm comfortable with everything,' I tell him, holding his gaze.

He nudges his glasses up his nose. 'Well, Eve, that's good to know.' Eyes on mine, always.

What's not good is the number of people filing in and out of the door at the back of the room as I try to conjure and keep hold of two-minute-long dynamic poses. Every time I begin staring at a spot on the wall, it's blocked by another intruder, most of whom just appear to be here for the peep show. Paul's standing by the door, ready to answer any questions and filter out any blatant frauds. A trio of red-faced schoolboys come trundling up to the threshold in their fancy private-school uniforms, hamster cheeks stowing laughter, ready to burst. Paul takes one look at them and sends them back down the stairs.

Without his regular reminders, I'm also having to keep an eye on the time, which means that no matter the position, my field of vision has to include the clock. I glance at its hands. Six, five, four, three, two, one. I stand square on, then bring my right knee up to my chest as if I'm stretching out my quads before a jog. I cling onto my knee with both hands and try to stop myself from wobbling (and thinking about the show down below). My left foot is faltering, back to front, side to side, my toes clawing at the wooden floorboards for a grip that doesn't exist. I glance at the clock – another minute and fifteen. I could swear the long red hand is out to get me. As my eyes move, I feel my body following suit and hop to the left. *Tsk.* A tut from the woman closest – mouth open, lips slack. Either truly artistic or trying way too hard: a pencil stabbed through her wiry hair, pinning it back.

You know, you say, this might be my favourite bookshop ever.
  I know, I smile. Mine too.
  At the top of the stairs, two girls with frowning faces and French haircuts are auditioning books to be their latest accessories. Ulysses, Infinite Jest, The Second Sex.
  We pause in front of a table of new hardbacks and wait for one of them to mention Hannah Arendt.
  When it comes on cue the other asks, Hannah who?
  Um, are you joking? She's iconic.
  Of course . . .
  We start to laugh and they shoot us deathly looks.

Finally. Three, two, one. I turn to face the window and – one arm up, one arm down, both bent at the elbow – reach my fingertips together across the length of my back. An escape, or at least a distraction, by way of my bum, for them. I look out over the tiled rooftops, puffing chimneys, circular dishes and spiky aerials. The sky looks extra blue against South Kensington's red-brick buildings and there are zero clouds today – a snapshot of summer midwinter, as long as you're snug inside, away from the chill. Thankfully we're sufficiently high up for my full-frontal display to go unnoticed by the outside world, save for a leery sparrow on the windowsill.

My eyes readjust like a clever camera lens, retracting to focus on the studio's interior. I zoom in on the windowpane, just a metre away from the tip of my nose. It must be cleaned on a regular basis – no blurry marks on the glass – but there's a spider's web outside. I trace the lacework, dewy in places with droplets of water, trying to locate its maker. No sign, though I'm sure she'll be back in time for dinner. Stuck to one silken thread is a swollen fly.

'OK, everyone, let's take a break.'

What?

'Eve, all OK?'

I whip around and look at the clock: ten forty-five. We're not supposed to take a break for another fifteen minutes. I have no idea how long I've been staring out of the window. I'm not sure what we're even on – thirty seconds, two minutes or ten minutes. 'Yes, all fine,' I say, snapping my hands together, trying to regain my composure. 'Sorry.'

Paul apologises too, though to the students and by way of a scrunched-eyes smile. He may as well be raising his hands in the air, palms upwards: What can I say? She's new! I'm pretty sure he's mouthing something about an extra fifteen minutes the other side. You'll get your money's worth, folks. So that means I have to keep still for an entire hour.

This used to happen at school. A history teacher moved me away from a street-facing window because I found watching couples arguing about how best to navigate a parallel parking space more entertaining than the black-and-white videos beamed onto the whiteboard. His beady eyes would lock with mine from behind his glasses, the lenses thick and smeary.

'Eve?'

'Yes?' I'm still naked onstage and he's standing right in front of me, offstage, his height matching mine. There go my pelvic-floor muscles. I cross my arms in front of my nipples, suddenly stiff, stabbing at him, and consider reaching for the blanket.

'I asked if you want some tea?' He smiles, tilting his head slightly.

'I don't like milk.'

'OK then, tea, no milk,' he says, turning and heading for the door.

'I prefer coffee.'

'Coffee it is,' he says, pausing. 'Oh, that's it for the Open Studios. You can relax now.'

'I'm relaxed,' I say, bending one knee and awkwardly holding my hands together in front of my pubic hair.

He laughs, nods his head and steps out into the hall.

I really am relaxed up here, at least most of the time. I feel alive, my skin magnetic, but it's mainly quite a pleasant sensation. I don't mind Paul's eyes on me, intent and difficult to read, from the back of the room. Even so, I throw on Karina's robe before I hop down off the stage. She asked if I'd seen it the other night but has since either forgotten or given up.

On the easel directly in front of me is a charcoal drawing of my last position – hands reaching for one another vertically across my back. I don't know how long I held it, but it must have been at least ten minutes for the level of detail here, the contouring and shading. My profile just on show as I turn my head, chin slanted upwards, raised in defiance. Loose strands of hair running like salty beads of sweat down my upper back. Shoulder muscles straining, winged blades at oblique angles. A dark channel along the length of my spine, down to the curves of my bum, not especially round. Arms moving in ways they shouldn't, on the brink of dislocation, knuckles highlighted white, fingers clinging to stay connected.

'Oh, I'm sorry, Eve, I'm no good at backs.'

'What?'

Annie.

'It must be funny, seeing yourself on the page.'

'Yeah, I suppose it is.'

She smiles politely.

'I think you're good at backs,' I add, stepping beside her so we're observing her drawing together. 'I mean, I don't often see mine so I can't tell whether you've captured the likeness, but you've definitely got the light and dark down.'

She laughs, absent-mindedly starts twirling her wedding ring round on her charcoal-smudged finger. 'Hey, I was wondering. I'm picking Molly up from ballet after this, just down the road, and I wondered if you might like to meet her?'

Because?

'If you're still considering babysitting, that is?'

Babysitting, I'd forgotten. I'm not sure I'm up to it, to be honest, on top of life-modelling and the bar work.

She looks at me hopefully, still smiling but nibbling her lip.

'OK. Yes, great.'

'Oh good, I'll meet you outside after class.'

The door flings open and Paul's leather boots clank across the wooden floorboards. The toes look a tad too polished. 'Eve, I almost forgot that tea of yours.'

I know I said coffee.

'Here you are,' he says, smiling and giving himself a mental pat on the back as he adds: 'No milk.'

'Thanks.' I take the hot china mug and quickly rotate it around in my fingers so I can hold it by the handle.

'How are you, Annie?' he asks, raising his hand to her shoulder.

Maybe he's like it with everyone. I don't know if that makes it better or worse.

'Very well, thanks, Paul. Just apologising to Eve about my poor draughtsmanship when it comes to backs.'

Your poor draughts*woman*ship.

'Not at all, it's wonderful,' he tells her, looking at me.

After the second half of the class and, to make up for lost time, a bonus round verbally dissecting their drawings and my body, we're released. Annie's waiting on the pavement by the time I'm down the stairs, gazing at an amorous couple hailing a taxi, between kisses, across the street. She turns towards me as the door clicks to. 'Quick glass of wine before we pick Molly up?'

I hesitate, staring at her, so composed and flawless, trying to work out what she sees when she looks at me.

'Unless you have plans, of course,' she says. 'I'm sorry, I should have asked before. I'm sure you do.'

'No, that's OK. I'd love to.'

'Great.' She says she knows a nice wine bar nearby and promptly heads off in that direction.

I'm about to ask her if she lives in the area – she seems to know her way around – when she receives a phone call. She picks up and starts talking at high-speed, the phone lodged between her ear and shoulder as she holds her handbag in one hand and her sketchbook in the other.

'There should be fourteen round tables, each with ten chairs, plus the head table with space for nine: the groom's grand-mother finally gave up the ghost last week. Eight vegetarians, two vegans, one nut allergy (peanuts, pistachios and cashews are deadly; the rest are fine), plus one gluten-free. OK?'

OK.

'Quickly, Jade, find a pen.'

Oh dear, clearly Jade didn't quite catch that.

I follow as she turns off the high street. It's getting a little greener. The trees are either completely bare or covered in dried leaves that have shrivelled and turned a deep red-brown, but every other block here has its own neatly manicured communal garden lined with freshly painted black railings. In one garden, a man and a woman are strolling with two snuffly French bulldogs trotting about off-lead. She's dressed all in beige like an expensive walking Rich Tea biscuit. As we pass by, she bends down to give the bulgy-eyed Frenchie a treat.

'Here we are,' says Annie as we turn the corner.

I didn't hear any goodbyes and wonder if she hung up on poor Jade. I send up a silent prayer for the nut allergy sufferer.

Up ahead is a small bar that looks Parisian. Even though it's December, and this is London, wooden tables and chairs are arranged on the pavement under a burgundy awning with golden lettering. As we pass beneath it, I feel the warmth emanating from two fiery-faced heaters. Frondy pot plants frame the entrance.

'This is my favourite bar in London,' she says, holding one of the squeaky swing doors open for me. 'After you.'

Inside it's all wood-panelled walls and, over in the more formal dining area, squashy red leather banquettes, vast mottled mirrors and oil paintings in gilded frames. We stick to the bar and take a seat at one of the tables for two by the window, with a view out on to the street corner. Tables for two. I picture Max sitting opposite me.

'What do you fancy, Eve?'

I hadn't noticed the bow-tied bartender approach and now both he and Annie are eyeing me expectantly. Despite my 'career' to date, I know very little about wine besides how to pour it. I like it when it's drinkable. 'I'll have the same as you,' I reply, putting on a smile. I spot her French manicure and shift my dry hands from the table to my knees. She's wearing the same necklace as before – three rows of silver beads – strung around the collar of a blue shirt. Over the top a loose slate-grey jumper that you probably have to wash by hand.

'Two small glasses of Cabernet Sauvignon, please.'

I nod along as she orders. Fucking hell, Eve. Say something. 'What do you do, Annie?'

'Oh, I work in events,' she says, shaking her head and smiling. 'Weddings, parties, that sort of thing.'

'Sounds fun,' I reply, wondering what's so embarrassing about that.

'If you're invited and not organising, sure.' She smiles. Another twirl of the wedding ring.

'And you're married,' I say. Good one, Eve. 'Your ring.'

She opens her mouth but says nothing, then glances down at it and nods, like she'd forgotten it was there. 'Oh yes, I am. You?'

'No, just me.' I shrug.

'Well, count yourself lucky.'

She sounds like she means it.

'And you, Eve? What do you do?'

'You mean besides life-modelling?'

'Yes.'

'I'm a barmaid.' Keep it simple.

'Oh, how lovely.' She opens her mouth as if to ask, And what else? Because of course that can't be it, bartending and life-modelling. She wants to hear the goals, plans, dreams.

'Two glasses of Cabernet Sauvignon,' announces the bartender.

'Thank you,' says Annie, raising her glass to cheers me. 'So, tell me about you, your family.' I must pull a face because she adds, 'No judgement here.'

'Well,' I say, taking a gulp of wine, 'I never knew my mum.'

'She died?'

'She left.'

A Youla-like exhale. 'I'm so sorry, Eve.'

I raise my shoulders.

'How old were you?'

'Almost five.'

'Wow, that must have been hard.' She pauses and then, when I stay quiet, asks tentatively, 'Do you know what happened?'

'Not really,' I say, the familiar reasoning loop running around in my head like a home video. Perhaps she suffered from post-partum depression or even psychosis. Perhaps she met someone and wanted to throw everything into the new relationship, their future together. Whatever the reason, cowardice must have played a part. And even if she's outwardly happy, she's surely grieving in secret, racked with silent guilt, grappling with the fact that she left her child behind. 'I tried talking to my dad about it a few times, but the drink gets in the way.' I hesitate. 'His way of handling it.'

A grimace.

'It's fine, really, he's not that bad,' I lie, remembering when, as a child, I thought it was funny that he occasionally drank Ribena from a wine glass for breakfast. 'And I have lots of friends.'

She gives me a knowing smile.

Before she starts to feel too sorry for me, I redirect the attention to her. 'What about you?'

Her turn to take a gulp. 'My husband and I have been married for six years now,' she says, tugging at her ring, two little frown lines emerging between her eyebrows. 'We're actually spending some time apart at the moment.'

'Oh, I'm sorry.'

She shakes her head like she's erasing an image. The frown lines melt away as she tells me about their daughter, Molly. 'She's six.'

'Can I ask how old *you* are?'

She laughs, takes another gulp. 'Thirty-two.'

Just a little more time on this planet than me and look at her. Job, husband (for now), kid. Nice clothes, expensive jewellery. Everything about her. What do I have to show for my twenty-six years? This woman is the walking embodiment of the life steps I'm never going to take.

'My mother's remarried,' she offers, pointing out that her parents aren't perfect either. 'My father lives in Palma. His partner died earlier this year.'

She doesn't say how or why so I don't ask.

'I never really knew her so . . .' She trails off and the silence feels crackly and expectant. 'Anyway, he'll be fine, I don't feel too sorry for him.'

As we move on to a second small glass each, she tells me she's not sure when her own happy marriage became an unhappy one. 'We were so in love when it began,' she says, laughing – without laughing – about how now their life together seems to have been no more than a short-lived domestic arrangement.

'I suppose people always are in love at first,' I say, 'other-wise what would be the point?'

Maybe it was the same with Mum and Dad before I came along. Cocktail parties, romantic dinners in newly opened no-reservations restaurants, trips to the theatre to see satirical plays, weekends away that involved little sight-seeing and lots of staying in bed. Visiting galleries and museums, maybe. By the sound of Dad's stories, and the look of her clothes, Mum was creative. The arty one.

Annie tells me that even making a home together was fun in the beginning. 'But we had Molly too young,' she says, swirling her red around the glass. 'I was about the age you are now.' She lifts the glass to her lips, tinged purple, and swallows the last few sips in one. 'I said yes to marriage mainly to avoid being a single mother,' she adds, staring straight at me for just a few seconds before looking away. 'I know that sounds awful.'

'I'm sorry, Annie.' I don't know what else to say. I have no experience with this. I can't imagine ever being married, let alone being in a marriage that's breaking down.

'That's OK,' she says, miming a signature to the bartender and reaching into her handbag. 'Come on, time to meet Molly.'

There's a huddle of women lingering outside the ballet hall, more than a couple pregnant, touching their tummies as they talk, and most with a second child either running riot or strapped securely into a buggy. I wonder how Molly feels about being an only child, whether she'll go through a stage of pretending she has a twin sister from whom she was separated at birth. When I told Grace about my childhood fantasy, she hugged me and said, You were right, here I am.

A woman in a long black skirt and matching black ballet shoes opens the door, peering out at the parents and then calling their children forward one by one. As she locks eyes with Annie I hold my breath. I'm trying to remember the last time I interacted with a child. I held my friend Sal's latest when she was born. But that was easy. I didn't have to say anything, just support her tiny head. How to talk to a six-year-old? She might not like me. I might do something wrong. Annie bends down. Chattering. I realise I'm not breathing and quickly gulp a lungful of oxygen.

'So, Molly, this is Eve, my friend who I've been telling you about.'

We're friends? I smile at the thought, and then at the little girl, skinny with a centre parting and two blonde plaits hanging either side of her heart-shaped face. She rubs her nose, small as a button, then looks up at Annie, not frowning but not smiling either. Her eyes are the same blue as her mum's.

'Hello, Molly.'

'Hello.'

'Did you have a good ballet class?'

'Yes.'

'What did you do in your class?' I crouch down so we're closer in height. Under her unbuttoned coat I see she's wearing a jumper printed with daisies without stalks.

'We practised our nativity play.'

'Wow, that sounds fun. What part are you?'

She gives me a toothy smile. 'I'm an angel.'

An angel. When Grace died, I briefly entertained the thought of her watching over me. But not in a halo-wearing, fluffy-white-cloud kind of way.

'Moll, do you want some juice?' Annie hands her a squeezy carton.

Molly frees the straw from its plastic packaging but strug-
gles to pierce it through the silver hole.

'Here,' I say, 'let me help you.'

'Thank you.'

My heart thumps.

'OK, Moll,' says Annie, 'shall we drop Eve off at the
station on our way home?'

She nods her head, plaits bouncing.

As we walk, Molly chatters away about her class. She
remembered all her sequences today. Someone or other
didn't. I nod and smile and tell her that sounds good or
bad. Talking to a six-year-old is easier than I thought.

As we round the corner to the station Annie gives her fifty
pence to buy something chocolatey from the kiosk. Molly
skips up to the counter, then stands and wriggles her fingers
in front of her chest, agonising over her choice.

'What do you think?'

'She's lovely, Annie.'

'I knew you would be great with her.'

'You did?'

'I did.'

'You know I've never done this before?'

'Eve, I trust you.'

Of course I trust you.

It feels like she's slapped me.

'So you'll do it? You'll babysit?'

Molly returns with a big grin and a packet of chocolate
buttons. 'Do you want one, Eve?'

I take a deep breath. 'I'd love one, thank you, Molly.' After receiving a button, I look up at Annie. 'I'll do it.'

'Oh, Eve, thank you. Here, put your number into my phone and I'll text you.'

She hands me her shiny iPhone, the latest model, and I tap in the digits.

'Thank you again. You're a life-saver.'

Grace, wake up. Please wake up, Grace. Please.

Nine

'So who is this woman?' asks Karina, drizzling a smidge of olive oil into a pan in a wobbly zigzag.

'I told you, I met her at work.'

'And she just waltzed up to you and asked you to babysit?'

'Yes. Why's that so hard to believe?'

She closes her eyes and sniffs.

What did I say? Ah.

She tosses in a handful of diced onions. 'It just seems a bit odd, asking the life model to look after your child.'

Well, I think it's odd that you'll only eat a couple of spoonfuls of Thai prawn curry, but I'm keeping my opinions to myself.

She squeezes the red paste out of its sachet and into the pan, notes of coriander, chilli and lime drifting into the air. 'What's the plan then?'

'The plan?'

'What are you going to do with her daughter?' She rips open plastic packets of corn and mangetout. Considers cutting the corn in half, then decides against it.

'I don't know, it's not until Saturday.'

'Well, you want to be prepared.' Lastly, the uncooked prawns, blue-grey maggots with wiry veins swimming in their bodily fluids.

'What would you do with her?' I ask.

She prods at the prawns submerged in the sauce. 'Drawing, reading, maybe some make-believe.'

I stare as their skin turns from blue-grey to pale pink. 'I like the sound of make-believe.'

She nods her head and smiles. 'Yes, that's probably the most fun.' She has a nephew and a niece, which is how she knows these things. 'Tiring too.'

'That's OK,' I say, turning over in my mind a scenario where we've toppled into a book of paintings and have to perform a series of tasks to return to the real world. The Picture Hoppers.

'I think you'll be great, Eve.'

I smile back, with teeth.

When I arrive at work Max is already behind the bar, buffing up the marble with a threadbare cloth. 'Hey, you,' he says as I shake off my coat.

I say 'hi' back, noting the way my breath catches just slightly at the sight of him. He's wearing a white T-shirt that shows off his strong arms. I scoop up a handful of salty peanuts and sidle onto one of the bar stools.

'Nice of you to join us,' he adds, skimming a couple of spilt nuts off the bar and into the open rubbish bin by his feet. He chucks the cloth into one of the sinks and squats down, out of sight, popping up a moment later with a crate of pint glasses in his hands, still steamy from the dishwasher.

'I'm not late, am I?' I swallow another handful, rub my palms against one another and slide my phone out of my pocket to check. Damn, twenty minutes. I hope Nina doesn't keep close tabs on her staff. I start to formulate an excuse about how it's the boiler man's fault – it's not inconceivable that he'd be coming round, seeing as our boiler's been on the blink, and Max might be glad to see me showing some initiative when it comes to the flat. There's something wrong with the fiddly time-setting needles. Bill keeps saying he's going to look at them but never does. Or I could say that I've been to see my dad. Max is always going on about the importance of family, how his own dad often mentions mine, wonders how he is. 'Well, you see—'

'Eve, my office, please.' A narrow-eyed Nina.

I look longingly at Max; he shrugs his shoulders, bends down again and starts sorting the clinking bottles of beer in the bottom fridge. I lick my salty lips and run my tongue along the fronts of my teeth, hoping there are no nutty bits lodged between them.

'So,' she says, before I've even made it into her office, which today smells oddly of vanilla essence, 'why are you late?'

I stand, greasy hands clutching awkwardly at my sides, and curse myself for taking off my coat – need pockets. She gestures to the chair opposite. She's all in black, of course, except for two lime-green hairslides shaped like shooting stars – the kind I might have worn when I was ten, if Dad had ever bought me hair accessories or, better yet, given me pocket money. Pinning her short hair back on each side, they make her features seem even more petite and pointy. In a good way.

124

'Eve?'

'Yes, sorry.' I look down at my shirt and brush away some crumbs.

'So?'

On her desk is a cream-coloured candle, its flame alight, presumably the source of the vanilla scent, syrupy-sweet up close. Funny, Nina doesn't strike me as the smelly-candle kind. Maybe she's also a secret fan of floral soap and bath bombs. A hoarder of toiletries in every flavour and colour like Karina. 'I lost track of time.'

'And last week?'

'I was late last week?'

'Half an hour.'

'Wow.'

'Yeah, it's not great.'

I glance at the rota on the wall and see that it ends with December. I'm not sure my body could handle life-modelling every day of the week.

'Don't worry, your name's due to make an appearance in January,' she says, her eyes steady on mine. 'But only if you get your shit together.'

'I will – I am,' I blab. Then, more slowly, accidentally taking a deep inhale of the saccharine stench and spluttering a little, 'I'm working on it.'

'Work faster, work harder.'

'Yes, right, will do.'

I sit back in my chair as she starts tapping away on her shiny MacBook, eyes fixed on the screen. Her fingers dance across the keyboard like honeybees flitting from flower to flower, knowing intuitively where to land. She's proably writing up a report of our conversation. Emailing the already-got-her-shit-together girl who was ready to replace me and saying that, sadly, there isn't an opening after all.

I'm sorry, Grace, it must be a bore, always having to lend me stuff.

I'm lying on your rug, tummy down, as you search your wardrobe. I need something smart for next week's ball.

Tell me about it, you say, exaggeratedly, pulling a face at some pink frills your mum must have bought you.

I guess it's only a matter of time before you give up on me entirely, huh?

Oh, it's inevitable, you say, slipping something shiny off a hanger. But don't worry, I've drawn up a list of proxies so I won't be lonely.

No! I cry, wrapping my arms around your ankles, I won't let you go!

You laugh, try to wriggle free. Fine, you win!

And the proxies?

I'll tell them I don't need them anymore. Now shh!

I sigh, satisfied, and relax my grip.

'Eve?' asks Nina, still tapping, still staring.

'Yes?'

'Work.'

'Right.'

The Christmas parties are becoming unbearable. I scan this evening's merry scene and count the number of spangly dresses (sequin, rhinestone or otherwise) on show: twelve. What is it about Christmas that makes grown women want to look like human disco balls? Actually, that one in green is more of a shimmery fish or lizard. Keep your skin on, lady.

And there's always one in holly red – there she is, with a smile that stretches too wide to be natural. She's wearing glittery eye shadow and dangling from each earlobe is a felt Christmas tree decked with tiny pompoms.

The men aren't any better, in their blaringly festive jumpers, shirts and ties – a rotund reindeer here, a squad of scarf-wearing snowmen there. And they're particularly chatty.

'One for me and one for you!' the twenty-something guy in front of me proclaims, as I hand him two flutes of very expensive champagne and a bowl of plump green olives.

'Oh, that's kind but I can't, thanks,' I say, accepting his card.

He has long brown hair that parts on the right, a lopsided smile and kind almond-shaped eyes, which are now downturned.

'I'm sure you'll find a taker,' I add, with a smile. I think about advising him to ditch the Father Christmas tie but sense Max behind me, reaching for a bottle, quietly close, and lose my train of thought.

He's busy shaking up all manner of colourful cocktails and, by the looks of things, also batting away his fair share of bleary admirers. Two women – one wearing a white shirt with ruffles, the other a squeeze-me-in dress – are trying to talk to him as he's making a pair of pornstar martinis.

'Uh-huh', 'yes' and 'oh right' are the only words I can hear coming from his lips as he concentrates on his liquid measurements. Vodka, something else clear, vanilla syrup (Nina's new favourite), passion-fruit pulp (could pass for baby food), Prosecco.

'That'll be eighteen pounds, please,' he announces, placing half a passion fruit in each glass and passing the luminous cocktails across the bar.

Squeeze-Me-In pulls a pen from her handbag and scrawls something onto a napkin. She folds it, first in half and then in quarters, before leaning forward seductively and sliding it towards Max as if it contains top-secret information regarding his next mission. Next, a crisp twenty. 'Keep the change, darling.'

I laugh as Max fumbles with both napkin and note, nodding mutely, eyes darting in my direction.

'Right,' I say, turning back to my own thirsty customers, 'who's next?'

The man in front – implausible overbite – raises a hand and knocks over his empty wine glass in the process. A crack emerges between the top of the stem and the rim. Apologises under his tobacco breath.

Christmas brings out the worst in everyone.

After a couple of post-shift drinks with the team, Max and his bike walk me to Waterloo. This time he doesn't have to offer. Our eyes have been finding each other along the bar all night. We stroll across the bridge and decide to get something to eat when we reach the station, which is brightly lit and still busy. He parks his bike and I nip to McDonald's to buy a burger for him and a bag of chips for me.

We sit on the stone steps, quiet, a mini tub of ketchup between us. A sputtering street light reminds me of the dodgy bulb in the bathroom at the flat, which I spent the morning whacking with Karina's loofah. I turn to face Max, opening my mouth to ask whether he has a loofah, and find him smiling at me, his burger long gone. 'What's so funny?'

'Nothing's funny. You're cute.'

This is a bad idea.

I watch with interest as my hand reaches across to find his, my thumb brushing his leg. 'Why don't you come back with me tonight?'

He doesn't say anything. Instead, he kisses me, and I forget all reason.

Ten

Maybe we shouldn't have done it, but God, it was worth it. By the time we were back at the flat I was worried I'd freeze when we got to my room, find myself unable to undress in front of him, despite all my recent practice. But when he started kissing me again, drawing back once or twice, checking this was what I wanted – a flicker of a smile on his lips – I felt entirely uninhibited. It was just Max and me.

After, we lay next to one another, me on my front, Max on his side. His fingers were tracing my back and my heart was hammering. A little while later, he whispered that he'd missed me and I had to bite my lip to stop myself from crying – happy tears. I've missed him too. After a while I fell asleep, a deep sleep, his body warm beside mine. The best bit: in the morning he was still there.

We didn't talk about it. Instead, he lifted up his arm and I slid underneath, laying my head on his chest and listening to his heartbeat. I wrapped my arm around him and threaded my legs through his, relishing the cosy feeling. A niggle in my head told me it couldn't happen again. That this would only end in tears. I ignored it.

Two days later and I'm eager to get to the gallery. I heard two front-door slams while I was reading – a meditative book about a woman who's mysteriously hospitalised and visited by her estranged mother (I should be so lucky) – so I've got the flat to myself. I pull on *my* estranged mother's baggy jumper and wander into the kitchen. A sticky note from Karina on the fridge:

> Please can you clean the bathroom today, Eve? Also, I still haven't found my dressing gown. You're sure you haven't seen it?
>
> K

I go to make myself a coffee but decide against it. I've been feeling jittery since Max left the other morning, anticipating a text or phone call suggesting we do something. Not in a why-hasn't-he-called-me? kind of way. More because the niggle in my head is growing louder and the thought of not being with him again stings like an insect bite. I shake it off and rootle around in the cupboard beneath the sink: we're low on cleaning supplies.

The temperature drops as soon as I enter the bathroom – someone (probably Bill) left the window open after showering. I pull it to and squirm my fingers into the rubber gloves. A distraction, this is what I need, even if it is germ-related. Before I attack the sink and the bath, I swirl some bleach around the loo, turning its insides azure blue. I move to the mirror, wiping at the grubby fingerprints grouped along one side; behind the mirror is a small cupboard and this is where it opens. Karina must have bought more lipstick. There, standing tall in its jet-black case, sealed with a golden band. I swipe it, like I did the one before, a shot of adrenaline rushing through me, my jitteriness forgotten. People are always losing lipstick.

'Oh, hi, Eve.'

Bill? I whip my head around and find him standing behind me in his dressing gown and crab slippers. The bathroom feels a lot smaller with two of us in it. I curl my fingers around my loot and squeeze past him. 'How come you're not at work?'

'Not feeling too good,' he says, following me back into the kitchen, sniffing.

'That's a shame.'

He holds onto the back of a chair, winces.

'Is everything else OK?'

'Not really.'

'What is it?'

'I think we should tell her.'

I start to feel light-headed. 'What? Why?'

'Because I don't like lying to her.'

'Can't you just forget it ever happened?'

'That's not how life works, Eve.'

'Actually, Bill, sometimes it is.'

He sits down and rubs his temples, as though keeping the secret is putting pressure on his brain.

I sit down opposite and look him in the eye. 'Bill, you can't tell her. I need you to promise me.'

Eve, I have to tell you something, but you can't tell anyone. This is just between us.

Of course, Grace, you can trust me.

I'm not supposed to go anywhere near secrets.

My phone vibrates as I climb the stairs at the gallery.

A text from Max. My heart thumps as I read it. *The other night was fun. Let me know if you're around on Saturday.*

Another vibration.

Annie: *Still on for Saturday, Eve? Twelve pounds an hour ok? A x*

Maybe it's not just the niggle that's against us.

I type out two replies.

To Annie: *yes, great, let me know where/when*

To Max: *sorry, babysitting annoyingly. see you at the bar*

I begin to hear murmurs of chattering and, as I walk into the first room, I find a rough semi-circle of seven or eight schoolchildren sitting cross-legged in front of the painting of Adam and Eve. I scan the group overzealously, just in case Molly's among them, and feel an unexpected flash of disappointment when there's no sign. Oh well, maybe being around children is good practice.

A teacher in a peppermint-green dress and red-rimmed glasses is standing beside the frame. I wonder if the wood panel has always been curved or, like a human spine, grown crooked with age.

'Yes, Josie?'

'I like Eve's squiggly hair.'

I look at the painting and nod. I hadn't paid much attention to those long, golden ringlets radiating from her head. It's probably supposed to be some sort of holy symbolism, a halo. Reminds me of the Wi-Fi symbol on my laptop screen, forever searching for our flaky signal.

'Very good, Josie. Yes, Amber?'

As their teacher talks her nose twitches up and down like a skittish rabbit's. I squint at her front teeth.

'I like the animals, especially the silver horse peeking out from behind the leaves.'

I prefer the bristly warthog myself.

'Actually, I think it's a unicorn.'

Oh, Amber, be serious.

I continue through the next few rooms: three and four are empty except for a couple of lone gallery-goers, but five is occupied by some more sprogs. I have to say – and this is coming from someone who's never been particularly fond of children, until Molly – I'm quite impressed. Granted, one boy's tunnelling north in search of bogeys (please don't pick and flick) and two gossiping girls are on the brink of a giggling fit. But on the whole these tiny people – without uniforms but all carrying the same see-through plastic wallet, containing blank sheets of paper and coloured pastels – are incredibly focused.

'Miss, I need the toilet again.'

OK, perhaps not *incredibly* focused.

I wonder if Molly likes art, who she draws when she's asked to do a family portrait. I included my mum, always, I just made her really small – a mini person in the corner of the page like she was standing in the distance, somewhere faraway. Very nosy, teachers. I also remember being asked to draw my home and my carefully crafted black splodge of bathroom mould causing some confusion. Maybe, before I go, I'll drop by the gift shop and get Molly a colouring book.

I reach room six and half suppress a sigh. A slightly larger group is huddled in front of Suzon. I'm about to ask if it's necessary that they sit so close to her, to my barmaid, with their sticky fingers, but a boy with helmet hair butts in.

'Is it a circus?'

'What makes you think that, Ren?' This tall and thin teacher is towering above her class in a carrot-coloured jumper and turquoise trousers that barely skim her bony ankles. It must be a thing, wearing flamboyant colours when you work in a primary school. Something to do with stimulation. I park myself on the bench behind them. The kaleidoscope has got me feeling dizzy.

'The person standing on the swing,' replies Ren, shooting up onto his knees and pointing to the upper left-hand corner of the canvas.

Dangling at the top of the painting are two pale legs, their feet clad in minty slippers – their owner, out of sight, balancing on a trapeze.

'That's a brilliant observation, Ren,' says the teacher, clapping her hands together and holding them there as she explains that the Folies-Bergère wasn't a circus but a café-concert hall, a place of entertainment.

'Is that why there are spotlights?' chirps a puny girl with a limp ponytail.

'Yes, Jo, well done!'

Wow. She sounds so excited I'm surprised she doesn't throw in a fist pump.

'The ones you're talking about are electric,' she adds, gesturing like a weather girl to two white spheres hanging from rectangular columns. 'They have a white glare, compared with the more dull and yellowy chandeliers – here, here and here.'

Or an air hostess? I feel beneath the bench for my life vest. Dried chewing gum.

'Manet was one of the first painters to depict such modern lighting,' she continues, shooting me a troubled look. 'In fact, he . . .'

I zone out, a talent I seem to be nurturing, like I'm wearing the odd-one-out headphones at a silent disco and moving to a different beat. I scan the painted crowd for more signs of the spectacle, swiftly looking away when I catch sight of the shady reflection of the man in the mirror. I try to avoid that face – full of menace. My gaze moves to the left but all I can see are smudgy impressions of onlookers. Wait, there: beyond the barmaid is a lady in long white gloves, holding a pair of shiny binoculars (opera glasses?).

I lock eyes with the barmaid: good day?

As usual, she's not in the mood to talk.

Another troubled look from the weather-girl-cum-air-hostess.

Again, I start to imagine what she would look like naked – Suzon, that is. If she has a birthmark. Whether her pubic hair is straight or curled. How wide her waist is when it's released from her tightly bound corset; in between her chest and hips, it looks unnaturally narrow, giving her that hourglass figure that men apparently find irresistible. If you can see the veins pumping blood around her tits too. Her belly button – if it sticks out or dips in. I've started to undress her.

'Excuse me, may I have a word?'

Out of nowhere, the teacher's standing beside me.

'Oh, hello,' I reply, shifting clumsily on the bench. 'Take a seat.'

She crosses her show-and-tell arms beneath her breasts like a shelf. 'This is a private lesson, I'm afraid.'

'Oh, that's OK.'

'Actually, it's not.' She gestures towards the door. 'Would you mind?'

'Actually, I would,' I say, leaning back, making myself at home. 'I paid my entrance fee too – seven pounds. Bet these kids got a discount.' I cringe at how pathetic I must sound.

Her face reddens and she bends down to whisper in my ear: 'I'm trying to teach a class and you're sitting behind us talking to yourself.'

'What?' I shake my head. 'I was not.'

She quickly reverts to upright as the semi-circle of tots lets out a load of squeaky affirmatives. Traitor tots. 'That's enough, children, come on. I want you to pull out your paper and pastels and copy a small section of the painting.' They do as she says and she turns back to me, lips pursed.

Crap. Am I losing it? Loopy, always was. That's what Dad said about Mum when I finally found the courage to ask why she left. Said it staring straight ahead at the TV – I can't remember the show, but I can still see the reflective glow on his already-red face. Said it was a disgrace. But dads leave all the time, I thought.

After checking that there isn't a small child sitting behind me, waiting to be squashed, I stand up and move to the side of the bench, forcing the teacher to take a step to the left. 'Just make sure they don't touch her.'

Eleven

On Saturday afternoon, I return to the flat after a trip to the supermarket and hear raised voices coming from Karina and Bill's room. Louder, louder.

'I do everything around here!'

'Everything except for the bins!'

And the dishes, laundry, hoovering, plunging.

The clonk of the curling iron hitting the radiator. 'You know the smell of bin juice makes me nauseous!'

'You almost hit me!'

'You deserve it!'

I freeze: he's told her. Why? I dump the food on the side and start scanning the room for essentials.

The voices become more muffled.

I'm busy planning an exit strategy when I hear the bed creak.

Either all is forgiven or they really were just arguing about cleaning.

I plug myself into my phone and make a coffee. I need it: I didn't get back from the bar until almost two o'clock in the morning. Before I started, Max told me that some of the staff like to unwind with a stiff drink and it turns out

Borrower-sized Nina's big into her expensive vodka. Last night, after closing, we hung around for about an hour, sipping drinks, telling jokes. At one point, Max leaned over and kissed me and everyone cheered. By the end of the night my cheeks ached from smiling.

My music is turned up so loud that I only realise Karina's asking me a question when she's standing right in front of me. She's wearing Bill's dressing gown and her hair is messy. A whiff of cigarette smoke.

'What?'

'For God's sake, Eve, take out your headphones. I asked where you're going.'

'Oh, nannying,' I say, swallowing the dregs of my coffee. She bought a new pack that smells oddly like Oxo cubes. I push the thought to the back of my head and pull on my shoes. I've decided nannying sounds more serious a profession than babysitting.

'Wow, bar work last night, nannying this evening. You're keeping busy.'

'Yep.'

Bill appears behind her in his grey tracksuit bottoms. 'Good practice, hey, looking after children, for when you have your own?' He's smiling and nodding as if his encouragement will free me up to enthuse about motherhood.

'Hm, I'm not sure I'd make a good mum. Bad parenting's probably hereditary.'

His smile is still there, just a whole lot smaller, lips locked.

'I think you would be a great mum,' says Karina softly, with a straight face that tells me she's being sincere.

My insides twist and turn as I smile and head for the door. No comment.

Standing outside a tall white house in South Kensington, I reach into my pocket for my phone and double-check the address. I'm in the right place. I glance around at the square, three sides of which are lined with identical Victorian terraced houses. At the centre is a secret garden, cloaked with evergreen bushes and bare lofty trees.

I take a step towards the black door, sandwiched between two columns and well-watered pot plants, and ring the bell.

A ding.

A bark.

The hushed sound of Annie saying something as she walks towards the door, shoes clipping on a tiled floor.

'Eve, hi.' She leans forward and gives me a peck on each cheek.

Must remember that for next time. Left, right. 'What a beautiful house.'

It is. It's big and beautiful and brimming with expensive-looking stuff. Framed paintings and prints on white walls. Terracotta tiles in the hall. Straight ahead a solid staircase with a beige runner – like most people round here, she'd probably call it 'neutral' – and a smooth black banister. To my immediate left a mirror and opposite, a wooden rack hung with coats. I take off my own and unfurl my scarf.

'Hello, Henry.'

Who's Henry?

'Aren't you a good boy?'

I swivel round to find a leggy Dalmatian with a dopey face and an idle left ear. He's nuzzling lovingly into her shoulder as she bends down to greet him.

'Do you like dogs?' she asks, turning to me all of a sudden. 'Great companions.'

No. 'Of course. Hello, Henry.'

'He won't give you any bother.' Turning to Henry: 'You spend most of your time catching up on your beauty sleep, don't you?'

I've never understood people who talk to animals.

'Now, what else. Let me give you a quick tour of the downstairs.'

She's clearly not ready yet – in leggings and a soft-looking jumper, probably cashmere, plus her loafers – so it really is quick. A peek in the dining room on the right, table topped with an abundant flower arrangement, then into the living room opposite. At the centre of the far wall is a fireplace, bookended by two upholstered armchairs and crowned with a row of candles; the smallest is little more than a stub, a puddle of melted wax solidified beside it. The fire has all but died – at the centre lies a lone log, glowing red – but I can still feel the warmth as I walk towards it and greet it with my fingertips. Annie has switched off the overhead light and, instead, turned on two lamps, one on the shelf beside the mantelpiece and the other on a low table by the door. She shows me how to work the TV as if I've never watched one before.

Loo beneath the stairs – more terracotta tiles on the floor; I'm not a fan of the painting of birds of paradise – and beside it a door to what must be a back garden. Lastly, at the end of the hall, the kitchen. A real family kitchen. Elsewhere, at least on the ground floor, the house is devoid of family photographs and the only paintings are mostly abstract. Well, this is Molly's gallery. The fridge – 'help yourself to anything to eat or drink' – is covered with her colourful creations, tacked on with alphabet magnets. A row of stick figures suspended between spiky tufts of grass and a single line of mouthwash-blue sky stamped with a yellow sun. A symmetrical square house topped with a triangular roof and surrounded by trees with thick brown bottoms and fluffy green tops. A diplodocus with a snaking spine and beady eyes. The imprint of half an apple that was slathered with red paint and pressed onto the page.

Henry's curled up in a bed in front of the cream-coloured Aga – the first I've ever seen in the city. Above it are three metal rails topped with saucepans and from hooks below their bases hang an assortment of utensils.

Annie shows me where to find the tea and coffee, and pulls out a mug from the middle shelf of the dresser, accidentally clinking a couple of its neighbours in the process. 'Right, which just leaves Molly. I'll go and give her a shout.'

I hear Annie climb halfway up the first flight of stairs and call for her daughter. In response, the stairs grumble with the sound of scurrying footsteps. I bite my lip. Children can be fickle. What if she decides she doesn't like me today?

Annie walks back into the kitchen, holding Molly's hand. 'Moll, you remember Eve, don't you?'

Molly nods her head. Her hair is in plaits again and she's wearing a white top stitched with tiny people linking arms across her chest.

'Well, lucky you, Eve's going to babysit this evening.'

'Where are you going, Mummy?'

'I'm going out, sweetie. Are you going to say hello?'

'Hello.'

'Hello, Molly.'

Silence.

'Maybe you can show me some of your favourite books and toys?' I press up onto my tiptoes awkwardly, waiting for her reaction.

'I got a new book for my birthday.'

'You did? That sounds great. Shall we let Mummy get ready and we'll go and take a look?'

'OK.' She lets go of Annie's hand and heads for the stairs, tapping the banister and sneaking glances at me as she climbs.

Annie gives my arm a quick pinch. 'Knew you would be a natural.'

Two floors up and I'm in kiddie territory. This is what a child's bedroom should be. A door labelled with painted wooden letters, the final Y of MOLLY hanging wonkily at the end. A bookshelf of children's classics: *The Wind in the Willows*, *Charlotte's Web*, *Peter Pan*, *The Wonderful Wizard of Oz*. A doll's house, self-decorated by the looks of it – painted flowers along the base of the façade and wooden shavings (presumably intended to resemble tiles) glued unevenly along the pitched roof. Carpet samples from John Lewis as rugs. Fancy furnishings mixed with matchstick-box beds.

Molly's babbling away about birthday presents. 'That dress. Some Playmobil. Also this colouring book.'

Damn, I forgot to go to the gift shop the other day. Oh well, it doesn't exactly look like she needs more stuff.

'Eve?' Annie's voice floats up from the downstairs hallway.

'Hang on, Molly, I'll be back in a second.'

She plonks down on the floor and starts playing with some plastic figures.

'Coming!' It takes almost a full minute to get down to the ground floor.

Annie's in front of the mirror by the door, giving her hair a final run-through with a folding brush. As I reach the bottom step, she snaps it shut. She clips her hair back and starts applying coral lipstick. She hasn't mentioned where she's going. Rude to ask? Perhaps it's a date. She smells of spicy perfume.

'Can you do my buttons, Eve?'

You're standing by the window, the back of your dress gaping open, your frilly white pants on show. No bra, just the hint of a tan line from the bikini top you wore on holiday in Greece this summer. I still can't believe your parents paid for me to go.

Eve?

You look back at me over your shoulder.

Yes, sorry, coming.

I stand up too quickly and, to make up for it, cross the room extra slowly.

Thanks, they're impossible to do on your own, too fiddly.

You twirl your hair between your fingers, a nervous tic.

No problem. Looking forward to your date with Niall?

I start at the bottom and work my way up, the dress moulding to your body, a perfect fit. Your skin is soft and even.

I guess, you say, twirling faster. Do you actually think he likes me?

I linger on the last button, looking at the baby hairs on your neck, trying to figure out how to tell you that yes, I think he likes you, but that doesn't mean he's right for you.

'Eve?'

'Of course, sorry.'

'I should be back no later than eleven,' she says as I make a start. 'Molly's had her tea but if she gets hungry later there's some sliced mango in the fridge.'

How sophisticated. 'Going somewhere nice?'

She looks like she is, in a stripy grey tunic and a pair of straight black trousers, coral kitten heels peeping out the ends that match her lipstick. A silky bra, the back of which I got a glimpse of pre-buttoning. She's busy checking the contents of her handbag, hovering in a square patch of light in the doorway to the living room, and either doesn't hear my question or chooses not to answer.

'You're good to go,' I say, pushing the final button through its hole.

'Thank you, Eve,' she says, smiling. 'See you later then. In bed by eight.'

'No problem.'

'Bye, Moll!'

'Bye, Mummy!'

As she slips out the door, I spot a car waiting.

I expect getting Molly into bed to be a battle, but she's as well behaved as Henry, who's sitting quietly at the foot of the stairs. After pulling on her flannel pyjamas (white with multicoloured polka dots), she brushes her teeth with an electric toothbrush. It flashes red after two minutes to let her know she's finished, just as toothpaste begins to foam over her bottom lip like a science experiment gone wrong. I read a chapter from her new book – about three sisters who mysteriously appear on a stranger's doorstep – to both her and her favourite teddy, Percy, who's missing a patch of fur on one ear. Then I half close her door, leaving her room basking in the lavender glow of her bunny-shaped night light, and head downstairs.

I pause on the first floor and cast my eyes over the corridor leading to a string of rooms on the left: study, bathroom, bedroom. The bedroom door's open so I tiptoe in.

It's a grown-up bedroom, no inside-out pants on the floor like in Karina and Bill's. No musky smell lingering in the air. A painting of a house in the country hangs above the neatly made bed (display cushions, of course). Opposite is a dressing table, with a stool tucked under it and only a few items on its surface: a couple of glossy magazines, a thank-you card, a small framed photo of Molly, another hairbrush and a glass bottle of the spicy perfume, which I spritz on the underside of my wrists. I pull open a couple of drawers to the left of the mirror and find a handful of little velvet boxes. One by one, I crack them open and try on the contents: diamond earrings, a gold bracelet, a pearl on a delicate chain. A single baby tooth, nubby and yellowing at the edges, makes me shudder. Inside the penultimate box is Annie's wedding ring, a plain gold band. I slide it onto my finger, wondering when she stopped wearing it.

A peek inside the chest of drawers, the top one a tangle of silk and lace. I feel around, expecting to find something secretive, but all Annie keeps in her underwear drawer are bras and knickers.

When I open the doors to the oak wardrobe I spy men's suits lined up alongside women's clothing. He must be between places, moved out but yet to collect his things. I wonder what Molly thinks – if Annie's told her what's happening. I leaf through every item like I'm in a high-end shop, testing the material is up to scratch before I try anything.

Finding a silk shirt I like, I slip off my top and put it on, enjoying the way it clings to my skin, charged with static.

'Mummy?'

Fuck. I twirl around and find Molly behind me, rubbing her eyes.

'I can't sleep.'

No time to take off the shirt. Hoping she doesn't notice, I cross the room and – when she stretches her arms out towards me, fingers wriggling – pick her up. 'That's OK, Molly, it's Eve. I can read you another chapter.'

She nuzzles against my neck. 'Why are you in Mummy and Daddy's room? I went downstairs and you weren't there.'

My heart does something strange in my chest. 'I was just putting some bits away,' I say, carrying her back upstairs and lowering her into bed.

Seemingly satisfied, she snuggles down and clings onto my arm as I begin to read. By the time I'm done, she's having trouble blinking open her heavy eyelids. One at a time, I unfurl her fingers, hoping that by morning all will be forgotten.

I hurry back to Annie's bedroom and take off her shirt, which now has a snotty stain near the collar – I dab it with a wet flannel then return it to the wardrobe. I turn to head back downstairs, but the bedside tables are calling out to me.

It's easy to tell which is Annie's, home to a jumble of receipts, spare buttons in mini plastic bags and nail varnish in every colour. I swipe a deep burgundy just to see what it feels like, having nails like hers, to see if it makes a difference. I creep back downstairs, remembering halfway that I'm still wearing her ring. I tiptoe back up, wary of waking Molly, and – after a brief flare of panic when I can't get it off my finger – return it to its box.

I'm half asleep myself when I hear keys in the front door and Henry grumble half-heartedly, without lifting either ear, from his second bed beside the lifeless fire. I turn off the TV and dab the inner corners of my eyes.

One shoe knocks against the wall, followed by another. A coat is slung on the rack. Annie walks into the living room, her toes visibly scrunched in her nude pop socks, and flops into the armchair opposite. I'm not used to seeing her creamy skin on show. She rests her heels on the coffee table, with hardback books on everything from gardening to interior design artfully arranged beneath the glass.

'All good?' she asks.

'All good,' I reply, eyeing up her rosy cheeks. From the cold or drink? I get up and head towards the door, assuming this is my cue to leave.

'Cup of tea before you go – or a glass of wine?'

I hesitate, taken by surprise.

'I'm going to have a glass of red. You?'

'Same, please.'

I follow her into the kitchen and stand awkwardly, hands held together, as she reaches for two crystal glasses from the oak dresser; there are different ones for water, white and red wine, champagne and whisky.

She slides a half-drunk bottle across the counter from beside a row of cookbooks, slips the cork out with a pop and pours. She hands me my glass. 'Oh, nice nails,' she says, gesturing to my fingertips, painted deep burgundy. 'I have a similar shade.'

I smile, my skin tingling. 'Thanks, it's my favourite.'

She leans up against the Aga, warming the backs of her legs.

'Did you have a good evening?' I ask.

'I did, thank you.'

'Go somewhere nice?'

'You don't give up, do you?' she smiles.

'Sorry, I'm being nosy.'

'No, no, it's all right.' She takes a big sip of red.

I can't help but stare at her elegant neck, visualising the wine spilling down.

'My first date in years.' I must make a face because she adds: 'An old friend who's known things have been over in the marriage for a while.' She goes to say something else but changes her mind and instead unclips her hair.

'Wow.' My turn to take a big sip, maybe more of a gulp. Too big. I cough and splutter into my hand. When she looks away, I wipe it on a tea towel. 'So your husband has moved out.'

'Yes, he's gone – staying with a friend.' Another big sip. 'Nothing's sorted – his clothes are still hanging in the cupboard, for Christ's sake – but it's over.' Her eyes well. I get the impression she thought this would all have blown over by now. Nothing more than a blip, a small bump in her otherwise smooth road. Then, with a shake of the head, her face hardens. 'I'm determined not to let it break me.' A lot of grit on that road of hers.

'How does Molly feel about it?'

She looks at me over the top of her glass. 'Moll's fine. She's resilient. Children are, I think.'

Are they? I may not remember much about Mum, but I do remember how I felt when a week went by and she hadn't come home. How much I missed her when I was growing up. It was a sort of hollowness – still is, some days. Like feeling hungry all the time. Or knowing you've forgotten something but struggling to put a finger on what it is. Always patting your pockets to check you have your keys, phone, wallet.

'Eve? Are you all right?'

'I think I should head off.'

'I'll call you a taxi,' she says, placing her glass on the counter and going to grab the house phone. 'Normally one of us would drive you, but David's clearly not here and I've had too much to drink.'

And you wouldn't want to leave Molly home alone, I think, surprising myself with the sudden leap to judgement. Annie's been nothing but kind to me and there's no sign that she's anything but a good mother. 'I'm happy to catch the bus, really.'

She holds up her index finger and speaks into the receiver. 'Hello, yes, I would like a taxi as soon as you're ready. Annie . . . yes, that's the one. Thank you.'

Must be a regular.

'Someone will be here in five minutes.'

'Thank you.'

'No, thank you. You've really helped me out this evening. Did you and Molly have fun?'

'We did. She's lovely.'

Twelve

Karina was still up when I got home from Annie's, lounging on the sofa, which, beneath the black-and-white checked blanket, is speckled with a smorgasbord of stains – some tea-like, others more suspect. She was wearing nothing except for an extra-large T-shirt stamped with a hand giving a peace sign, exposing her fair, elongated limbs. Oh, and a freaky face-mask sheet.

'How did it go?' she asked, lips squashed through one of four holes.

'It went well, I think. I actually really enjoyed it.'

She cocked her head at me, a satisfied smile spreading across her face. 'And the girl?'

'She's great.'

The sheet crinkled on her cheeks as her smile widened further still.

I sat down beside her and she handed me a rice cake, which tasted as dry and flavourless as it looked.

On the TV, a comedy chat show was replaying a viral clip of the head of government dancing. A few minutes later, some car advert was playing. When the young mum and dad strapped in their little girl and kissed her on the forehead, my eyes unexpectedly started to fill with tears. Karina must have noticed because she offered to give me a face mask too – apparently pampering is therapeutic. I smiled, said I was just tired and took myself to bed.

It always creeps up on me around Christmas – the feeling of being alone. I'm not in denial about my lack of a solid family unit, but this is the time when it hits me most. It doesn't help that Karina and Bill have disappeared to Norway. They flew first thing and won't be back until just before New Year's Eve. No cereal bowls on the side, but Bill sweetly left a half-filled cafetière by the hob to remind me of him.

One solace: apparently I'm good with kids. Who would have thought it? Molly's the kind of child I'd want to have – if I were to have any, which I won't. I don't like the idea of carrying another human being inside me. I don't have the itch, the ache, the longing. That therapist I never visited would surely have told me it's all about Mum, if she even is my mum anymore. Maybe motherhood comes with a sell-by date, and a leave of absence this long disqualifies her as a parent. Strips her of her motherly rights. Either way, I'd rather not have children than have them and change my mind later.

Molly's fizzy with excitement, like a shaken-up can of Coke, and yet polite and patient – well, to an extent. She wants to know every minute detail. Sometimes scarily pratical and perceptive. At one point she asked whether my name had anything to do with Christmas Eve and I told her (because it doesn't count as lying if it's fun for children) that I'm one of Santa's little helpers. What followed was a series of extremely specific questions:

– Exactly how many people, including elves but not including reindeer, work for Father Christmas, Christmas Eve?

– What does he like for tea and does he eat ice lollies even though the North Pole is cold and snowy?

– How does Father Christmas decide who delivers the stockings? And did he also send you to our house to babysit?

– Does Father Christmas have to brush his teeth for two minutes every morning and two more minutes every evening? (Said with a mouthful of toothpaste, nodding her little head in vigorous agreement at my answer before swishing and spitting.)

More than anything, though, she made me feel at home – and so did Annie.

I walk to the studio in Karina's black boots, the tops of which cut into my calves and are probably branding them with two red marks like a farmyard animal's backside. I pull her second-warmest coat tight around me; she's taken the warmest with her.

I arrive with just a couple of minutes to spare. Most of the students are already in their seats, gazing at blank sheets of paper or chatting among themselves. The rest are standing in the corner, sharpening pencils. I watch as the coils of shavings fall into the bin. When I undress, it's just as I predicted: two straight lines are scored on the backs of my legs.

'OK, Eve, I would like you to adopt some poses half-clothed today.' Paul snakes between the easels and joins me, a bundle of fabrics in his arms.

Been raiding the dressing-up box, have we?

'Silk, wool, felt.' He leafs through them before letting them float to the floor. 'Just play around with these, draping one over your shoulder, wrapping another around your leg. Make sense?' He asks the question as he loops the thinnest fabric around my waist, tying it in a bow at the side. His poorly circulated fingers brush against my skin.

'Makes sense.'

'What we're doing here is tapping into an age-old tradition,' he says, turning to the students, 'the practice of half covering a naked model in order to draw attention to her nudity.' He launches into a mini lecture with more art history in it than usual. 'The concealment of one breast draws attention to the exposure of the other. The placement of loose cloth over the bottom half invites the observer to imagine what lies beneath, to imagine peeling back that cloth . . .'

Inserting a finger.

'Viewer becomes voyeur.'

OK, let them get on with it. They're probably just happy to draw something other than flesh and bone. A little layering. Some ruches. Pleats, please.

'Eve, whenever you're ready.'

Still standing, feet hip-width apart, I keep hold of the narrow fabric and pull it taut across my nipples, imagining the words 'NO ENTRY' flashing across it in electric red writing. Next, I make a fist and wrap the material around it; I look at the clock, fist pulled back behind my head, a slingshot ready to be released. I exchange this cutting for a rectangular swatch of wool, which I hold up in front of my body, concealing one half of me. Two minutes later, I wrap it around my middle and tug it tight. Clingfilm, a corset, a tightly bound bodice.

'OK, moving on to the ten-minute poses.'

Annie's sitting further forward than usual and I notice for the first time that she purses her lips as she draws, jiggles her left leg (not an entirely satisfactory date, then). She catches my eye and smiles. I keep a straight face, trying to ignore the tingling sensation breaking out in my right leg. I should know by now not to choose such a contorted pose to hold for this long. I try to subtly shift the balance from toe to heel. Still tingling.

I wonder what's going to happen when she and her husband are divorced. If Molly will spend time with each of them. Divide her days between two houses, two bedrooms, two sides of London – presuming they both stay in the city. Alternate Christmases, Easters, birthdays. A small weekend bag forever tucked under her bed. Maybe she'll even have two toothbrushes.

'OK, Eve, moving on.'

I stumble as I put weight on that same leg but manage to catch myself before crumpling into a pile on the floor along with the fabrics. OK, a seated pose. I straddle the chair, turned away from the students and their scrutiny, my elbows resting on the back, my chin in my open hands. At least this way I can relax my facial muscles. On the windowsill, my speckled sparrow friend is hopping to and fro on its teeny legs, so skinny they'd surely snap like breadsticks. I lower my eyelids.

I remember writing letters to Mum in the beginning and asking Dad to put them in the post. I'd fold them neatly in half and he'd promise, or at least agree, to slip them into an envelope with the correct postage – the stamps to ferry the letter to wherever she might be. Come to think of it, I never asked whether he had her address. I never even asked where she was, what she was doing, who she was with. All I asked was, She'll reply this time, won't she? Each time he'd give me a vacant smile, take the folded piece of paper and shrug. Maybe.

I'd draw things I'd seen that day at school to keep her up to speed. A boy with a red river running from each nostril; I'd never seen or had a nosebleed myself so that was fairly alarming. A big-booted fireman, who came to talk to us about the London Fire Brigade, and his snaking hose spraying cold water over the badly behaved children (artistic licence). A giant cake, with a runny layer of seedless raspberry jam in the middle and a thick coat of fondant icing on top, made from scratch by some girl's mum for her birthday – would my mum be home for mine this year? A fish tank, swimming with wavy pieces of seaweed and more fish than could possibly have lived together in such a small volume of water (never mind the purple crab and the black starfish with yellow spots).

'One more, Eve.'

I can't be bothered to turn around so instead I interlace my fingers and stretch my arms overhead. I picture a couple of students bristling at my laziness. The sparrow pauses for a moment, eyes on mine, then takes off.

She never did reply and after a while I gave up. I stopped writing her letters, stopped drawing her pictures. I forgot I'd ever done it, too, until I packed up my things at Dad's to move to Vauxhall. Up in the attic, alongside a widowed shoe, some dusty books and a stack of CD cases, most of them empty, was a medium-sized cardboard box. When I lifted the lid, the stale smell made me nauseous. Neatly piled inside were sheets of plain paper covered with my childish creations and curly, yet-to-be-joined-up handwriting. Instead of just throwing them away, he'd kept every single one. My welling eyes took me by surprise. It's good I never asked for her address, I thought, because then he'd have had to admit that she never gave it to him; she upped and left and now he had no clue where she was. Not coming back. Beside that box was another, containing my old notes about Suzon.

Maybe Molly will be fine without her dad. I've come this far without Mum – not that I'd recommend it. I wouldn't go as far as to say it's worked out well. I may be able to afford my monthly rent thanks to Karina and Bill's semi-generous discount. But I don't have much else to show for my lack of an upbringing. My upbringing brought low. My downbringing. Grace was the first person to believe in me, other than Max.

'OK, everyone, let's take ten.'

Who else do I have? What else? A couple of hundred *nude* drawings, at least – and even those don't belong to me.

Alone in the studio, I squeeze between the easels, alert, eyes peeled. Cosying up to one leg – long-forgotten, I'm sure – are some knotted headphones, the wiry white kind designed for iPhones. I could do with a new pair because the left-hand speaker of mine is broken. Makes me feel lopsided, my left ear left out. I bend down and swipe them.

'Eve, how are you doing?'

Annie.

Karina, why are there no pockets in this damn robe? I crumple up the headphones inside a fist, little finger reaching for a dangling bud. 'Good, thanks, and you?' Got it.

'I'm fine.' She physically brushes away the question with the back of her hand as she might do some leftover crumbs. 'Thank you again for last night. You were a big hit with Molly.'

'I was?' The thought makes me feel woozy, in a good way. Without thinking, I blurt out that I'd love to help more. 'If you need me, that is. Don't worry if not.'

'Oh, that would be wonderful – thank you, Eve. Molly's going to be thrilled.'

Something along the lines of a 'yay' escapes from my lips before I lock them together. When I trust myself to open them again: 'So, fun plans for Christmas?' As I ask the question, I nip back up onto the stage, fishing one sock out of a shoe and bundling the headphones into the toe.

'I'm not sure "fun" is the word I would use.'

I laugh before I have time to read her expression. She looks sort of sad, the whites of her eyes tinged with crimson.

'I thought it was just going to be me and Molly, but David called earlier.' Worry leaks into fine creases on her forehead. When her voice cracks, she taps her chest as if she has a tickle. 'He's insisting that we all spend the day together.'

Without thinking, I hug her, even though she's not the hugging kind and neither am I, and she pats my back like I'm the one being consoled. A squeeze and I let go. 'I'm sorry, Annie, that must be weird for you. I'm sure it will be OK, though.'

'I hope so. I just hate the thought of him being in the house after what happened, playing happy families.'

'It's just one day,' I say, wondering what exactly did happen and whether she's going to tell me. 'You can do it.'

The other students are filtering back into the studio, Paul bringing up the rear and glancing in our direction.

'You're right,' she says, putting on a smile. She shakes her head as if to say, I'm overreacting, and goes to sit down.

I'm fine, Eve, don't worry about me. You force a smile that fades as quickly as it appears.

The class ends with a forty-five-minute seated pose. I have my left foot on the seat, knee bent, left forearm resting on top, wrist slack. My right leg is outstretched at a slight angle, my foot flexed. My head hangs to one side, as if it's lolled that way in my sleep. I feel like a ventriloquist's dummy, post-performance. I also feel sorry for the woman sitting straight ahead. Tunnel vision between my legs, a place that's now used to being on show and no longer tingles. When she gets home maybe she'll sit in front of a mirror, legs spread, and compare.

When it finally gets to twelve o'clock – I swear time slows down in the studio – Paul decides we should carry on with the same pose next week, give the students a chance to build up a more detailed portrait. As they pack up their things, he kneels beside me and places pieces of masking tape behind my right heel and along the sides of my thighs and bum cheeks. I watch him as he tears at the tape with his teeth, which, up close, are more yellow than I expected. He's the type of person I could have imagined using whitening strips.

He glances between my legs and goes to rip off some more. He looks up at me. 'Hold still just a moment, Eve.'

Chatter has erupted as the students resume their conversations about Christmas. Really, you're cooking for fifteen? How lovely to spend it just the two of you. Will the children be up at the crack of dawn? I'm sure it will taste just fine, don't you worry.

He tears off another piece and sticks it to the seat, along-side my inner thigh, fingers inches away from me.

When I reach the bottom of the stairs I pull out my brand-new headphones, shaking them loose as I open the door. There's a rush of cold air. The naked trees are quivering, especially their most slender, exposed branches – shivering to keep warm. Despite the sun, it's bitterly cold. The roads and pavements will probably be icy by this evening. I exhale and watch my breath swirl up and away.

In the living room of the town house opposite, a man and woman are sitting down to Sunday lunch in front of the TV. Plates piled high with something to warm your insides. A show to make you laugh, a dog at your feet. I blink and look away.

I find a steady beat and plug myself in, ignoring the group of carol singers – the tallest standing at the back and the smallest in front, the way we used to line up each year for school photos. 'Good King Wenceslas'? I can't tell from the movement of their mouths, but that man at the rear looks like he's singing deeply, his brow furrowed and his chin tucked into his neck. Other people's parents actually bought those school photos, framed them and hung them proudly for all to see.

My phone buzzes as I'm walking back along South Lambeth Road.

I tap the green button. 'Hi, Max.'

'Hey, you, how's it going?'

'Good, thanks.'

'You sound like you're walking.'

'Yes, just heading home from work.'

'Work, hey? I know you're not at the bar, so which job is this?'

'Well, I actually have three jobs now.'

'Really?' He lets out a whistle. 'What are the other two?'

'Babysitting,' I say, 'though I think I might have mentioned that one.'

'Oh yes, you did. How old are the kids?'

'Kid. Molly. She's six. And surprisingly sweet.'

'I'm glad,' he laughs. 'I bet you're great with her.'

I feel a twinge of happiness. 'I like her a lot.'

'And the other job?'

OK, time to come clean – if it is even something to come clean about. 'And life-modelling.'

'Life-modelling?'

'Yes.' I angle the phone away from my mouth as I breathe deeply, waiting for his reaction, wishing I could see his facial expression.

A moment's silence and then: 'Wow, I'm impressed.'

'You are? You don't think it's . . .' I rub my fingers together, searching for the right word, '. . . debauched?'

'Ha. No, Eve. I think it's great. It must take guts.'

I smile at the ground.

'So, before I lose my train of thought to images of you posing naked—'

Now it's my turn to laugh.

'I have a question to ask you: do you have plans for Christmas Day? Someone you're spending it with?'

'Oh, I haven't really thought about it,' I lie.

'It doesn't have to be your dad, Eve, just someone.'

I bite down on my lip. I texted him earlier telling him that Karina and Bill had left, so he knows that's not an option.

'Why don't you come and spend it with me?'

'Really?'

'Really. We've got the whole family coming – aunts, uncles, cousins. It'll be fun.'

My smile wanes. 'That sounds like a lot of family, Max. You're sure I won't be in the way?'

'Not at all. I want you there.'

A warmth swells inside me. 'OK, why not? Thanks, Max. Count me in.'

Thirteen

At the foot of my bed, which is tucked up against one wall of my room, in a sort of nook, is a print Karina gave me last Christmas. She bought it in the gift shop at Tate Modern after seeing an overpriced, overcrowded Picasso retrospective. I refused to go – besides the fact that the Courtauld is the only gallery I visit these days, Picasso was a misogynist who abused women and I told her so. She sighed and said, That doesn't mean we can't appreciate his work as an artist. I semi-conceded but still stayed home. *Good Art by Bad People.* That's an exhibition I'd like to curate.

It's a print of *Le Rêve* (The Dream), a portrait of the then fifty-year-old painter's then twenty-two-year-old muse and mistress, Marie-Thérèse Walter (he started sleeping with her when she was seventeen). Karina was drawn to it because of the palette – yellow, red, lilac, blue, green. She liked the patterned backdrop and the beaded necklace. I thought it would cheer you up, she said. (She knows Christmas is my worst time of the year.) What she didn't realise, until I pointed it out, was that Picasso painted Marie-Thérèse mid erotic daydream with her hands shaped like a vagina and a flopped-over penis forming the top part of her head. Karina gasped, hands comically covering cheeks. Bill chortled, only quieting down when he became the object of an icy stare. I thanked her profusely and went in search of Blu Tack. Said I knew just the place to hang it. Prime position: it would be the first thing I'd see each morning when I woke up.

I've always wondered what Marie-Thérèse thought when she saw that print. Surely she didn't recognise herself? Come to think of it, I didn't recognise myself in any of the drawings the students created the other day, not really. Some made me look old – accidentally, I assume – with sagging skin, a willowy frame, and knobbly knees and elbows. Others gave me the gift of daily workouts and good genes, with a peachy bum and toned stomach. To them, I know I'm not much more than a collection of sketched lines, a still life of flesh and bone. I may as well be a bowl of softening fruit or a chipped block of wood. A half-filled vase of flowers or a pile of dusty books. They can rub me out with a few flicks of the wrist. Here one minute, gone the next.

We've got into a habit of having a drink with Niall after closing, but tonight my feet hurt and I want my bed.

Here you go, babe, says Niall, filling up your shot glass. Get that down you.

You laugh and, unlike you, knock it back.

You've been seeing each other a lot lately. When I pointed out your new nickname a couple of weeks ago, you smiled shyly and said he calls all girls that.

He looks at me and raises the bottle in the air. Eve?

I think I'm fine, thanks, boss. (His new nickname.) Shall we head off soon, Grace?

I think she's fine too, he says, draping his arm around you.

Your eyes are glinting, either from happiness or sambuca. I might stay a bit longer, you say. See you tomorrow?

Sure?

He kisses you on the cheek.

More laughter.

He looks at me again, this time no offer of a drink. See you later, Eve.

It's Christmas Eve, my last chance to see Suzon for a few days – the gallery always closes on the twenty-fifth and twenty-sixth, which is fairly selfish. Some people may enjoy shutting themselves off from the outside world as they gorge on dry turkey and buckets of red. But some of us would appreciate having somewhere to go that's tinsel-free. Someone to talk to if we suddenly need them.

Speaking of which, Annie had a last-minute lunch date last week, so Molly and I had one too.

Standing in the hallway at their house, Annie widened her mouth to comic effect – faux fear in her eyes – when she told me it was a second date.

'Mummy, why are you scared?'

'Oh, Moll, I'm just joking.' She stroked her daughter's cheek and headed for the door. 'If you ask nicely, Eve might make you some fish fingers.'

In the kitchen, I asked Molly where the fish fingers lived.

She giggled. 'In the freezer, of course.'

'And what would you like with them? Maybe some peas?'

'Yes, peas, please.'

I kneaded the icy bag with numb fingers as I tried to squeeze joined-up chunks of frozen peas through a too-small hole into a stainless-steel saucepan. Giving up, I whacked the bag on the kitchen counter once, twice, then three times, until I finally felt the solid clusters give way. Eve 1, Peas 0.

'OK then. How many fish fingers do you normally have? Two, three . . . ten?'

She giggled again. 'Two.'

'Right. And which door of the Aga does Mummy use?'

At this point she thought I was plain ridiculous. Too many giggles to speak. Clutching her belly. Nodding her head.

'The longer you take to tell me, the longer it is until you get these fingers.' I wagged a pair of them at her button nose.

'This one!' She pointed to the top door.

'Thank you,' I said, sliding in the tray. I twisted the timer to fifteen minutes. Henry startled at the ticking, circling round in his bed before settling down again, this time facing the wall to block out the sound. 'OK, what's next?'

I turned around and found Molly's little fingers burrowing in and out of the bag as she pincered one pea at a time and popped it onto her tongue, green on pink.

'Not too cold for you?'

'I like frozen peas.'

I poked my own fingers in and came out with a couple. 'Me too.'

I decide to make an edible contribution to Max's family Christmas, which is probably a mistake because his Irish mam's a terrific cook and anything I bake will taste tolerable at best. Still, I can't turn up empty-handed. So before going to the gallery, I nip to the corner shop and buy the ingredients Nigella tells me I'll need for her Christmas chocolate cookies – 'a doddle to make' apparently.

Maybe for some. Halfway through the recipe, with more cocoa on myself and the floor than in the mixing bowl, I take a selfie. I consider sending it to Max, along with the caption: 'Look what you've done to me.' I'm wearing Karina's apron, which is strangely girly for her, white with a profusion of pansies. I laugh at the blurry image – Eve, an unexpected housewife in the making – then raise my eyebrows at myself. I hit delete.

Now I can see why Nigella calls the cookies 'dark, fat patties'. Mine go into the oven looking like little cow pats and emerge cracked and uneven. She assures me that it's this 'cosy, homespun' look she loves, so without giving it a second thought I slide them from the tray to the cooling rack. Exhausted by my efforts, I decide the topping can wait until this evening.

Marjorie's mid nose blow when I walk through the glass doors. She looks up, embarrassed, realises it's me and continues.

'That time of year,' I say.

'Hm.' She stuffs the tissue up her sleeve and I try not to think about it squelching against her skin. 'Seven pounds.'

When I was Molly's age, I was friends with a girl called Suzie who was always blowing her nose with soft white tissues that her mum had taught her to tuck into her top for safekeeping. One lunchtime, when I was bunged up myself, she surreptitiously pulled one out and passed it to me beneath the table. I felt lucky, like she was sharing a secret.

'You have something on your chin,' says Marjorie.

'I know,' I lie, resisting the urge to rub it off while she's watching. 'I've been baking.'

'Three pounds change,' she says, just before she sneezes.

'Thanks.' I drop the coins in my bag. Breathing lightly through my mouth, I turn away and climb the stairs, running my palm along the polished banister.

I wonder if Suzon would prefer to go by Suzie. School friend Suzie's skin was ashen, except for a plummy splodge shaped like a banana on her left cheek – a birthmark, she said – and more freckles than either of us had ever seen. Another lunchtime, when persistent rain prevented us from hurtling around the playground after we'd finished the gruel on our plates, we played dot-to-dot along her forearm, from the tip of her middle finger to the knob of her elbow (we called it a funny bone). When our teacher saw it, she shouted at us to go and scrub it off. Poor Suzie's arm was blotchy all afternoon, even more than her nose. But we giggled: no one knew that, in the bathroom, we'd created a constellation of freckles around her belly button.

Suzie it is, I think to myself, as I glide through the first two rooms.

It's busy today: in each room leading to mine are a bunch of gallery-goers. I check out the competition in three and four.

Standing in front of a defunct fireplace is a bearded man in ugly orange-and-brown trainers. He's pincered by a pair of chunky headphones and appears to be enjoying it, tapping his toes in time to the tinny song leaking out between the mini speakers and his peculiarly long ears. He's also mindlessly swiping through something on his phone. Girls? Boys? Both? I strain to see the screen but fail.

An inch to his left but seemingly a world away, a woman with glossy hair that smells of Elnett is staring so intently at Mrs Gainsborough that I worry she's trying to burn a hole in her forehead. She's either playing through an important presentation she has to make or analysing an uncomfortable conversation she had with her beautician flatmate this morning. Always achingly slow in the bathroom.

In room five I roll my eyes at a girl taking photos of every artwork she sees. She's spending less than a second in front of each piece. Looking at it through her camera lens – *click* – then moving to the next. Heathen. I continue to room six, giving Badger a greeting-by-way-of-nod. He looks worried, opens his mouth to say something, then snaps it shut like a lid.

I squeeze through the human wall assembled before the barmaid and sit down in front, ignoring the whispers and one sharp clucking tongue, disapproving. That's when I see it. Nothing: I see nothing. A blank wall. Suzon vanished. Disappeared. The bar gone. Not even a clementine left behind as a consolation prize. The eyes of the human wall on another painting. Beside it, a tour guide. I scramble to my feet.

'Where is she?' I ask the question to no one in particular and yet:

'Miss.'

I turn around and find Badger walking towards me, slowly, his arms outstretched, like he's approaching a wild animal prone to spooking at the slightest ruffle of leaves.

'Where is she?' I ask again, eyes flashing between him and the empty space on the wall. The air hums with anticipation. The tour guide keeps talking.

He says nothing. Slowly points to a small, laminated card bordered by a thin black line. A death notice.

I walk to the blank wall where the canvas should be and read, in tiny font, the words:

Édouard Manet (1832–1883),
A Bar at the Folies-Bergère (1882)
This painting is on loan to the Musée d'Orsay, Paris.

'I'm sorry, miss. It will be back in just a month.'
   It? A month? Four weeks? Without seeing her?
'Miss?'
Erased in a flash.
'Miss, can I do anything?'
I have no memory of leaving. Just a heavy weight inside me.

I creep into your room to borrow a book and find you fast asleep beneath the duvet. Your hair is wet and your face is red and smeary like you've scrubbed it too hard. I thought you were staying at his – did something happen? I'll ask you in the morning. It's late and you must be tired. I listen, just for a moment, to you breathing in and out, so evenly.

A heavy weight and at the same time emptiness. It was the same with Grace. All of a sudden I was half-formed, fractured bones. Half a set of shared memories, fragments.
   I'm supposed to be working at the bar this evening, the Christmas Eve rush, but I call in sick. Before going to bed, I take the tray of cookies and tip them out onto the pavement for the foxes to eat.

Fourteen

My bedroom window looks out over our downstairs neighbour's neglected garden and beyond his rickety fence on to
a quiet through-road lined with lamp posts – the meeting
ground for a group of local teenage boys. I peer through the
glass: no sign of any teen swagger this morning. Must all be
opening their stockings or, more likely, sacks of coal. With
the first flecks of stubble beginning to develop around his
knife-sharp cheekbones and pointed chin, the oldest can't be
more than about fifteen. Another boy – with close-cropped
hair and spiky studs that have nothing to do with his soft,
boyish face – lives next door with his working mum. I suspect
she doesn't know that her son and his mates skip school once
or twice a week to hang out behind the house. She's never
home to hear the base-heavy tunes sounding from a booming
speaker or to smell the skunky scent of weed.

I see our downstairs neighbour – the one whose garden
it is – so rarely that I can never remember his name. Not
a huge problem since I'm probably never going to introduce him to anyone. His garden is overrun with spindly
blades of grass that fall forward, bowing to a lone tree with

peely bark and pointy branches. There's a push lawnmower propped up against the left-hand side of the fence, separating his patch from the next, but unsurprisingly it's rusty with age; happened to the hand-me-down bike Dad's neighbour gave me when her own daughter was ready for a Barbie-pink upgrade. Nearby is an old barbecue, the small, portable kind, shaped like a flying saucer and perched on four legs like it's just landed from outer space; a dog bowl, full of slimy water and hunks of moss (never seen a dog); a flimsy deckchair with white-and-blue stripes; and a washing line, the one thing that appears to be in use, pinched at uneven intervals by plastic pegs.

If I had a garden, I like to think I'd keep it trim and tidy, though I've never been into horticulture (you can lead a whore to culture . . . Grace would tell me I'm a wit). It would be my own private park, a sliver of the great outdoors that belongs to me. I'd have pots of peonies and dahlias and Max would be there. Together, we'd sit in the garden drinking late into the evening, him sipping a cold beer, me the gin and tonic with extra lime that he'd made me. He'd be there and I'd be happy.

Not today, though. I picture his Christmas morning. Him spending time with his parents and younger brother – just the four of them before the rest of the family descend, presents in tow. Grandparents. A gaggle of younger cousins. A shrill aunt. An inappropriate uncle – why not? A family friend who has nobody? That could be me. I try and fail to smile back at their beaming faces.

I glance at my phone, which tells me I have a text from him. I open it. *Hey, Happy Christmas! I hope you're feeling better? Looking forward to seeing you. Come anytime from midday.*

I press my lips together and, before I have time to change my mind, fire off a quick reply: *sorry, still not feeling well*

Followed by another, saying what I should have said first: *happy christmas! hope you have a good day*

Before he has time to reply, I pull Mum's jumper over the two layers I wore in bed last night and pad into the kitchen, my feet snug in thick knee-high ski socks (I've never been skiing, but Bill has). The boiler's playing up again, but Karina has decided that's a good thing because it means there's no chance of us frittering away money on something as ephemeral as heating. Another thing that's ephemeral? Life.

I make myself a cup of instant coffee and curl up on the sofa, staring at the wilting fern in the corner and wondering how Suzon is. I think about Max, about how his morning is going and whether he's angry with me, whether I've made a mistake. Then Dad pops into my head, drunk and dreary, making Christmas Day memorable for all the wrong reasons. Making it miserable with one vacant stare or cross word. No, it's the right decision.

I manage a half-smile when I imagine the lunch Max and his family are preparing. I can see it now. It's a feast! A giant turkey, juicy meat and crispy skin, fluffy potatoes roasted in duck fat, Brussels sprouts fried with chopped-up chestnuts, carrots cooked in honey, chipolatas wrapped in crisp rashers of streaky bacon, and his mam's famous stuffing, laced with herby sausage. Both cranberry sauce and redcurrant jelly, as well as velvety-smooth bread sauce and freshly made gravy. For dessert, a traditional Christmas pudding set alight and served with vanilla ice cream, rum sauce, brandy butter or all three. I look down at the muddy dregs of coffee in my mug.

The floor begins to vibrate beneath my bare feet. I spy his name on the screen of my phone, glowing green. Hi, Max, I think to myself, just to test whether he can hear my thoughts. More buzzing. He'll be calling to check up on me, to convince me to come over. I kick the phone away with my toes. Trust me, I'm not good company.

I stand abruptly and turn on the radio, flicking through the crackly stations until I find something other than carols and fucking Michael Bublé, something that will distract me, clear my clouded head. My phone vibrates again, just once. A text. Or maybe he left a voicemail. I sink back into the sofa, hugging my knees into my chest.

My eyes flicker towards the phone before I have a chance to stop them; my fingers loosen their grip around my shins. I close my eyes and picture my hands in his instead. His make mine look childlike. Against his skin, my own feels soft, feminine. His palms are warm, but not clammy. I raise one to my cold cheek.

Max came over one Christmas when we were in our early teens with a baking tray covered with foil – his mam had 'accidentally' made two lots of stuffing. I'll never forget the way Dad patted him on the back as he walked him to the door, the way he told him he was a 'good lad'. Not like the guys I met at Oxford. Or the girls. Except one. Just don't go falling for any of those creative types, Dad told me, the evening I came home from school and – inspired by my brilliant teacher – told him I wanted to study art history. None of them can be trusted, he said sadly, shaking his head, not one of them. I assume he was talking about Mum.

I need food. I stretch my neck and stare fixedly at the boy behind the counter in an attempt to hurry along our order.

Do you think Niall was being a bit off with me last night?

I give up and rest my chin on the table, contemplating what to say, how to tell you what I think of him without pushing you away.

Eve?

Yes, I think he was, I say.

Maybe he was tired.

Maybe. Or upset about the football. Or hungry. Or even, maybe that's just what he's like.

One grilled cheese and one bagel with smoked salmon and cream cheese?

Thank you, I say, sliding the bagel towards you and catching a glimpse of your downturned eyes. Look, Grace, maybe you should take a break? I really don't know about him, some of the things he says, the way he treats you. Do you trust him?

You don't?

You want my honest opinion?

You don't answer. Instead, you flick the capers out of your bagel and say, I'm sure it's fine.

I force myself into the shower, twisting the stiff metal dial to turn the temperature right down. I gasp as I step beneath the torrent of icy water but resist hopping immediately back out. I breathe in through my nose and out through my mouth, as Youla would have me do, imparting wisdom in her husky foreign accent (Greek, I think). After a while I get used to the cold and end up staying under the nozzle for a quarter of an hour. When I get out I pick up my phone and, without looking at the screen, hold down the power button.

Karina texted me first thing to tell me where she'd hidden my present. She must have thought I'd have been too excited and unwrapped it early if she'd handed it over before they left. Before I head out for a walk, I wander into their bedroom and, as instructed, rootle around in their wardrobe. Stuck to the inside of one door are photos of their friends, most of whom I don't recognise. That girl in the halter-neck with the angel curls, I've never met her. Nor that guy in the hipster hat with fuzzy facial hair and a floppy cigarette slung between his lips. The one cheers-ing with a frothy pint looks vaguely familiar, but I've definitely never laid eyes on the 'fashion' brunette sidling up to him. Karina features in about five photos, Bambi-like with her long, skinny limbs. Is that Bill? The sandy-haired one in a white shirt, who she's kissing, an inch above the doorknob. Surprisingly photogenic.

In the bottom right-hand corner, on top of some shoe-boxes, is a soft square parcel wrapped in lilac tissue paper and finished with a matching ribbon tied up in a bow. I slide it towards me and rip it open, letting pieces of purple fall to the floor like confetti. Inside: one silky robe.

Prince's Court is the kind of quiet you experience when you're underwater in a swimming pool. As I lock the front door, smack-bang in the middle of the craggy brick building, I look left and right to see if any of our neighbours' lights are on. The hazy windows into each flat are the same shade of grey as the front doors. Either the residents are huddled in their living rooms, lights dimmed, falling asleep with full bellies in front of a festive film, or they're out of town visiting loved ones. Because everyone has someone: families to feast with, friends to give gifts to, future husbands and wives to flirt with. People enjoy spending time with them because they're fun to have around. As far as I can tell, I'm the only one here.

'Oh, other than you, of course,' I say, with a wink, to the stone toad perched outside our front door. A monosyllabic laugh. I still can't wink without screwing up one side of my face. I try again and fail. Spasm.

'No plans for Christmas?'

He stares at me with his beady eyes, sunken above bulging bags and beneath weighty lids. His lips are long and thin.

'I see, you're on your own now.'

Nothing, not so much as a blink.

Apparently Karina and Bill found him here when they came to pick up the keys. The old owners must have left him behind, whether intentionally or by mistake.

'Well, have a good one.'

Like grief, he's been squatting here ever since.

It's not a white Christmas but I'm not complaining. Inevitably, when the sky does decide to shed its skin it changes its mind an hour later and you're left sloshing through skew-bald pulp on the pavement. The air is sharp but it feels good after so many hours indoors. A Christmas Day stroll – it's something people do.

I turn left onto Fentiman Road, lined with terraced houses, and glance through the windows as I walk. Strung-up cards, spangling lights, ribboned presents. Crackers, jokes, charades. Wreaths hang on most front doors, dried flowers in silvers, reds, blues and greens – probably artificial. The street looks like it's signalling to a far-off ship: fairy lights flash on and off at numbers twelve, fourteen and eighteen.

I hear the Fentiman Arms – one of Karina and Bill's favourite pubs – before I reach it. Various families are enjoying Christmas meals cooked for them by harried chefs whose own families are missing them at home. It's cold outside and the sun's calling it a day, a cool embrace around the pub's golden glow. Is that an open fire? A woman with honey hair reminds me of Annie.

I try to picture her Christmas Day. Her husband, or ex-husband, there to keep things as normal as possible for Molly. I can see Annie now, smiling, going on with the show. Holding back tears until she can get away with nipping to the loo again. I feel a nick in my stomach, like skin caught on barbed wire. What if Molly picks up on the tension? One broken glass or some spilt red wine is all it takes for the carefully maintained balance to tip. For happy to turn to sad. For us, it was always just as we sat down to eat. Wait, Dad, you have to wear your paper hat! Chair legs would screech, footsteps recede, a door slam. I'd be left alone, fingers knotted in my lap, as I watched the food slowly cool.

When I get home, I close every curtain – keep the outside world out – and open a bottle of red. I read my book, about a sad and lonely girl who decides to sleep for a year when things get tough, and contemplate the benefits of following suit. Two or three glasses in, I fold over the top corner of the page I'm on, close the book and reach for my phone, now concealed under the coffee table. I turn it on. Another message from Max: *Hope you're feeling ok, Eve. Call me if you want to talk.*

I also have two texts from Annie. I take a glug, wipe my lips with the back of my hand and read.

The first: *Merry Christmas from me and Molly, Eve! A x*

The second contains a snowman emoji, presumably from Molly.

I smile, and I'm still smiling a few seconds later when Karina's calling. 'Merry Christmas!' I call in my jolliest voice.

'Yeah, you too.'

She sounds strange.

'Everything OK?' I ask.

'What do you think, Eve?'

Anxiety starts to nibble away at my fingers and toes. Please, no.

'You know, for some reason, I'm OK with you taking my things. My necklace, my robe, my lipstick.'

I go to speak, but she gets there first.

'But my boyfriend is a step too far, Eve.' She starts to sob.

'Karina—'

'No,' she says, sniffing, 'I'm still talking.'

I close my eyes. Fucking hell, Bill. Christmas Day?

'We let you live with us for half the rent we could get from someone else. We make an effort with you – to be friends, not just flatmates. We put up with all your moaning, your moods. The way you zone out when we're trying to talk to you. Well, what a waste.'

She's crying properly now and so am I. In a raspy voice, I tell her I'm sorry.

'Yeah, me too.'

'God, it was nothing, Karina. Less than nothing.' When she doesn't say anything, I add: 'We were drunk.'

She laughs, but not in a happy way. 'That's a crap excuse and you know it.'

Of course I do, but this can't be it. 'Karina, please. I'm so sorry. I can fix this.'

'It's time you left anyway.'

'But—'

'Please can you pack up your things?'

'Can't we just—'

'Now, Eve. There's been a change of plan and we're coming home this evening.'

When I don't reply, she says: 'I don't want you there when we get back, OK?'

'OK.' I pull a cuticle so hard it bleeds.

It doesn't take me long to pack, partly because I focus on the fundamentals but mainly because I don't have much stuff. I purposely ignore the Picasso print and a shelf full of books, hoping that if I leave some bits behind, I'll be able to come back and make amends.

Out on the pavement, I phone a few friends, but either they don't pick up or they tell me, their voices feathered with regret, that they're sorry, there isn't room. I don't phone Annie because she has enough to worry about, or Max because I can't bear to explain to him what's happened. I try to imagine how he might react. Protective, disappointed, angry, jealous. Maybe he'd show up in Vauxhall, unannounced, and challenge Bill to a duel.

I walk to the station, forgetting that the tube isn't running. Two Ubers cancel on me. The third arrives fifteen minutes later. The driver's chatty to begin with. I turn and face the window. Christmas songs sound from the radio.

By the time we reach Finsbury Park it's around ten. It would be pitch-black were it not for car headlights and kebab-shop interiors shining bright. We pull off the main drag and pass through more residential streets to Dad's flat. The living room looks on to the street and, through the shut-tered blinds, I can just about make out the gentle glow of the lamp that hovers above his armchair.

'Merry Christmas to you too,' says the driver when I fail to thank him.

I linger outside the front door for a few minutes before ringing the bell, telling myself I don't have a choice. I have to do something I learned early on never to do – I have to ask my dad for help. When I press and hold my finger against the metal button, he doesn't appear. I try the knocker. Still nothing. I feel beneath the faux-terracotta plant pot, with a crooked crack working its way down from lip to base, and find the spare key. After a moment's pause, I turn the lock.

The smell is almost unbearable. A pungent mix of stale carpet, booze and perspiration. It wouldn't be a bad thing if my dad took up smoking. Cigarettes smell better than sweat.

Nothing has changed since I last visited in the summer. The coat rack is bare except for his ratty Barbour, shiny with age and ragged at the hem and cuffs. The bumpy wallpaper is peeling back on itself like a pre-opened envelope that won't re-stick. Ignored post has piled up on the doormat. I dump my bags and start to flick through it, just in case there's anything addressed to me. I give up when I see a women's clothes catalogue – no name but clearly directed at Mum – and rub my chest to get rid of the pain. Sometimes I don't blame him for wanting to dull his own. I start untoggling my coat, then change my mind. When I brush my fingertips against the radiator, it's stone cold.

The door to the living room is closed so I creep past it into the hole-in-the-wall kitchen. Every surface is hidden beneath empty or half-drunk cans of cider and dirty dishes streaked with brown sauce, breadcrumbs, solidified puddles of fat, gooey orange. The pedal bin is overflowing with rubbish and standing upright in front of it are empty whisky bottles. Beside them, a mousetrap with no cheese. I peer inside the fridge: nothing but more cans, a half-eaten packet of that kiddy ham that looks like it's made of plastic and a bunch of sauces. In the cupboards, tins of tomato soup and baked beans. The calendar on the wall is stuck in July, every square blank apart from the second Wednesday, which contains my handwriting: *nine o'clock, doctor's appointment – please don't forget*. I grimace and flick through the sheets to December.

The old springs in his armchair wheeze. I wonder whether he's heard me and turn around to face the hallway, bracing myself. A minute goes by and nothing happens. Must have been shifting in his seat. I wash my hands, even though there isn't any soap and I haven't touched anything, and go to greet him.

I knock on the door before turning the handle. 'Dad?'

He's fast asleep, facing a blank TV screen. His legs are outstretched, his ankles crossed – if he weren't wearing baggy moss-coloured cords and his holey slippers, the pose could pass for elegant. His elbows are supported by the worn armrests, his palms clutch his favourite mug, which is propped up on his paunch. As always, his face is the shade of a plum, purplish-red, as if there's been a leak from the capillaries dutifully pumping blood beneath the surface. Below his eyes are spidery lines of a darker shade, a sign that other vessels have burst.

'Dad?'

His nose twitches, like I'm the bad smell. Tiny grey hairs sprout from his nostrils. The hair on his head is, strangely, still fairly dark. He could do with having it cut.

'Dad!'

This time his entire body jumps. He opens his oval eyes, which I've always thought appear kind – even when they're blood-red.

'Evie.'

Only he calls me that.

'What a nice surprise.'

In spite of myself, I feel the sting of tears, something solid in my throat.

'What are you doing here?' he asks, heaving himself into a more upright position, all the while clutching onto his mug.

'I need a place to stay, Dad.'

He keeps shuffling, not content.

'Dad?'

'Hm, what's that?'

'I—' I falter, determined not to cry. 'I need a place to stay.'

'What about your own place?'

'I had to leave.'

'Why?' He cocks his head, confused rather than concerned.

'Does it matter?'

He mumbles something about his lumpy chair and, after one final shove, sits still. He raises his mug to his lips, then peers into it, frowning. A groan.

'Dad?'

'What's that, Evie?'

I swallow the desperation rising inside me. 'I don't have anywhere to stay.'

He looks at me with faraway eyes. He sighs aloud, strokes his stubble, from his cheeks and chin down his neck to his chest. 'Oh dear.'

'What do you mean, "Oh dear"?'

'Oh dear that you have nowhere to stay.' He says it sadly, like it's a real shame, then he picks up the remote.

I feel the tears again, stinging in my eyes, on the verge of spilling. 'It's Christmas Day, Dad.'

'Well, look, love, I'm sure you'll find somewhere.'

Almost inaudibly, I ask, 'Here?'

He puffs out his cheeks. 'I just don't know where you'd stay here. You know what it's like. I haven't had a chance to—'

I look away and, as I do so, hear a conversation start up on the TV. Some game show that can only have one winner.

'Evie?'

I look back at him.

He's looking at the screen.

'Yes?'

'Grab me a top-up from the kitchen, would you?'

In my mind I'm screaming but my mouth's not moving, there's no sound.

'All right there, Evie?'

'Goodbye, Dad.'

An hour later, I'm in Kilburn. As a last resort I tried phoning Paul, but there was no answer – probably a good thing, except now he's going to think I was drunk-dialling. On Christmas Day.

Max's lights are off. He must be in bed. By himself or with someone? Standing outside in the cold, my thoughts start to unravel. No, we haven't had 'the chat', but Max isn't like that. I tell myself to get it together and press the buzzer.

A few seconds later his voice sounds, a little groggy: 'Who is it?'

'It's me.' I force a smile at the speaker in case there's a camera. 'Eve.'

'Eve?' He sounds surprised, unsurprisingly. 'Come on up.' As the door opens he reminds me that it's the second floor.

I transfer my bags into one hand in an effort to make them less conspicuous. It doesn't work. As soon as Max sees me his face drops.

'What's happened?' He's wearing a navy jumper and a pair of tracksuit bottoms, not unlike the ones Bill had on before we fucked up. His hair is tousled from being in bed and his eyes, though open wide, are specked with sleep. 'Eve?'

I try to unhook one bag at a time. I fail. Without warning, tears are trickling down my face. He steps towards me and releases the entire load from my grip.

'Thanks,' I say, unfurling my fingers and rubbing my palms together to iron out the strap marks, wiping the wet from my cheeks as I work out what to say. I decide to go with vague: 'Karina and I had an argument.'

'And she kicked you out?' He raises his eyebrows, either with pity or disbelief. 'Must have been a pretty serious argu-ment. Isn't she in Norway?'

'It was. She is. She was.'

We're hovering in the doorway, which makes me wonder whether he does have another girl in there. More tears spill over my lower lids.

'OK, come in.' Still holding my things, he moves aside, then closes the door behind me. 'Do you want something to eat or drink? A bath?'

'I think I just need to get some sleep.'

'Of course.' He goes to move, then pauses. 'I can sleep on the sofa bed if you want your own room.'

'If it's OK, I'd rather be with you.'

Fifteen

The next morning, it takes me a few minutes to remember where I am. The light's different, brighter thanks to a nosy street lamp sidling up to the window. The temperature feels different too, warmer, like the heating is on. Of course, that could also be down to Max lying beside me.

I wish I'd come straight here. I wish I'd never gone to Dad's. Before, even if I didn't really believe it, I could at least tell myself that he cared, that he'd be there for me if I ever really needed him. I try blinking hard to erase the memory – the old habit, apparently faulty.

I hear a mewing. I slip out of bed and creep towards the window. A sooty cat is prowling along the brick wall by the rubbish and recycling bins, a communal dumping ground for all who live in the building. It pauses, crouching close to the ground, its back end slightly raised, eyes locked on an invisible (to me) target. Mouse? Rat? Beetle? Bee? Don't do it, it'll sting! Too late. It catapults itself into the air and lands with the grace of a prima ballerina. A brief pause and then it continues on its way, pride intact by the look of that strut. No sign of the prey.

'Eve, what are you looking at?'

I turn around to find Max propped up on his elbow, squinting at me through sleep-filled eyes.

'I'm sorry,' I say, sliding back under the duvet. 'I heard a cat.'

'Mmm, ginger or black?' he asks, wrapping an arm around my waist, his face pressed between my shoulder blades.

'Black.'

'Ah, the alpha male. Always prowling around the bins, that one. Ginger's a little more elusive.'

I yawn and settle back down beside him, focusing on the feeling of his breath on my skin.

Before Max heads to the gym, he makes us both some coffee.

I haven't been to his flat for a while, not since shortly after he moved in. He paid the deposit with all his savings and some inheritance, and now has a hefty mortgage. Even though most of his furniture probably comes from IKEA, it gives the place a satisfying Scandi look: plenty of wood and a palette of greys and creams. Blue cushions on the sofa add a splash of colour, as does the family of house plants, one towering above the boyishly big TV. A couple of prints on the walls. One of those kelim rugs. A compact bookshelf with room to spare. I feel a bud of hope inside me.

'I know it still needs some work,' says Max, eyes glued to mine, trying to gauge my reaction, 'but it's getting there.'

'Oh, Max, it's great. I'm impressed, really.'

He smiles and nods. 'I don't know what you like to eat for breakfast, but there's cereal in there, bread on the side.'

I follow his pointing finger towards the cupboard by the fridge and fish out the giant box of Shreddies; a yellow banner informs me that it's a BIG 1KG PACK. I decant some into a mug and start nibbling.

Max looks at me like I've gone mad.

'What?'

He laughs. 'Nothing, I just forgot you don't like milk.'

'So, Christmas was good?'

'It was fine, fun. It would have been even better if you'd been there.'

I nod and smile tightly, imagining the casual affection and gentle chaos of his family gatherings. The steady hum of chatter and laughter. Homey smells wafting through the air. I think of the silence strung out between me and Dad, broken only by his guttural cough. The scent of whisky that hit me when he lurched forward in his chair. 'It would have been great.'

A few seconds go by, in which I consider asking where his gym is. Or what exercise he's planning to do. Anything to avoid the question I know is coming.

Then he squints. 'Are you going to tell me what happened?'

I shovel a few Shreddies into my mouth, buying time.

He passes me my coffee and waits.

I start picking at my fingers. 'I can't. I'm sorry.'

A flicker of disappointment and then: 'OK, you don't have to talk to me, as long as you're talking to someone.'

I manage to keep still, but my insides are squirming.

'Are you still seeing your therapist?'

I wince. I'd forgotten that fib. 'I am,' I say, 'or at least I was.' I look down at the floorboards and spy a Shreddie lodged in a crack. I bend down and pick it up, pop it on the side. 'She's away at the moment.'

When he smiles it feels like someone's stuck a nail in my chest.

'It's great that you're still seeing her, Eve, I'm glad.'

I attempt a smile too.

'Will she be back soon?'

'I hope so.'

'Well, you're obviously on it. I'll stop interfering.'

'I like it when you interfere,' I say. 'It makes me feel like you care.'

He walks towards me, holds my face in his hands. 'Of course I care. And you can stay here for as long as you need.'

The following day I decide it's too far to walk to life-modelling from Kilburn so I hop on a bus to Edgware Road, then catch the tube. Probably a good thing: it's icy out, the coldest day of the year. I breathe deeply as I walk up the road to the studio, imagining the diesel particulates working their way up my nose and into my brain, clouding my thoughts.

Annie catches up with me on the stairs, a little out of breath. 'Eve! How was your Christmas?'

'It was good, thank you.' No need to go into any detail. 'And you?'

'Mine was fine.' She smiles, a sad smile that wobbles on delivery.

I stop at the top of the stairs and so does she. 'Is everything all right?' I feel I should ask. Her blue eyes are lake-like, calm on the surface but full of uncertainty.

'Oh, ignore me,' she says, her voice cracking. She pauses for a moment before continuing. 'I'm just being silly.'

'No, that's silly. What is it?'

She's twiddling the woven leather strap of her handbag between her fingers. She opens and closes her mouth a couple of times, searching for the right words. The third time: 'It's

David. I had my suspicions before, but now I'm sure of it. He—'

'Ladies, how are we doing today?' Paul pokes his head around the studio door. His chin and cheeks are covered with more stubble than usual and he's wearing a beige cable-knit jumper I don't recognise. A gift from someone.

'Wonderful, Paul, and you?'

She's a good actress – knows deflection is key. Was she about to tell me that her husband cheated? Or has a new partner? Or maybe he's unwell. They've reconciled but now he's dying – the doctors caught it too late, no time for treatment, six months to live.

'Oh super, super.' His eyes squint a little behind his glasses as he says it. 'All good, Eve?' He nods his head, pre-empting my response, and rocks between toes and heels.

'All good.'

I'm half undressed by the time he reappears with a worried look on his face – mouth open, teeth clenched, forehead crumpled like newspaper. My Converse are kicked off to the side and my leggings are folded over my bag, quite tidily for me. He knocks on the screen – asking without asking, Are you decent? But really there's no need. He can already see me, and he knows I know it. He swings his hands together, clapping but not.

'Everything OK?' I ask, avoiding his gaze as I unbutton my denim shirt. I slow my finger work, still unsure about being naked in front of him out of character and in such close quarters. To avoid strap marks I've stopped wearing a bra on my way to the studio. He still hasn't said anything, so I give him a fleeting look. Fingers slow further still.

Luckily these buttons are a little stiff. I'm a third of the way down.

'Oh yes, all fine. Just a slight mix-up.' He looks over his shoulder and chews the inside of his cheek. I haven't seen him like this. I haven't seen him as anything but in control.

'What kind of mix-up?' I can't stall anymore. I undo the bottom two buttons and whip off my shirt, thankful I'm still wearing my knickers, then throw on Karina's robe, silky against my skin. 'Paul, who's that?'

An old man in a white dressing gown – the fluffy kind you might find in a fancy hotel room, along with a pair of matching slippers – is zigzagging between the easels, greeting some of the students by name. He's heading our way, a little hunched over, carrying a plaid cushion. What the actual fuck.

'Yes, so, as I was saying . . .'

I glance at him sharply.

'. . . we seem to have double-booked. Ralph was hired for this evening's session back in August, before you started. He's in demand so we try to nab him as far in advance as we can.'

I glance over at Ralph, balding on top, with leathery brown skin. Looks like he's spent too much time in the sun – like clothes laid out to dry, turned crisp when forgotten. In demand for what?

'Eve?'

'OK, so what do you want me to do about it?' I hate it when I'm like this. Moody teenager.

'Well, I was thinking it might be fun – and challenging for the students – to draw the pair of you. Have you pose together. What do you think?'

I exhale, too loudly. A deflated balloon at the end of a birthday not worth celebrating.

'No touching, of course,' he adds, quickly but quietly, resting his hand on my shoulder as he says it. 'Just sitting or standing side by side.'

Ralph's onstage – lucky the step up is shallow, probably has dodgy knees – and approaching, the floorboards creaking beneath his old-man weight. I put on a smile.

'You, young lady, must be Eve,' he says, extending a hand well and truly mapped with the lines of age.

'Nice to meet you, Ralph,' I say, keeping a wary eye on the scrap of material securing his dressing gown.

'Well, as I've said to you both, I think this is going to be great,' says Paul, turning on his heel and inching towards the stage's edge. 'We'll start off with some gestures, as usual, then move on to two-minute and then ten-minute poses before the break. OK?' He's looking at me as he says it, still assessing my reaction.

Like a second-rate dad leaving his child alone in the flat for the first time, aged eight, not to return until the next day. No telephone. Barely any food in the fridge. What if I'd had an accident? Burnt my wrist on the stove. Sliced off the tip of my little finger. Slipped in the bathroom and cracked my head on the sink.

'OK,' I say, straight-faced. He doesn't deserve my reassurance.

As Ralph tugs at his gown, I avert my eyes to the window. They skate across the sharp outlines of overlapping jagged roofs and chimneys standing on end. Plumes of smoke, a couple of loosely spun clouds (must have run out of thread), a plane overhead. I consider where the lucky passengers might be escaping to. Take me with you.

Bill was hairier than I thought he'd be – when I tugged off his T-shirt, his chest was covered with little brown hairs. The memory of his fingers on my skin makes me queasy, the way they grabbed at me. His lips hot with chilli. I remember that strange, slippery sensation of drunkenness descending, my body surrendering control over certain limbs, my tongue tripping over my teeth. But Karina's right – that's a crap excuse. It was still a betrayal.

Why the fuck I'm thinking about this now, with Ralph bare-bottomed by my side, is beyond me. Up close, I discover that his brown skin is in fact floury-white skin made to look dark by hundreds, thousands, no, hundreds of thousands of joined-up sunspots. I squint, then stop, in case any of the students are focusing on my face. In fact, some of the sunspots are moles, raised and sprouting fine grey hairs. There, to the left of his belly button.

'Change.' Paul's guiding us today to save one of us keeping an eye on the other as that other keeps an eye on the clock.

I cross my legs and wind my arms together up above my head. Who needs Houdini when you have Eve, The Impossibly Tangled Human Plait? Ralph's also standing, arms stacked in front of his chest and legs bent, our very own Morris dancer in the buff. My thighs would be trembling by now so he must be fitter than he looks.

'Change.'

He slips between positions as smoothly as a tai chi master. No sudden movements. I suspect he's been doing this for some time – an old hand, among other things. I find a stance that lets me focus on his face.

It's a field of ridge and furrow. Dead-straight grooves run from his nose to the corners of his mouth while dog-leg wrinkles frame his chin. His eyelids droop down over his eyes, making him seem sad or tired. His neatly combed hair – missing on top – is thin and has shed any lingering flecks of colour. Brown, perhaps.

'Great job, Ralph and Eve.'

Eve and Ralph.

'Now how about something symmetrical?'

Ralph suggests two seated poses.

Good idea, I think. Definitely preferable to lying by his bare side for forty-five minutes like we're lost in post-coital bliss, the older man and the young mistress. I grab a chair and position it so I'm facing the students, trying to sense if they look at him the same way they look at me. Or is it gendered looking?

'Oh, I wondered if we might face one another?'

'Quite right, Ralph,' says Paul. 'Much better.'

At least the intensity of their looking is spread a little more thinly.

I resist mentioning Marina Abramović and that lengthy performance piece I read about at MoMA. Apparently she sat still and silent for seven hours a day, six days a week, over a period of almost three months, as intrepid visitors took turns sitting opposite. A child asked her mother if the artist was made of plastic. A beautiful young man wept. At least one person stripped her bare. Fortunately my torture should only last for three-quarters of an hour.

'Perfect. Hold it there.'

To begin with, I avoid eye contact altogether, looking everywhere other than Ralph's face. I'm turned away from my modesty screen, towards the peeling exhibition posters tacked straight onto the wall. Matisse at the Royal Academy, Caillebotte at the Musée d'Orsay, something about portrait miniatures at the Met. The Courtauld is often overlooked but I like it that way – helps me keep her to myself. *Helped* me keep her to myself. Below the posters are pigeonholes rammed with pencils, brushes and papers. When I look out of the window I must move my head because Paul encourages us to 'keep holding the pose, please, looking straight on'.

I try the trick of staring at Ralph's eyebrows (my favourite schoolteacher taught me that one, before my unexpected Oxford interview). I trace the wiry hairs from left to right, reading them like a book, the bridge of his nose the spine. Punctuating the middle of the second eyebrow is a mole. When I finally do drop my gaze to Ralph's eyes, I find them closed.

I don't know why but I drop it further, down his chest, crawling with little white hairs, and between his man breasts, not as saggy as I'd expect. It keeps dropping, out of my control now, too heavy for me to hold up, past his stomach, which seems rounder now he's sitting. Down, down, down. Oh God! Like an elastic band, my gaze pings back up to his eyes, now open and twinkling with delight. Again, I think of Bill, his lazy eye and his terrible jokes. Sometimes he actually made me laugh. So did Karina, though I'm not sure she intended to. I close my eyes and will them to be laughing together again.

By midday I'm drained. Mind and body kaput.

'Good.' Ralph stands there for a moment or two, still naked, stretching left and right, surveying the room.

I slink back into Karina's robe, which I didn't return, even though she busted me. My own robe, the one they gave me for Christmas, is neatly folded in my bag at Max's.

'Lovely working with you, dear,' he adds, at last covering himself but not before giving me a full-frontal.

Even now they're concealed, I can still see his slack balls – it's like I have X-ray vision that won't switch off. This must be how the students feel when they see me before and after class. I pull my own robe tighter.

I expect Annie to stick around but she's the first one out of the door, yanking her phone from her bag and pulling with it a grey notebook that falls to the floor. She doesn't notice, already up and out of her chair. My fingers start to itch. Others follow, among them Ralph, who must have left his clothes in the loo.

I nip behind the screen and slip on my things. By the time I'm dressed, I'm alone. I make a beeline for the notebook – a Moleskine with a hardback cover, about the width of my handspan – and open it at a random page.

Anyway, I'm not desperate – or was it fragile, feeble-minded?
It's hard to remember precise put-downs from that barrage.

A diary. I tried to keep one after Grace – write it down, people said, it's cathartic – but it ended up being one long letter to her, twirling around the subject, telling her banal details about my day instead of how I felt. What I'd eaten for breakfast. The colour pants I was wearing. The weather report. If I had toothache. I close and reopen my eyes, and flick through the pages.

Each is filled with Annie's graceful, elaborate handwriting. I glance towards the open door, adrenaline flooding through my veins, an instant shot. I can't. Can I? Holding my breath, I slide it into my bag. A piece of Annie. No wonder she's wounded. Dickhead.

'Eve?'

Paul.

He closes the door behind him and walks towards me. 'I'm sorry I missed your call the other night.'

Fuck, I'd forgotten. 'That's OK.'

'I would have called you back but it was my turn to take the kids this Christmas, so I didn't have much alone time.' He takes off his glasses, rubs his eyes, then puts them back on.

Kids? Plural? 'How old?'

'Seventeen and fifteen.' He smiles, like them reaching their teens is something to be proud of.

'Wow.' Which makes you?

'Their mother and I got divorced two and a half years ago. They live with her, but they come and stay with me every other week, sometimes more.' There's that smile again.

'Right.' So how old exactly? I suspected his Dumbo ears might make him look younger than he is, as if he hasn't grown into them.

'Anyway.' He takes another step towards me, reaches out and takes hold of my side, just below my hip bone. Lower than usual. 'Maybe you would like to come and model for me on Thursday evening?'

'Model for you?'

He drops his hand. 'I would like to draw you.'

Is that a euphemism?

'I'll pay you, of course. Same rate.'

Maybe not. 'Yes, OK.'

'Good, I'll message you.' He smiles, nods once, turns to walk away. 'Oh, I have to head off now so can you let Ralph know that I've left the payment by the door?'

My eyes flash to two envelopes sitting side by side.

'Eve?' He's lingering in the threshold.

'Yes, will do.'

'Thanks. Bye, then.'

After he's gone, I check there's no sign of Ralph and, curious, carefully unpeel the back of his envelope, his name neatly written in pencil. Forty pounds. That can't be right, unless we've been paid more because of the mix-up. I tuck the top into the bottom, hoping he won't notice it was stuck down before, and check my own: thirty.

'Everything all right over here?' Ralph's now fully dressed in his maroon cords, black coat and beret – *bonjour*. All that exercise has got his blood pumping: his scarf's hanging smartly over the crook of one arm.

I hold my chin firm. 'Yes, everything's fine, nothing out of the ordinary to report.' I stuff my envelope into my pocket. 'Goodbye, Ralph.'

The diary's burning in my bag, a small but wide-open window into Annie's life. I can't wait until I'm back at Max's – it's too long. Also, he'll be there. Instead, I walk to the Natural History Museum and wait five minutes. I can read on the bus.

Tapped in and sitting at the front of the top deck, I open it at page one.

> *I've decided to do something I was sure I never would:*
> *pay a stranger to listen to me talking about my feelings.*
> *So American. So self-indulgent. That's what I always*
> *thought. Anyway, now I'm diarising – at her suggestion.*

She's in therapy. I'm surprised and apparently she is too. Like me, she doesn't seem particularly open when it comes to sharing how she feels. I did suggest it to Dad once, when he was coherent – a brief spell of sobriety one weirdly warm March, back when he still had the odd period of drying out. He scoffed, said I should have seen Mum, that he was nothing compared to her. In bed at midday, the covers thrown over her head to block the rays of sunshine seeping through the blinds. One day she couldn't bring herself to face the world, he said, not even us, her family – no, Evie, not even you. The next she'd bound into the kitchen and suggest pancakes for breakfast and a trip to the coast.

Now that I've sat in the chair, with the long pauses and the tissues, I understand why it's called the talking cure. Of course, it's going to take time. It's hard to unravel.

After Grace, they practically rammed it down my throat like I was some French goose. Not Dad, of course. He was oblivious and had already expressed his views on the subject. But my unbelievably brainy yet socially incompetent tutor, our equally awkward professors, the student welfare officers: they were all for it. They recommended I visit the college counsellor. Just try it, what's the harm? They were the ones who pushed the diary idea too. I told them I wasn't ready to talk to anyone. Ignore the problem, I thought, and it'll go away.

I no longer feel the urge to shout when he skips a family dinner. When he says I'm nagging him, I keep my mouth closed rather than wasting energy. I resist asking whether he would prefer to stay in, just the three of us, on a Sunday evening rather than go to the pub. Now I just have to conquer that lurch my stomach does every time he goes outside to take a phone call – we both know he's seeing other women.

I knew it. Even if I ever did manage to navigate those life steps – house, husband, kids – it wouldn't be worth it. It would never last because nothing ever does, even if you're Annie. Everything falls apart in the end.

I close the diary and stuff it back in my bag, scratching at my fingers.

Sixteen

It's Wednesday and I don't know what to do with myself. Max went out early on his bike and I'm not due at Annie's until midday. I try staying in bed but I can't get back to sleep, Suzon's face tattooed on the underside of my lids. I pick up one of Max's books but I'm struggling to focus, my attention span defective. I google the painting but it's not the same, not after years of weekly sessions face to face, in the flesh. I even try to vaguely recollect my non-conversations with Marjorie – a weekly exchange of a handful of words at best.

After showering, I brush through my hair without holding it at the roots, yanking the brush from top to tip and detaching entire knots of soggy strands in the process. I bundle them up into a ball and shake them into the loo, wondering if it's normal that so many fall out each day. I brush my teeth, then floss between the cracks – something I never normally do, which is probably why they bleed.

When I'm done, I stand and stare at myself in the mirror. I tilt my head to the left, bite down on my lower lip and pinch my cheeks.

Annie must have noticed her diary's missing. She writes in it every day by the looks of things, a ritual, a routine to keep her going. That graceful script, almost calligraphic. It reminds me of a medieval manuscript, big and small letters swirling and looping across the page. Too bad it's not illuminated with miniature illustrations, portraits of her and her family in vibrant colours and gold leaf.

Her house looks extra bright against the mousey-grey sky, which is mottled with stringy clouds and has been shedding tears non-stop since this morning. Shading my eyes from the sparkling white stone, I climb the steps and ring the bell. Within seconds I spy ten little fingers wriggling through the letter box.

'Oh dear,' I say, crouching so low that my teeth are only inches away. 'I hope Mr Crocodile doesn't eat these worms. He's feeling peckish and this is the sort of squirmy snack he fancies.'

'No, no, Mr Crocodile, please don't eat us!' cries Molly, retracting her juicy offering and retreating down the hall.

'Eve, hi,' says Annie, opening the door.

She's well dressed, as usual, in a thin black jumper, straight jeans and her loafers. She looks intimidatingly together. Is she hurting? She must be, feeling vulnerable after what her husband has done, bracing for the divorce, but the perfectly made-up face – there's that coral lipstick again – doesn't give much away. I've never known someone who can switch their emotions on and off so easily. Just press the red button.

'Everything OK down there?' she asks, laughing.

I realise I'm still bent at letter box height. 'Oh, hello!' I stand up and, in the process, almost wobble back down the steps. I imagine a bloodstain defacing her squeaky-clean façade. I lean in to hug her; she takes control and we end up pecking on each cheek.

Standing before her, it strikes me – not for the first time – just how different we are, and how she turned out a lot better than I did. Since that first proper conversation we had when we went for a drink, she's opened up about the fact that her father left when she was fourteen, that he was too young, too curious, too selfish – and he proved it by starting again with a younger woman with fewer greys and more eggs. He missed out on her adolescence, an absent father, barely wrote or called. I don't know, maybe losing a father isn't as bad as losing a mother. God, I hope she can't smell that over her spicy perfume, the reek of jealousy. Although, I've lost both, haven't I?

'Well, come in.'

I close the door behind me, brushing her dopily affectionate dog's fur the wrong way.

Just as I go to take off my coat, Annie reaches out and clutches my arm.

I hold my breath. She knows.

'I forgot to mention, I'm hosting a workshop at home today so I was wondering if there's any chance you could take Molly to yours?'

'Oh, sure,' I say, exhaling, though of course there is no mine. Nor a Karina and Bill's. Which leaves Max's. I'm sure he won't mind but, just in case, I fire off a text. 'Molly,' I call, 'do you want to choose some toys to take with you?'

'Yes!' With that, she scampers up the stairs.

'Thanks, Eve,' says Annie, smiling and heading back upstairs herself. 'Text me the address and I'll come and collect her later.'

'You're sure? I can bring her back if that's easier.'

'No, no, it's fine. Besides, it would be nice to see where you live.'

I rack my brain, trying to remember if I ever told her I lived in Vauxhall.

Molly reappears a moment later with enough things to keep her occupied for a week.

'OK, Molly, let's put these in a bag. It's cold outside so you're going to need a coat.'

She points to a yolk-yellow parka on the rack, too high for her to reach.

I help her into it. 'Do you have gloves? A hat and scarf?'

Below is a woven basket full, it seems, of all of the above.

'Do you want to borrow some, Eve?'

Who, me? Wouldn't dream of it.

After a tube and bus ride, we're back at Max's flat.

'Is this your house, Eve?'

'This is where my friend Max lives,' I say, rootling around in my bag for the spare key he gave me on our way back from a fairly sedate shift at the bar on Monday. 'I'm staying with him at the moment.'

She looks up at me with hunched shoulders and a half smiling, half wincing face. 'Is he your boyfriend?'

I laugh, wondering how it would feel to say the word: this is Max, my boyfriend. 'I'm not sure about that.' I let us in and direct her towards the stairs. 'Up two floors, Molly.'

'Just like at home!'

'Hm, not quite.'

She races ahead and by the time I reach the second floor she's waiting to jump out at me from behind a wall. I pretend to be scared, even though I can see the toes of her winter boots peeping out.

'Is Max going to be here?'

I laugh again. 'We'll see, shall we?' I unlock the door. 'Hello, we're here.'

Molly beams as Max emerges from the kitchen.

'Well, hello there,' he says in a phony posh voice, bending down and holding out his hand. 'You must be Miss Molly.'

She giggles as they shake, amusingly firm from her, her entire body jostling up and down.

'Allow me to introduce myself.'

More giggles.

'I'm—'

'I know who you are,' she interrupts, arms now crossed in front of her chest, a know-it-all look on her face. 'You're Eve's *boy*friend.'

I feel my cheeks colour as he turns to look at me, a question mark dangling from his lips. 'Is that right?'

'Molly, how about we do some colouring in the living room?'

She nods, easily distracted.

I can feel Max's eyes on me, his mouth still grinning, as we tip the pencils out of the tin.

After cobbling together a Molly-friendly lunch of peanut butter and banana on toast, I decide to give Max a break – it turns out that, of all the books and toys she has with her, he's her favourite. He told me about a park around the corner when he replied to my text, saying he'd love to meet her and listing fun things we could do and see in the area.

'Don't we need the key?' she asks as I close the door behind us.

'What key?'

'For the park? Like the one we have on the tree key ring.'

'Ah, I don't think it's that kind of park.' She must be talking about the one in the middle of their square.

The air feels colder after spending time in Max's snug sitting room. I look down at Molly, whose round cheeks are already a little rosy. We walk to the end of the road and when she spies the park opposite she scoots ahead.

'Wait for me, Molly,' I call. 'We need to hold hands as we cross the road.'

She slips her mittened hand into mine.

'You say when it's all clear, but remember to look both ways.' No cars in sight. Just two women limbering up for an afternoon run in gaudy Lycra.

'Clear!' She bops up and down with enthusiasm.

'Great, let's go.'

'Can I do the gate?'

'You can.'

After struggling with the latch for a moment, she removes a mitten.

Although you can't see it from the road, the trees and bushes surrounding the park are double-glazed: two rows sandwich a hidden path of wooden shingles. In the middle of the grass is a stone sundial and at the outskirts are wooden benches, each with a brass plaque in memory of a loved one.

Now what? I didn't think to bring a tennis ball, a skipping rope – something to pass the time. I desperately search my brain for games to play with little people. What did I used to do? Sit in my bedroom with my books.

'Do you want to play hide and seek, Eve?'

That one I know. 'OK then.'

'I'll hide, you seek.'

Before I can answer, she's darted off. 'OK, Molly, but you have to stay in the park.'

She doesn't respond.

I breathe in and out and count, aloud, until I get to forty. My hands grow cold as I hold them over my eyes – wish I'd said yes to a pair of gloves. I hear rustling for a short while and then, abruptly, silence. Unsettling silence. 'Thirty-eight, thirty-nine, forty. Right, ready or not, here I come!' That last bit came back to me out of nowhere, like remembering the lyrics to an old favourite song.

A peep behind the sundial and all four benches, for her amusement. Then in between the two rows of bushes and trees. I creep to begin with, the shingles foamy beneath my feet. Then I start calling her name, telling her I'm on my way.

A-ha. Her parka wasn't the wisest choice. It stands out, bright yellow amid the tangle of bare branches.

'I've found you!'

No reply.

'Molly, I can see you.'

Still nothing.

Fuck. 'Molly?' I lurch forward and grab onto her shoulder. It crumples in my palm. She must have taken it off, hooked it onto a low branch. 'Molly?' I call, louder this time. 'Molly, it's time to come out now.'

Why isn't she saying anything? I spin around on the spot, nausea clawing at my insides. My breath's running away with me, too fast to keep up. 'Molly, please!'

The sound of someone really running, across the grass in the middle. I turn around and she's standing behind me, her cheeks so rosy it looks like someone's dabbed them with face paint. 'Molly, thank God.' I wrap her coat around her and hold her close. 'You must be freezing.'

'Didn't you think it was a good decoy?'

I lean back and look her in the eye. 'How do you know what a decoy is?'

'We learned it at school.'

'Well, yes, it was a very good decoy.'

'Shall I seek this time?'

I close my eyes and manage to slow my breathing. 'OK, just one more time, though. Then let's go inside and warm up.'

She nods, tongue between lips, then puts her mittens to her eyes and starts counting.

I walk away to hide, hand on my chest steadying my pounding heart.

Does someone hear me scream?

Back at the flat I make Molly some tea, then tell her she can watch TV while I do the dishes. Just as I go to turn on the hot tap, the buzzer sounds. Annie.

'I'll get it,' calls Max.

I haven't told her about him, but then she hasn't really told me about the guy she's seeing either. Not that I'm *seeing* Max. I squirt some Fairy Liquid onto Molly's plate and, again, rack my brain trying to remember if I ever mentioned Karina and Bill.

A knock at the door.

I run the tap, but not so loudly that I can't hear Molly calling 'Mummy' and telling her gleefully that 'this is Eve's *boy*friend'.

'Oh really?' I can tell Annie's smiling from the tone of her voice.

Nothing from Max, which makes me think he must be raising his shoulders – perhaps his hands – in disbelief.

'It's a pleasure to meet you,' she adds.

The voices become muffled as they move into the living room. A few minutes later, as I'm drying my hands, I notice Annie lurking by the kitchen door, watching me. I scrunch my fingers into my palms, nails testing the skin. She does know about the diary and she's going to confront me. I brace myself, stiffening my arms by my sides and digging my nails in deeper.

'Thank you for today, Eve.'

OK, lulling me into a false sense of security. 'You're welcome.'

'Molly sounds like she's had a ball.'

And . . .

'And Max is lovely. You kept him quiet.'

I swallow, anticipating the segue.

'So, I have an idea. How would you feel about making this a bit more official – perhaps helping out two or three times a week?'

I try not to baulk, but then I realise my mouth's hanging open. She wants me to spend more time in her house, with her things? With Molly?

'I've been thinking about you a lot recently . . .'

You have?

'. . . and it might be nice. I know you don't have much family and the fact is, right now, I could really do with an extra pair of hands.'

My hands?

'Look, Eve,' she says, closing the kitchen door behind her, 'things are worse with Molly's dad.'

I keep quiet. What to say? I know. I've read all about it. The other women. The insinuations, smirks, hand gestures. I clumsily clear my throat.

'We've started the divorce proceedings,' she tells me, apparently oblivious to my blockage. 'I know it's the right thing to do,' she continues, full of resolve. 'I just don't know how to explain everything to Molly, how she's going to cope.'

'She'll be all right,' I say, though I'm not sure I believe it. 'You turned out pretty well.' That much is true.

'Well, that's very sweet of you,' she says, brushing some stray hairs away from her face, which changes as she adds, 'Things are also getting more serious with the man I'm seeing.'

This is unprecedented sharing from Annie.

'Anyway, please feel free to say no if you're too busy or simply not interested. I know you've just been doing me a favour.'

'No!' I almost shout it, hands out to keep her from retracting the offer. 'No, I'd love to.'

'Oh, Eve, that's wonderful. Moll will be so pleased.'

I feel a soft glow of pleasure.

'Let me grab my phone and we can lock in some more dates before we leave.'

I follow her into the hallway, inspecting my palms: four mini crescent moons branded on each.

'So, boyfriend?'

Max and I are lying in bed, my head on his chest, our legs interlinked. He's running his fingers up and down my back, half massaging, half tickling.

'Oh,' I say, closing my eyes, 'I'm sorry about that.'

'Don't be, I enjoyed it.'

'You did?'

'I did.'

I press my lips together and silently pull the duvet over my head. 'What does that mean?'

He throws the duvet onto the floor and I cover my face with my hands, the rest of me naked.

'It means,' he says, peeling one finger away at a time, until my face is exposed and the only cover I have left are my eyelids, 'that, one day, I'd like to be your boyfriend.'

I open my eyes, left and then right.

'One day?'

'Yes, one day, when we're ready.'

Seventeen

Last night I couldn't sleep. Max drifted off almost immediately, his arms wrapped around me. I felt hot and sticky, my skin starting to itch, but I didn't want to wake him. Soon I was struggling to breathe, so I had no choice but to untangle my limbs from his. I slipped out of bed and cracked open the window. By the time I got back in he'd rolled away, which for some reason made my eyes sting. I shuffled as close to him as I could, pressed my body against his. But when he moved away again, onto the very edge of the mattress, I did the same. I lay there for a while, on the opposite side of the bed, still but alert, listening to his breathing, steady and untroubled. When finally I fell asleep, I had a dream that I was standing at the bottom of a long flight of stairs, shouting his name louder and louder, but he couldn't hear me.

I wake up to a text from Paul: *Six o'clock? Nine Hansard Mews.*

My stomach tightens. I assumed he'd want to draw me in the studio. It's not a problem, me going to his house. It just feels a bit overfamiliar. Then again, we are a bit overfamiliar. How could we not be when he sees me naked twice a week? Watching me, lingering by the door, one arm crossed over his chest and the other bent upwards, his palm cupping his cheek as he tilts his head. More. Yes. There. The tightness creeps up into my chest.

Grace, are you sure this is what you want? I thought you two were having an argument.

You glance up from your packing, but you don't stop.

You said he was putting pressure on you.

Only because he wants to see me more, you say. And he apologised anyway. He understands that I have exams coming up.

OK, but still. Why doesn't he come over here? We could all hang out, the three of us.

You smuggle a scrap of black lace in with a T-shirt and I pretend not to see.

I suggested that, you say, zipping up your bag. He said we can all hang out at the bar next week.

I try to smile. OK. As long as you're happy, Grace.

You smile back, though there's worry in your eyes. I am. I should go.

I hug you goodbye. Text me if you need anything.

'Hello, you.' Max walks in, hair wet from the shower, towel slung around his hips.

I expect the tightness to subside, but instead it morphs into something sharper. I tentatively ask if he slept well and he tells me he did.

I sit up. 'What time will you be back this evening?'

'Oh, it's going to be a late one, I'm afraid,' he says, pulling on a pair of jeans.

Some club night, I remember.

'You're welcome to join.'

'That's OK, you go ahead,' I say.

'All right, well, text me later if you change your mind.' He leans over and kisses me goodbye. 'Fun plans today?'

'Just life-modelling.'

'Mm, what better image to take away with me.' He flashes me a smile before slipping on his shoes and heading out of the door, helmet in hand.

Being with Max like this, day after day, feels like rolling along the motorway in a good car: comfortable, reliable, reassuring. But somewhere under your feet is that dark, insistent hum – one twitch of the wheel and it's all over. Annihilation.

I turn back to my phone and type out a perfunctory reply: *see you then*.

Hansard Mews is lopsided. That is, there are only houses on one side of it. I join the road at the wrong end. Twenty-seven is the first number I see, with a beakish porch that looks like an afterthought – a nose job gone wrong. Twenty-five, twenty-three. Lawn needs mowing. Twenty-one. I walk slowly, gazing through the mostly open curtains at the interiors of happy families. Go back to work, will you? Nineteen. An upended sofa on the road either saving a parking space or ready for the tip. Seventeen, fifteen. An odd one out, all metal and glass. Must belong to a monochrome-wardrobed architect, who designed it herself. There she is, reading some journal published on matte paper, wearing her thick-rimmed glasses. Thirteen. NO JUNK MAIL. Eleven. Pebbledash painted candy-floss pink. Really?

Number nine is nondescript. Inoffensive and uninteresting. I'm not sure what I expected. Something special, it being the home of an *artiste*?

No bell but there is a knocker. I lift it and let it fall – one quick hit. Rather than being in the middle of the house, the front door is set off to the left. Above the letter box and either side of the knocker are two frosted panes of glass. I squint. A bookshelf. A big green plant, triangular slatted leaves. Some stairs. Coming down them, a smudge of colour. Closer, closer, until . . .

'Eve, welcome.'

I'm still bending forward when he opens the door, straining to see signs of life. 'Hi, Paul.'

'Come in, come in.'

I don't know why he says it twice. He also beckons with one hand as he holds the door ajar with the other. Desperate or just very keen.

'Thanks.'

No shake, no hug, no kiss.

'Oh, shoes off.'

Is he kidding?

He gestures to a smart wooden shoe rack by the door.

Evidently not.

As I tug at my Converse he asks if he can get me something to drink. 'Gin? Glass of wine?'

Drink-drawing. I want to ask if it will affect his vision, his judgement. 'Gin and tonic, please. Lime if you've got it.'

'Coming right up.' He closes the door behind me and pads into the kitchen, his bare feet shod in supple leather slippers.

I prefer Bill's crabby ones. Oh, I forgot to bring Karina's robe with me.

'I have to tell you, Eve,' he says, measuring out two single shots of gin and tipping them into two heavy-bottomed glasses, 'I'm excited to finally draw you myself.' He diligently rinses the stainless-steel measure, then opens the freezer and scoops a handful of ice out of an open bag. The drawer makes a screeching noise as he pulls and pushes.

'Well, I hope I don't disappoint!'

He smiles, says nothing. A lemon and a lime sit in a finicky metal fruit bowl. After adding a splash of tonic, he grabs the lemon and cuts it into wedges.

I try to ride out the silence, then I give up and ask where the studio is.

'Upstairs.' He hands me my drink.

To calm my nerves, I gulp down half of it in one go.

'Hold on: cheers.' Looks me in the eye.

What is it with posh people and cheersing? To us. To you. To our success. Fuck off, the lot of you.

There's that smile again.

'After you.' He nods towards the stairs, wood painted white.

I expect them to creak, like the ones at the studio, but they don't. He follows, a couple of steps behind me. The backs of my legs burn, a tingle of apprehension, like prickly heat.

Grace, how long were you lying in the sun?

You turn your head to face the wall. I was waiting for him, you say, your voice sounding small. You start to say something else but trail off.

I smooth the lotion up and down your calves, normally milky white, now more strawberry milkshake.

Grace, you have to end it.

Not yet, you say, reaching back with one hand. It's too much. After exams.

I interlace my fingers with yours. OK.

216

I don't really know Paul. And there's something weird about him. He's oddly neat and tidy for an artist, like he's hiding something. What if he's a psycho killer? *Fa-fa-fa-fa-fa-fa-fa-fa-fa-far better.* Another of Dad's favourites. Just in case, I run through a roll call of potential excuses in my head. Forgot I have to work this evening. Period pain. Dodgy tummy. Maybe I should have asked Max to call me at a certain time with a faux emergency.

'Round to your right.'

His bedroom – bed made, lamp lit – and, opposite, a small bathroom. Between the two, a white-walled studio hung with drawings and paintings, all nudes. I can't tell the quality from here but there are men as well as women, which I suppose makes me feel a bit better. White wooden floorboards with a few stray spots here and there, tinned and squeezy paints lined up on a counter, glass jars on the windowsill stuffed with pencils, pens and brushes. At the centre, an easel, a lot smarter than the ones the students use. On it, a few loose sheets of paper. Opposite, a lemon-yellow sofa, no cushions. A whiff of oil paint and turpentine.

'I thought we could start with a simple reclining pose and work our way up?'

Up to what? I smile and nod as I hold my breath in an attempt to suffocate the butterflies let loose in my stomach. I place my glass on the desk beside the sofa.

Right on cue, he slips a coaster beneath its cold and wet base.

I glance to my left and right.

'No screen here, I'm afraid.'

'Oh, that's OK.'

He nudges his glasses up his nose as he watches me remove my many layers. 'How about some music?'

'Sure.' I turn around as I undo the clasp of my bra, shaking it off, trying to relax.

Something classical sounds from the radio.

As soon as I'm naked I feel a greater change inside me, my heart pounding like it does before the doctor asks me to roll up my sleeve and takes my blood pressure, the cuff inflating around my pumping artery. My mind races like a shitty film on fast-forward. Like the songs Karina skips before they've come to an end, sometimes before they've even begun – drives Bill crazy. 'How do you—'

'Here.' He guides me towards the sofa and asks me to lie down. 'A little more on your side, facing me.' He holds onto my waist as he rotates my body, fingers frigid from his glass.

It's not unusual for him to touch me in the studio, but here it feels more intimate, more suggestive. Every muscle in my body seems to contract, from the tips of my fingers, up my arms, down my torso and legs, right to the balls of my feet. Even my nipples, which I'm sure he notices.

In a bid to distract us both from my discomfort, I force out a joke about wanting him to draw me like one of his French girls.

I'm not sure he gets the *Titanic* reference, but he smiles, clicking his fingers to the music.

Then nothing. He says nothing. Thank God for the piano tinkling away in the background. I don't know where to look but I'm not sure I want to look at him. Instead, I focus on a spot of red paint on the floor.

Can I borrow your nail polish, Eve?

After about five minutes, the rustle of paper. Still he says nothing. I can feel his gaze singeing my skin. It's not totally unpleasant. Kind of like lying in the sun for too long. You only really feel the effects the next day.

I keep quiet and focus on the red spot.

Thanks, I'll bring it back when I'm done.

The sliding of slippers across the room. He stands in front of me, blocking my view.

'We're going to try something a little different.'

It takes me a few seconds to realise he's talking to me – which is strange because of course we're the only ones here. I swing my legs round and go to stand up, but he gently lowers me back down. I'm facing him front on now, sitting on the sofa with my feet on the floor.

'Like this,' he says, holding onto my shoulders and pulling me forward.

I'm kneeling in front of him, my face inches from his waist. 'Well, this is definitely different!'

He smiles, he's calm.

I'm flapping.

'Now, put your hands down.'

All fours. 'Oh, my mistake!' I clamp my lips tight together, trying to get a hold of my nerves. I try to imagine I'm in a yoga class, practising my cat/cow, and instinctively arch my back.

The sliding of slippers.

Another five minutes passes.

Although less of me is on show, I feel more exposed, my tits hanging limp like tiny udders. I locate the red spot.

You wiggle your fingers in front of my face.
  Looks good, Grace.

Again, the sliding of slippers. This time, no instructions. He bends down, looks into my eyes and, once again, there's that smile. He kisses first my cheeks and then my lips. I laugh it off. He's messing around. He laughs too, then kisses me harder. I squeeze my eyes shut to conceal my surprise and let my tongue go limp as his spills into my mouth. His hands are in my hair, stroking then tugging. Mine remain planted on the floor, unresponsive.

I'm trying to work out what to do or say when I realise I need air. I pull back, lightly, not wanting to offend. I laugh again, though I worry I sound a bit hysterical. 'So, shall I—'

'Shh.' He walks behind me and starts touching my back, rubbing his hands up and down my arms. My chest starts to thump. He pinches my nipples. Squeeze and release, like a trigger. I moan, more out of pain than pleasure. Satisfied, he strokes then slaps my thighs, and pulls them wider apart.

The red spot.

Matching toenails.

His breath quickens, grows louder. I snap to attention at the sound of a belt buckle being undone.

A black leather belt buckled around your neck.

A button. Wait. A zip. It's too late. I feel him arrange himself behind me. My entire body tenses. He reaches round and touches my mouth, one finger pressing against my lips, which I part – because what else? The taste of charcoal in my mouth.

Was it a struggle? Throat closing, lungs gasping for air. Did it hurt?

Then he presses into me, groans and grabs at me, clumsily trying to get me going. I open my eyes and stare at the red spot.

Grace?

The only consolation: it doesn't last long. After rocking against me for half a minute, there's a rabbit-like rush and it's over.

He starts touching my back again, rubbing my arms, tells me it felt good.

I stay still until I can't bear it any longer. When I stand up, I realise he wasn't wearing a condom. 'Just going to the loo.' I say it so quietly I'm not sure he hears.

When I get back, he's inspecting his drawings, pencil in hand, adding one or two details. 'Oh, there you are. You're so beautiful to draw, Eve.' His voice is neutral, his body language professional.

I step back into my pants, then reach for my jeans.

'You're getting good at this.'

As I stuff my bra into my pocket and pull on my T-shirt I realise my hands are trembling. 'I should go,' I say, my voice still softer than usual. Shirt and jumper. What else? Coat and scarf, shoes, downstairs.

'Let me show you out.'

This time he leads the way and I experience an urge – so strong it scares me – to push him down the stairs. When he reaches the bottom, he passes me my coat and scarf and, as I throw them on, he opens the door.

'Everything OK?' he asks, extending onto his tiptoes, then bending at the knee.

I stuff my feet into my Converse, coax my mouth into a plastic smile. 'Fine.'

He smiles back and hands me an envelope. 'A little extra today.'

Eighteen

I can't remember the last time I had a bath like this – a boiling-hot bath that irons out every kink and lasts longer than six or seven minutes. I'm shielded on all sides by mountains of bubbles, each tinged with a single fleck of colour – green, yellow, purple, pink – reflected from the shaded bulb hanging from the ceiling.

I scoop up two handfuls of the tiny pockets of air and watch them seep through the cracks between my fingers and down my wrists. They trickle from the tips of my elbows back into the warm water. Closing my eyes, I lay back and rest my head against the end of the tub. The only thing I'm missing is a waterproof pillow.

Selling myself for 'art' is one thing. Now what? Selling myself for sex? The thought feels like a hefty punch in the lower abdomen. It's been a week since it happened and I still have a horrible feeling prowling in the pit of my stomach, a cruel mixture of carsickness, hangover, nerves and fear. I suck in my tummy to try to get rid of it and sink a little deeper into the water. I'm a shitty feminist.

I open my eyes and inspect my fingers, their pads wrinkled like aged cooking apples – the kind that used to drop from the wilted branches of the tree outside Grace's window in first year. I reach my right foot towards the hot tap, twisting it with my toes until it releases a steamy stream. The fresh water cuts a clear channel down the middle of the bath, a window on to my submerged body. My up-for-grabs body. My come-and-get-it body. My give-me-the-money-and-it's-all-yours body. Ouch, too hot. I scoot my feet back, away from the tap, and reach forward to twist it shut with my fingers. I look down again only to see that the bubbles have silently inched their way back across the window, my body ensnared.

I dry my hands on the nearest towel, then reach for Annie's diary. While the bath was running, I remembered I hadn't finished reading it. A welcome distraction. I flick through the pages until I find my place and feel myself relaxing.

> *I wasn't going to cry today – so much for that plan. I've never cried as much as I have in that sunny little room.*

She's still talking about therapy.

> *It's a weird relationship. I can't imagine not talking to her now, which scares me – especially when I haven't told anyone about her. I don't intend to either. Not my 'friends'.*
> *Not Mum or Dad. Not Paul.*

I sit up too quickly and send a load of water cascading over the back of the tub. Paul? Why would she even contemplate telling Paul? I skip ahead, eyes scanning her elegant script for further appearances of his name. Nothing. It could be nothing. A coincidence even. Paul's a common enough name. I place the diary on the closed loo lid and swallow, feeling suddenly queasy.

It's not inconceivable that he could be the man she's seeing. The 'old friend' who knew things had been over in the marriage for a while. But I've seen them together so often – could I really have missed it?

Before I can stop myself, I'm picturing them together. Alone. In his house. Him fixing her a drink. The two of them walking up the stairs, which don't creak. Having sex in the shower, against the kitchen counter, on the landing. I wonder if he's gentle with her. If they talk about life-drawing – if they talk about me, my life outside the studio. Eve has a boyfriend? Really?

Annie's Paul. It doesn't make sense. Still, he might have mentioned that he was going to see me. Would she mind me posing for him, I wonder, the way Suzon posed for Manet? Staring at him while his eyes skipped between her corset and the canvas. If they're not together, and he has nothing to hide, he might have even mentioned the sex. My breath catches as I imagine Annie on the other end of the phone, telling me that she and Molly unfortunately don't need me anymore.

I didn't want to. In those slippers, in that white room, wafts of white spirit lingering in the air. I splash my face with water. It's too much.

A knock at the bathroom door. 'Eve?'

I freeze, fingers to face. 'Yes?'

'Are you almost ready?'

'Oh, no, I'm not. Sorry.'

A moment's pause, during which I picture the pained look on his face.

'I'll see you there?'

'See you there,' he says, walking away.

I pull the plug and watch as a whirlpool forms at the base of the bath – a dark downward spiral. The foamy water starts to disappear down the drain. I stand up carefully. A nasty slip as a child – unsupervised, as always – taught me to hold onto the edges of the tub with both hands when boarding and disembarking.

I've been avoiding Max. I can barely look him in the eye, let alone talk to him. How could I, after what I did? Whenever I try, an image of Paul staring at us in bed, like he stares at me onstage, pops into my head.

My shifts at the bar are becoming a blur due to the amount of alcohol I'm consuming after closing. Too much wine. Shots of something cold and spicy spilling down my throat. Nina's still mad on vodka and now I need it too. At night I curl up on what's become my side of the bed, clutching onto the edge of the mattress, twisted with guilt but tanked up enough to sleep.

In spite of my behaviour, Max has been leaving his bike at the bar and catching the tube home with me; he probably doesn't trust me not to fall asleep and wind up at the end of the Jubilee line. It's not at all couply – more like he's my probation officer – but nonetheless he's there beside me, his arm brushing up against mine and sometimes holding onto it (for stability). I may have gone too far the other night. I was struggling to walk for more than a few metres in a straight line and he stopped and asked me if everything was OK. Instead of answering, I leaned in and up and kissed him. A drunken kiss with too much saliva and not enough feeling. He must have thought so too: he pulled away, leaving me standing there, lips puckered like a fish.

'I think you've got a problem,' he said.

*

The air is cold, head-achingly so, wrapping itself around my body and making me squint to shelter my leaky eyes. I wince when I see an empty sleeping bag outside Kilburn Station, wondering how Fred's fared down in Vauxhall this Christmas. I nip into the corner shop and buy a couple of packets of custard creams, which I poke into one of three plastic bags otherwise filled with tat.

When I arrive at the bar, Max looks and sounds concerned. 'Are you OK?' He stops whatever he's doing with the beer barrels and comes out to give me a hug. He smells clean and fresh.

'I'm fine, thanks, why?' I ask, resting my cheek against his chest and closing my eyes, suddenly sapped of energy.

He leans back, making my head nod, like it does when I fall asleep on the bus. 'Because you're almost an hour late.'

I cling onto him as if he's a buoyancy aid and I'm adrift in the middle of the ocean. Don't let go, please. I interlace my fingers.

He takes a step back, my fingers lose their grip and my arms drop down by my sides. I'm drowning.

'I covered for you, said you had an appointment. Eve, what's going on?'

'I'm sorry.'

'You're sorry? What does that mean?'

'It means I'm sorry I put you in that position.'

'That doesn't answer my question.'

'Max, people are arriving.' It's true. Three suited men are approaching the bar, laughing and jostling. 'Later? I'll explain later.' Once I've thought of an excuse.

*

Tonight, when I'm offered a drink by a man with a glum look on his face and half a dozen glasses of wine in his gut, I say yes. I catch Max glancing at me from the other end of the bar as I pour two large glasses of red and clink mine with the equally beetroot-faced punter after tapping his card on the reader. The earthy liquid slips down my throat and settles inside me, its warmth spreading out like central heating. When he returns half an hour later and offers to buy me another, I say yes again. Tonight, drinking on the job makes the job easier.

The steady stream of people ordering drinks means Max and I barely have a chance to speak. He sticks to his end, me to mine.

My second glass is nearly empty. Where's whatsisname? I stand on tiptoes in an effort to see him through the crowd but fail. If Nina's so keen on drinking after work, surely she won't care if I have a couple during? I'm about to pour myself another glass, unpaid for, when:

'Excuse me?'

Another option. Decent-looking, despite the receding hairline. Mid-thirties. No wedding ring.

'Evening, how can I help?'

'Pint of lager, please.'

'Coming right up.' I stare into his eyes until they stare back at me.

'Having a good night?'

'Oh, you know, it's not so fun this side of the bar.'

He looks at me blankly.

'I'd love to join you for a drink but . . .' I gesture along the length of the bar with a sweep of my arm.

'Well, I'm sure we can work around that,' he says, adjusting his tie and leaning forward. 'What will it be?'

'I'll have a gin and tonic, thank you.'

'Make it a double.'

'If you insist.'

By the end of the night, I've forgotten all about Paul and his paws, that stinging feeling I had between my legs afterwards. I've forgotten my missing Suzon. When I try to picture her face, it's as blurry as the crowd of onlookers reflected in the mirror. Maybe she'll have changed anyway. Got a piercing, dyed her hair. Got a boyfriend. Grace. When I close my eyes I see her, cringing at the phone numbers scrawled on paper napkins in front of me.

I crumple them up and toss them into the bin, then glance over at Max. I haven't spoken to him all shift, except when I needed him to make a cocktail for a skinny redhead, the name of which (the cocktail, that is) I was unfamiliar with. I've forgotten that now too. He handed it over without a word, without a smile.

'Max?'

He's busy cleaning his end of the bar, scrubbing at something sticky by the look of how much pressure he's exerting on the surface. Either that or he's more pissed off than I think. He doesn't answer. What's happened to our parallel dimension?

'Max, can you hear me?' I raise my voice and direct it through cupped hands.

He looks up at me and then over my shoulder. More scrubbing. The counter starts to squeak.

'What are you looking at?' I turn around and find Nina standing behind me.

'Eve, my office.'

It feels especially devoid of colour this evening, her office. Devoid of forgiveness, devoid of feeling. As I follow her across the threshold and take a seat in the chair opposite, I know what's coming. I know I have no excuse. But that doesn't stop me from grappling around for one. Silently, mind – I do have my dignity.

'So, Eve, I think it's time for you to take a break from bar work.'

She probably sits in here every night, watching us. How dare she. It's an invasion of our privacy. Like personalised adverts, the microphone in my pocket. I try to get a glimpse of her screen: a collage of cameras, documenting every angle. I shift my attention to her ears, scanning for a headpiece.

'Eve?'

My tongue feels thick in my mouth. The alcohol is hitting me at the wrong moment. I swallow. 'I'm sorry I was late. But really, I'm fine. I just had an appointment and forgot to tell you. It won't happen again.'

'Eve, that's only the start of it and you know it.'

I wonder if she has anyone waiting up for her at home. Covering a plate of something home-cooked in kitchen foil. Leaving the landing light on. Probably not, if she's cooped up in here every evening. That's why she's paying so much attention to me: she's lonely.

'So, I'll pay you your wages for the next two weeks, but I think it's best if you leave now.'

She's fired people before. Knows how to get in and out as quickly and painlessly as possible. I stare at my name in red ink on the schedule. She'll have to screw up the whole thing and start again from scratch. What a waste of paper, time, energy.

It's such a waste, she had so much going for her, he says. Your tutor, after the funeral, soggy cucumber sandwich in one hand, a plastic cup of cheap white wine in the other.

Maybe she could tidily cover every 'EVE' with a squirt of Tipp-Ex and then, once it's dried, etch my replacement's initials on top. At least my name is short, a trifle to obliterate. One syllable.

'Eve?'

'What about the new rota?' I point at the wall. 'It has my name on it.'

'You know what, Eve?'

I glance back at her, hopeful.

'Don't worry about it.'

Nineteen

The next morning I wake up with a sicky feeling in my stomach, the kind I know will continue to worm its way around behind my belly button until I give in and get back into bed this evening. It's my own fault. I shouldn't have polished off that bottle of red when I got back to the flat last night, especially when I didn't eat any dinner. Still, it was already open and I needed something soothing.

They used to snag at me, memories of Grace, a bodily response to seeing or hearing someone or something that reminded me of her. But ever since that day in the restaurant with her parents it's become more of a constant queasy flickering.

Last night as I rode the tube home – this time without Max – they came crashing into my head, one after another.

The weight of your door, heavier than normal.

The round handle, a shiny brass ball, cool in my palm like an unripe plum that's been kept in the fridge.

No response to my knocking so I call your name. Grace?

Something's in the way.

The sirens. Flashes of blue and white.

There's a lingering smell of freshly toasted bread in the kitchen. Max is eating breakfast while watching a cooking programme on TV. I sneak a glance at him: his brow is knotted, like he's working his way through a diabolical sudoku, even though the shakshuka recipe the chef's describing sounds relatively easy. I try smiling but it feels like I'm scowling.

I go to make myself a coffee and, by the time the kettle has boiled, he's finished. I keep my eyes on my mug as he walks towards me. When he stops in front of me, I stiffen, readying myself for words I don't want to hear.

Instead, he envelops me in his arms and holds me there for a moment, neither of us saying a thing. Then he lets go. 'Eve, what the fuck. Why didn't you return my messages?'

'Messages?' I ask, wavering slightly, my body suddenly wobbly without his. I clink the teaspoon against my mug and drop it in the sink.

'I tried calling you last night, sent a bunch of texts,' he says, rubbing his face. 'What was I supposed to do? You just left and when I got back you were out cold.'

'I'm sorry, Max. I didn't mean for this to happen.'

Misadventure, says your dad from the front of the church, although we both know that wasn't the ruling. There was nothing accidental about what happened.

A short and sharp exhale, like Youla has us do at the beginning of a yoga class, except his is accompanied by a 'ha' of
disbelief. It's weird how often she pops into my head.

'You didn't mean for this to happen?'

I'm not sure if I'm supposed to answer.

'You show up for work late a bunch of times and then, to
top it off, you get wasted and throw yourself at customers!'

'I was not wasted.'

'Come on, Eve.'

'Or throwing myself at anyone.'

'Right.'

'I think I'm sick.'

'Well, have you been to the doctor?'

'Not yet.'

Neither of us says anything for a few seconds. We just
look at one another. What does he see? Me standing here
in his flat, in an old T-shirt and leggings, hair and body
unwashed, face without the faintest lick of make-up. Crap,
I hope I don't smell. I can't remember if I put deodorant
on. At least I brushed my teeth.

He breaks the silence: 'Eve, I'm worried about you.'

I start to feel feverish. 'Max, come on.'

'No, I can't keep pretending everything's OK. You're
completely absent.'

That's not true. I'm right here. I reach out for his hand
to prove it, but he pulls away.

'Sometimes I talk to you and it's as if you don't hear me,
like you're somewhere else entirely.'

I remember the certainty that we had a special wavelength
and cringe.

'Eve, you need help. I mean, look at you.'

So I take it he doesn't like what he sees. The thought hits me like a smack across the face. His opinion matters to me. He matters.

'You need to talk to someone – someone else. Whoever your therapist is, she's clearly not helping.'

When I keep quiet, he continues.

'You need to talk about Grace.'

'Please, Max, honestly, not now.' I start to feel wobbly again and tighten my grip on the counter. He's the only person I've ever talked to about her.

'Have you thought about going back?'

I baulk at the suggestion.

'Maybe it's worth seeing if it helps. How are you ever going to be able to move on if you haven't faced what happened?'

'I'm fine, really.'

'Stop saying that. You're not fine. You're self-destructing.'

Another smack, this one twice as hard.

'I'll go to the doctor's today and get some medication, OK? Last time it helped.'

It's true: when I tried taking some pills, they did help – at least for a while. By the end I wondered if they were doing anything at all, but even so it took me a while to wean myself off them. It was like when I was a child and no longer believed in the Tooth Fairy; some older kids at school selfishly gave the game away, but I couldn't bring myself to admit it for another year or so, just in case. Dad never played along – no pound coins under my pillow – so it didn't matter anyway.

He holds his hands up. 'OK, that's a start. Do you want me to come with you?'

'I think I should go by myself.' As I say it, I reach out again to hold his hand and this time he doesn't pull away. 'Thank you, Max, I know you're only trying to help.'

I keep my promise and take the tube down to the doctor's in Vauxhall. I always expect my senses to be dulled after a heavy night of drinking, but every time it's the opposite. As I pass through the streets, everything around me is sharpened. The glare of a silver car pulling up to park. The whoosh of well-pumped bicycle wheels. The piercing cry of a newborn baby who's either tired, hungry or wearing a nappy squashy with shit. My skin itches at the thought of bumping into Karina and Bill.

I check in with the beady-eyed receptionist and plonk myself down in the corner of the waiting room, so strongly disinfected that breathing through my nose makes my nostrils prickle. I sit there for almost an hour, half reading my book – a story about a world where men are afraid of women (science fiction, apparently) – while listening to whiny children and rattly old folk. I draw in minimal air, trying to match the gentle wheezes of the whiskery man to my left.

I've just started playing a game of 'what's he/she/they got?' when my name flashes red on the digital screen above the reception desk and a cheery voice invites me to 'please go to room three, that's room three'. As I head through, I hear a man with no shame telling the receptionist he has a rash. He thinks it's fungal.

Clearly the cheery voice doesn't belong to the doctor waiting for me behind door number three: a po-faced woman with a runny nose (looks like they don't disinfect staff too) and a globule of mascara loitering in the corner of her eye. Night shift? On her desk is an overripe banana that smells fermented.

'OK, how can I help you today, Eve?'

'I think I need some more SSRIs. I've taken them before.'

'Right,' she says, scrolling through my electronic file. 'You've been feeling down lately?'

I nod and she follows up with a series of more probing questions. Do I have a steady job? Have I been keeping up with family and friends? What's my living situation? She's full of questions; I have no answers. Next, she checks my blood pressure, height, weight.

'OK, I'm going to prescribe you some more SSRIs as you've requested,' she says, rubbing her eyes and, in the process, transferring the globule of mascara to her cheek. Definitely night shift. 'A fairly low dosage so you shouldn't feel any side effects – mood, dizziness, insomnia, etcetera,' she continues, unaware, clicking some buttons that will make the pharmacist release the goods.

I contemplate mentioning the mascara but decide against it. We're not friends. Speaking of which, I wonder how my non-friend Marjorie is. Maybe she's on antidepressants too.

'That's it, you're all done.' She rubs her eyes again, then her cheeks. The globule's now on her chin.

Since I'm south of the river, I decide to drop in on Youla. I got an overenthusiastic text from her a few days ago telling me: *Come start the new year with new balance!!!* I ignored it, feeling sick at the thought of doing a downward-facing dog hung-over, but now I'm here and wearing leggings, so I might as well try to find a feeling of calm.

'Eve, so good to see you!' she says, greeting me like a long-lost friend.

I'm not sure we're friends either but, even so, I let her press her toned torso against mine and squeeze me tight.

'Where have you been?'

I don't want to have to talk about moving and I can't face the disappointment in her eyes as I explain I simply haven't wanted to come, so I lie. 'I've been away with work,' I say, bending down to undo my laces. 'A job in Paris.'

'Wow, what do you do?'

'I'm a lawyer, an art lawyer,' I say, switching feet. 'I deal with cases of stolen works of art.' I don't mention Suzon or Manet or the Musée d'Orsay, but I let the scenario play out in my mind.

She nods her head hard and fast, curls springing up and down, as I concoct a story involving a good art collector gone bad.

'It sounds like a fascinating job.'

I agree, it does.

The class is full. I settle for a spot in the centre of the room, giving myself someone to follow no matter which way we face. I'm rusty and I know I'll struggle to remember the sequences.

To begin with, though, I do feel calm. I almost forget that anything's wrong, that anything's missing. Anyone. Then that familiar blankness settles inside me and for the rest of the session I feel comfortably vacant.

On the bus back to Max's, I dry-swallow a couple of pills, shuddering as I picture them tumbling down my throat.

Immediately after, Annie's name flashes up on my phone.
Are you free to babysit on Friday? A x

I've got a lot of babysitting booked in over the next few weeks. Partly because I've made myself readily available – Molly talks back, so is proving to be a more reliable companion than my missing Suzon – but partly because Annie's so busy. I bristle, just a little, imagining Molly murmuring goodnight to me instead of her mum. Calling out for me when she has a bad dream.

A moment later, another text: *Oh, Molly drew this! You're part of the family now. A x*

I feel my heart flicker. I click on the image. A drawing of five figures standing in a row, each labelled neatly underneath. 'Daddy', with black laced shoes and a tongue-like red tie. 'Mummy', her yellow hair so long it's almost tickling 'Henry'. 'Me', surprisingly tall for six years old, with flowers in her hair. And finally, holding hands with 'Me', in the middle, 'Eve'.

I glance at my next six months' worth of pills.

You're not here but the others are. We're in our gowns, waiting to be let into the exam hall.

I need this – that's what they say with their sympathetically slanted heads. What they say with words is, Grace would've wanted you to ace these, she would've wanted you to move on.

I pause for a moment, fingering the open packet, then stuff it back into the paper bag with the others. A new beginning. When I get off the bus, I take two big steps to the edge of the pavement and dump the whole lot in the bin.

They have no idea what you would've wanted.

Twenty

Max and I had sex last night. It was the first time since I'd
been with Paul and, as soon as he started touching me, I
could feel Paul's hands on me too. I tried to shut them out –
the memories of his fingers in my hair, my mouth – but they
kept creeping back. It made me rush things with Max, who
seemed taken aback by my sudden enthusiasm but recovered
swiftly, his breathing quickening to match mine, his pupils
dark.

Later, he tentatively asked me how it went with the doctor.

I pictured the pills at the bottom of the public bin, by then
topped with used coffee cups, greasy crisp packets, a browning
apple core. 'It went well, thanks.'

He asked me what I planned to do about work and I told
him I'd already taken on some extra babysitting shifts.

He opened his mouth to say something, then stopped,
rubbed the back of his neck. 'That's great, Eve. I think you're
brilliant with her.'

I smiled at him, feeling that same contentment that settled
over me when I saw Molly's family portrait. 'We should
go away soon,' I said, higher-pitched than intended. In a

more level voice, I added: 'Maybe we can make a plan at the weekend?'

'That's a great idea.'

I arrive at Annie's house and hear a muted tapping sound. I look left and right, then up towards the sky. It's not bright but I automatically bring my hand to my forehead to shade my eyes. There: on the top floor, second window along, Molly's standing with her face pressed against the pane, her breath white on the glass. She greets me most days now, one way or another.

I wave up at her and she waves back before disappearing from sight.

I ring the bell and a minute later Annie opens the door, holding a tail-wagging Henry back with her outstretched leg. She has her sleeves rolled up and when she leans forward to kiss me her cheeks feel warm.

'Sorry, Eve, Moll's swimming lesson ran over. I was just getting her out of the bath.'

'Oh, no worries.'

'Do you mind taking over?'

'Absolutely.' I leave her to close the door and start climbing the stairs.

'Eeeeeeeeeeeeve!' Molly comes racing down and meets me on the first floor, pink-skinned, hair still soggy.

'Hello, you,' I say, bending down to hug her. 'I like your dressing gown.'

White with black splotches.

'It matches Henry.'

'I can see that.'

She takes hold of the two ends of the belt and stretches them out to the sides, twisting left and right.

'Have you had lunch?'

'No.'

Annie walks up the stairs behind me. 'Sorry, Eve, I meant to feed her before you arrived. I've left a note on the kitchen counter.'

'Don't worry, we're happy – aren't we, Moll?'

She angles the belt, pretends to be a plane swooping through the sky. 'Yes.'

'Well, have a nice afternoon.'

The doorbell goes.

Annie tsks.

'Who's that, Mummy?'

'Oh, no one, Moll, just a friend.'

I stare at her, searching for a glimmer of guilt, but there's no sign.

'Have fun,' she says, giving her a kiss. 'Thanks, Eve.'

I nod.

She heads back down the stairs and opens the door, closing it quickly behind her. I wonder if Paul knows I'm here – if he really is the one, that is.

As usual, the fridge is crammed with food, mostly very healthy, very green. I read Annie's note:

Plain pasta and carrot and cucumber sticks for lunch.

Molly scrunches up her nose when I read it aloud but says nothing.

'Well,' I say, rootling around in the cupboards, 'we could have plain pasta and carrot and cucumber sticks.' A-ha. 'Or we could have pancakes?'

Her eyes bulge. 'For lunch?'

'Why not?' I ask, plonking the plain flour on the counter and returning to the fridge for the milk. 'Just don't tell Mummy.'

She pinches her lips.

Flour, milk . . . urgh, eggs. But how many? There's a reason I hate them. I tried to cook poached eggs for Dad when I was a child, swirling the water, trickling in the vinegar, trying to get them just right like Mum did. I should have known he'd have passed out by the time I was done. I remember putting them on the floor in front of his armchair, hoping the smell would wake him up. The next morning I came downstairs and they were still there, except they'd been squashed by the sole of his shoe and dragged across the carpet.

'Do you know how to make pancakes, Eve?'

Can a six-year-old look sceptical? This one does.

'Oh ye of little faith.' I gently tap her on the head with my whisk. 'No, we need our friend Google.'

She runs from the room and returns with an iPad.

'Good work.'

I search for a recipe. 'Right, Moll, the first thing we need to do is measure out the flour. Where does Mummy keep her scales?'

She raises her shoulders.

'Never mind, let's guess.' I shake a load into the bowl and coat the counter – and Molly – in the process.

'Ohh, I'm a ghost!' she cries, waving her little white arms around. Now the floor's covered in flour too.

'Henry?' I call.

He wags his tail excitedly, then, after a quick sniff, turns up his nose.

I make a small divot and crack two eggs into the middle – expensive eggs from a local farmers' market, no doubt, with bright orange yolks. Then milk. May as well guess again. I glance up at Molly, who's been sidetracked by some yappy cartoon characters on the iPad.

'OK, Moll, want to learn how to flip a pancake?'

She cheers.

I heat up the pan and, after adding a knob of butter, pour in some liquid, a little lumpy. 'Right, are you ready?'

'Ready!'

'One, two, three . . .'

Pancake down.

'Henry?'

This time he politely obliges.

An hour later, Molly and I decide to go to Hyde Park. She asks Henry if he'd like to join us. He stretches out his spine, yawns and hunkers back down in his bed.

'Do you come here a lot, Molly?' I ask as we reach the park's outer fringes, muddy from the recent rain. How lucky to live so close.

'Sometimes,' she says, her little matchstick legs, clad in woolly grey tights, working double time to keep up with mine.

We overtake an outdoorsy-looking woman and her three-wheeler buggy, which reminds me what Annie once said about bringing Molly here as a baby. That she would push her around and around the perimeter until she finally, for the love of God, gave up her grizzling and fell asleep.

'We watch the boats or I play in the playground,' says Molly. 'I like the swings.'

We continue straight, strolling along a sodden path that runs alongside the main road. Molly picks up a stick and uses it like a crutch as we walk.

'Come on, Hobble.'

She giggles, tells me that's not her name.

Eventually we reach the lake and a lengthy overpass supported by arches. Molly asks if she can sit on the stone banister and I tell her no, it's too dangerous. I do lift her up so she can peer over at the water, its glassy surface dappled with reflections. The stone's golden glow is stirred up like food colouring with the greens of bushy conifers and burnt umbers from bare branches and crinkled and crisp winter leaves.

'Look, swans.' She points, jiggling in my arms.

They sashay towards the bank as ripples begin to appear in a steady pattern. Something's coming. I lean forward, holding tight around Molly's middle as she does the same, and spot a baby-blue rowing boat emerging from beneath the bridge. In it are two men: one keeping cosy in a hat, scarf and gloves; the other not even wearing a coat, warm from his exertions. Some tourists start snapping photos and, spotting the camera-toting gaggle, the rower sticks out his oars and smiles, making his partner – and Molly – laugh.

'Excuse me, doll, will you take our picture?'

It takes me a few seconds to realise that the copper-haired lady with the American accent and the smart black camera is talking to me. She's dressed for the cold in a floor-length milky-tea puffer coat – a duvet, naked without its cover.

'Sure.' I lower Molly down and she starts drawing a picture in the dirt with her stick. I move aside. 'Here?'

'Great, thanks,' she says, thrusting the instrument into my hands.

I throw the strap over my head and around my neck, then wait for the four women to bunch together. 'This way?' I ask, holding the camera landscape.

'One of each, please.'

They smile and I take two shots landscape, followed by two more portrait, in case anyone's caught mid-blink. They thank me, squinting down at the screen.

'Do you want us to take one of you and your daughter?' The first woman is holding a hand out towards me. 'Assuming you have a camera or a phone?'

My daughter?

It's getting dark and, though Molly had a big lunch, it won't be long before she's hungry for her tea. We take the first left off the main road and I check the time on my phone. Half past three. We'll turn back in the next five or ten minutes.

People are weaving in and out of the ribbed columns shouldering the arcade entrance to the Serpentine Sackler Gallery, catching whatever show's on before it closes for the evening. Molly and I size up the poster, which says something about artificial life, then lose interest. If I'm going to take her to a gallery, it won't be this one. I picture the two of us slipping through the automatic glass doors at the Courtauld. Waving hello to Marjorie. Gliding up the stone staircase. Past portraits, landscapes, pieces of furniture. Into room six. We sit on the patch of floor in front of the bench. I introduce her to Suzon. Molly politely extends her hand and the two of them are immediately friends.

'Henry!'

I look up just in time to see her run off, racing after a Dalmatian that's missing its owner. 'Molly, wait, it's not him.' They all look the same to me too. Though this one could do with having its portion sizes reduced.

A dull thud followed by a sharp cry. She's on her knees, hands splat in front.

I hurry over. 'Molly, what happened? Tell me what hurts.' I scoop her up in my arms and stare at her face, hot with snot and tears, avoiding the judgemental looks I imagine I'm attracting from all sides.

'I fell over.'

'Are you in pain? Where does it hurt?'

She holds out her palms, lightly grazed, and points at her knee. Her woollen tights aren't torn but one knee is stained a mushy cherry.

'Can you bend it? Is that OK?'

She reaches out to touch my face. 'Don't cry, Eve.'

What? I'm not the one who's crying. I put my hand to my cheeks. They're wet. 'I'm sorry, I'm just being silly.'

'Can we go home now?'

'Yes, let's go home.'

I heave a deep breath. She's fine.

By the time Annie's home she's more than fine, thanks in part to the Jaffa Cakes I gave her after tea. She nibbled the choc-olate, then the sponge, then ran around the kitchen waggling the orange jelly at me: 'Look, Eve, a jellyfish!' We played with the doll's house, I read to her and, when she claimed she still wasn't remotely tired, I suggested we watch a film.

Annie offers to book me a taxi but it's not late, so I tell her I'm happy to catch the bus. She says she and Molly will join me because Henry could do with a walk. After some persuasion, she manages to tear a totally absorbed Molly away from a briefly hospitalised ET.

We walk silently side by side through the dimly lit streets. I look up at the sky – now a deep, hazy blue, the sliver of moon a stark white toenail. The only sounds I hear are the closing of car doors, the speeding up and slowing down of vehicles and the occasional grumble from Henry, who just wants his tea. As we reach the end of the block, a squirrel darts across the pavement and up the thick trunk of a tree. Henry lurches forward, giving Annie a swift tug on the lead.

'Henry!' Molly chastises him.

She didn't mention what happened in the park and neither did I. That's another secret then. Annie either didn't notice her knee or chose not to comment. Although the panic has subsided, my insides still feel fluttery with worry.

We reach the bus stop, occupied by two strangers – one reading something on her phone, the other watching something on his – and see that my bus is arriving in three minutes. I sit at the far end of the bench, sheltered from the slight wind, and Annie perches next to me, Molly the other side of her and Henry curled up by our feet.

'Is everything OK, Eve?' Annie looks at me searchingly, frown lines appearing between her eyebrows.

Grace, what happened? Are you OK? I hold you close.
You try not to cry. You fail.

I look at Molly. With both hands, she's holding a book in front of her face, a cheerful story about a friendly park keeper and his animal friends. She has one ankle crossed over the other, her feet swinging back and forth against the bench. She nods her head, either in encouragement or agreement, as she whispers the story to herself – actually her own story, partly based on the one in front of her, partly fresh from her head.

'Eve?'

'Of course, why wouldn't it be?' I reply, turning my attention to the silver medallion on Henry's collar.

'You just seem a bit low. If you've got too much on and need to dial back the babysitting, I would understand.'

Please, no. 'I promise I'm fine.' I can't say anything else. I feel myself creeping closer to the edge. If I try to speak again, the tears will start and they won't stop.

'OK, well, if you're sure.'

I nod briskly, put on a smile, lean in and hug her, remembering too late that she prefers two light pecks.

Still, she doesn't move away until my bus arrives, its dazzling white headlights glaring on our cold faces. 'See you next week then.'

Twenty-one

My period came this morning. Hallelujah – I'm not pregnant with Paul's offspring. When I realised, I was so relieved I yelped. Max must have thought something terrible had happened because he came running and banged on the bathroom door, calling my name.

I remember the first period I ever got. I went to the loo and, when I pulled down my pants, there it was – blood, albeit more brown than red. I was angry that my body had deceived me, tricked me into this next stage before I was ready, mentally, physically. After fifteen minutes, Dad knocked on the door – not because he was concerned but because he needed to piss. I screwed up some loo roll and stuffed it in the crotch of my pants, which I'd throw away later that evening. When I unlocked the door, I didn't say a thing.

A baby, Eve? Reminding me what happened, every day? I'd have to tell people. I'd have to tell my parents. What would I do about getting a job? It's not part of the plan. I'm just not ready.

You pause, breathe.

I can't, you say, there's no way.

I got a text from Molly off Annie's phone first thing. No message, just a bunch of colourful emojis: a blue butterfly, two pink hearts, a bunch of flowers, a shoal of tropical fish. I texted back saying I had fun with her on Friday and was looking forward to seeing her again next week. I meant it.

After our trip to Hyde Park I'd almost forgotten about Paul and getting fired. I couldn't forget Annie's diary, though, tucked away in one of three drawers Max has kindly donated to me. No wonder I felt like I was wading through a thick and gloopy stew of guilt as I rolled back to Kilburn on the bus, thinking about her looping sentences staring back at me, judging me as I read. So, I've made a decision. Today I'm going to return it – well, not return it exactly, but somehow put it back in her possession. Yes, I'm going to return it. If I make it to the studio, that is.

My legs feel wobbly, brand new, like they might buckle and collapse at any moment. It's cold out, a stern wash of stone grey bruising the sky, but I feel hot and sticky, and not because I'm walking. I remove my coat and rub the corner of my left eye once, then twice; now it's itchy. When I go to yawn, my jaw locks and for a few seconds – feels like a few minutes – I can't close my mouth. I think I might be nervous.

I bump into Annie outside the studio and, as we walk up the stairs, she receives a phone call.

'Hi, Nancy, yes, everything's in order. No, I promise you . . .' She looks at me, mouths the words 'mother of the bride' and heads back down.

'Good morning, Eve.' Paul's standing at the top in his leather jacket. He must not realise that it doesn't quite go with his personality: leather loses its lustre when the wearer's a neat freak.

I persuade my feet to keep climbing. 'Hi, Paul.' Clearly he hasn't clocked that I hate myself for what happened and will never let it happen again.

'You look flushed, Eve. Everything OK?'

Always happens on the first day, along with the crunching in my womb, as if someone's ripped it out and is squeezing it like a damp sponge. 'Fine, thanks, just the cold.'

I expect some sleazy comment – well, if you need warming up, you know where to find me – but instead he just agrees. 'Mm, chilly.'

I turn towards the studio.

'Actually, Eve, do you have a minute?'

I look at him. He's had a haircut, his grey-black tresses a thin covering on his head, which now looks horribly bony. 'OK.' I follow him down the corridor towards what must be a classroom at the back, all desks and chairs. Annie mentioned that part of the building was owned by a language school. Maybe this is where they practise *le français*.

He opens the door – something that apparently requires a knack, a combination of push and pull – then closes it behind me.

I look at the whiteboard at the front of the room, stamped with words in green marker pen. *Dans la chambre . . . l'armoire, la lampe, le lit.*

'Eve.'

'Yes?'

Without warning, he's kissing me, his hands racing over my body as if they're searching for something. I clench my fists and stand firm, hoping he'll get the message. He doesn't. Instead, his thumbs turn white as he tightens his grip.

Another tack: 'We're going to be late.' I lean my head back as I say it and he starts at my neck, lips and teeth, sucking and biting. 'Paul.'

He comes up for air, breathy and red. 'You're right.'

I wipe away the fleck of saliva that just landed on my cheek.

He smooths down my duffle coat and pats the sides of my arms. Adjusts his glasses, which for once need adjusting. 'Later.'

If you can fucking catch me.

I can't tell whether the studio's stifling or if it's the presence of a bare mattress on the stage that's making me hot. A demonstration. A lesson. Don't let your life-drawing tutor fuck you. Either way, I turn off the portable heater and crack open the window, ushering in a tunnel of cool air.

A groan from the jabby-elbowed man, still wrapped up in his scarf, in the front row. I don't recognise him. Receding hairline, wonky nose, iron-creased trousers, brown brogues. Must be new.

'Sorry, just feeling the heat today,' I tell him, nipping over and whispering in his ear: 'That time of the month.' Smiling at his open mouth, I hop back up onstage and remove Karina's robe.

He cocks his head to check that I've tucked any string out of sight.

I keep watching him as he leans to one side to get a better look and, after about ten seconds, I catch his eye.

Clears his throat and looks away, sheepish. Crosses one leg over the other.

The last of the students filter in, Annie bringing up the rear. She's laughing at something Paul's said and he's walking

253

too close to her, his arm grazing hers. Once he's walked her to her easel, he gives her a wink and resumes his place by the door.

'So, everyone,' he says, glancing at the clock, 'today we're going to focus solely on horizontal poses.' He gestures wildly with his arms, like an amateur actor trying too hard. 'Closer, bring your chairs closer.'

Easel and chair legs scrape across the floor as the students hotch forward.

'Think of the reclining female nudes drawn by so many great men . . . artists.'

Fucking hell.

'Picasso . . .'

Sure, makes sense to start with the misogynist.

'. . . Modigliani, Matisse, Manet.'

Leave Manet out of this.

'All fascinated by the female form.'

I close my eyes.

'The sexual awakening, the ripening of the fruit.'

I consider plugging my ears but resist.

'Eve, over to you.'

I try to catch Annie's eye before assuming my first position, but she's busy leafing through the pages of her sketchbook and reaching into her bag for her charcoal and pencils.

The old mattress is a stale yellow, musty up close. Not for the first time, I think about how many models – and students – Paul might have had sex with. I lie on one side, elbow bent, head propped up in the palm of my hand. This is what he wants: a re-enactment, as if he has it on tape. Please tell me he doesn't. I can feel his eyes on my body, my neck rashy. My chest begins to burn, a roaring flame.

I remember as a child I'd thrash around before settling upon a comfortable position and slipping into a deep slumber. In a cocoon on my side, one arm tucked under my pillow feeling the cool underneath, the other arm clutching the duvet cover (which was a little big for the duvet itself) as if to stop someone from yanking it off. Flat on my front, arms resting by my hips, head turned to the left, then the right. On my back, like a beetle, except instead of waving in the air my legs would be clamped tight together, my hands clasped across my chest.

Today, in the studio, I move through all of the above before curling up like a foetus and closing my eyes.

Eve, will you come to the appointment with me?

In a bid to distract myself I adopt some more difficult poses. After a while I also ignore the mattress. (I can see him out of the corner of my eye, fidgeting, shaking his head at my dis-obedience.) Knees bent, one leg wrapped not once but twice around the other, arms held out in front, bent at the elbows, twisted. I feel a stretch so tight across my back that I worry my ribs might slice through the skin and I'll morph into some kind of freaky insect. On the chair, knock-kneed but feet spread, arms hanging loose, lifeless. Sitting on the floor with my back leaning up against the chair, legs outstretched; the chair isn't heavy enough and ends up sliding away.

Someone laughs.

I stand rigid like an early Ancient Greek statue, with the odd sense that any movement will give something away.

The sound of charcoal, still sketching.

A cough.

I'm losing focus.

A throat cleared.

I close my eyes and wait for it to be over.

A sneeze followed shortly after by some sniffing.

'OK, everyone, let's take ten.'

This is it. I stand up and go to grab Karina's robe from the screen, throwing it on while keeping an eye on Annie as she leaves the room. She has the same handbag with her, hopefully rammed with things. Could she have missed her diary if it were hidden at the bottom? Maybe I'd be better off waiting and planting it in her bedroom.

No time to deliberate. I reach into my own bag for the loot and hold it behind the screen as the last of the students leave the room. Now. I hop off the stage and head straight for her seat. Well, almost. There. Another handbag, open, a couple of ten-pound notes poking out of the inside pocket. I wouldn't normally take this much but now I could do with the money, unlike the owner of this racing-green Chloé. I should find out how much it costs to take this class. How much Paul pockets. I'm clearly not being paid enough, at least compared to Ralph.

I swipe both notes, hop back up onstage and stuff them into the toe of one shoe.

Come on, Eve, concentrate. Take two.

I dart over to Annie's bag. No. What? There's barely anything in there: a small packet of tissues; that fold-up brush of hers, golden hairs visible between the slits, trying to break free; lipstick; lots of keys on one smooth silver key ring; a mini box of raisins, presumably an emergency snack for Molly; a bottle of water. It's too obvious, surely. She'll know someone took it. She'll know it was me – because who else? She won't ask me back. I won't get to see Molly again.

The door opens and I drop the diary underneath her easel. Fuck. I look up.

'Everything OK, Eve?' she asks, walking towards me with a mug of steaming tea in one hand and a biscuit in the other.

How did she get that so quickly? 'Yes, fine, thanks. Just checking out the drawings.'

'Oh goodness, please excuse mine. Not my finest.'

She's right. She's given me stumpy legs and an elongated body. It's not at all flattering. 'Don't be silly, it's interesting.'

She laughs and so do I, though I'm sure mine sounds like it has come straight from a can.

'I have some news,' she says, gingerly blowing on her tea before taking a sip, followed by a nibble of biscuit. 'I'm planning a weekend away in February.'

'Oh, that's nice.'

'With the man I've been seeing.' This time a dip and a nibble, the biscuit crumbling against her lips.

Right.

'I wanted to talk to you about this on Friday evening, but Molly was there and, regardless, it didn't seem like a good time.' She pauses, lips pursed, then: 'Eve, it's Paul.' When I don't say anything, she clarifies: 'Paul's the man I'm seeing.'

'Wow.' What else is there to say? 'Really?' That bit wasn't intended.

'I know, it's probably a bit of a shock. I didn't want to say anything too soon because it's early days and we're just seeing how it goes, but he's been so supportive since everything went sour with David.'

257

I bet he has. I feel his hands on me, grappling at my skin. I part my lips to tell her that he isn't good enough, to explain what happened, but my throat contracts. I've already lost Karina and Bill because of too much truth-telling.

'Anyway, all this to say, I was wondering if you could come and stay with Moll? David will be out of town – work, he says.'

'Sorry?'

'While we're away.'

'Stay at your house?'

'Well, yes, if that's OK with you? I can ask Mum if not.'

'No, I'll do it!'

'Oh wonderful, Eve, thank you. It'll only be one night.' She pops the last piece of biscuit into her mouth and mumbles something about double-checking the dates. She bends down towards her handbag. Mug on the floor – Paul won't be pleased – then a delay. She stays perfectly still, crouched like a cat pre-pounce, before reaching out her hand and picking up the diary. Silently, still crouching, she turns the pages.

'Everything all right?' I don't know what else to say.

She turns to look at me, saying nothing but exhibiting frown lines full of questions. A clearing of the throat. 'I lost my diary a couple of weeks ago. I was sure I had it in my bag, but it vanished. And now it's here?'

An inflection.

Was it you, Eve? you ask on our way back from a seminar, eyelashes wet, cheeks pink.

I reach out to wipe away a tear, but you brush my hand away.

Grace, no. I didn't tell anyone, I promise. As I say the words, I try to ignore the sense of guilt crawling over my skin.

You shake your head, look down at the ground. No one else knew, Eve.

I follow your gaze, glance back up at your face. You know. I imagine a scenario when you no longer trust me, when we're no longer friends, and feel a coil of fear unfurl inside me.

Eve, how could you?

'Well, it must have just slipped out of my bag and been lying here all along,' she says, glancing around the room nervously.

She can't honestly believe that.

'Anyway, back to those dates.'

That's it?

She slides the diary into her bag and retrieves her phone. 'Ah, yes, so we're thinking the second weekend in February – does that work?'

Valentine's Day. I don't know what to say, apart from: 'Yes.'

'Great, I'll tell him he can go ahead and book.' She makes a squeaky noise, just another wide-eyed student who's fallen for her teacher.

A couple of the others are still drinking cups of tea when they reappear, a homey smell wafting through the air. Paul's the last to enter, closing the door behind him. Behind me, the window rattles in its frame.

'OK, Eve, I would like you to find your inner child for us and assume a position on all fours.'

He's joking, surely. A titter from the young girl with the fiery hair. I don't move, let alone loosen Karina's robe.

I feel dirty. Like I've been out all night and gone to bed with a face full of make-up: crusty eyelashes thick with mascara, lips cracked with too much matte lipstick, skin dried out with powder. Hair tangled and doused in rock-hard hairspray and second-hand smoke. My clothes still on from the night before, the gusset of my tights hanging loose, my bra straps digging into my shoulders. Furry teeth, bad breath. A vinegary smell. I glance around the room at the students, watching, waiting. They can tell. They know my secret.

'Is there a problem, Eve?' He looks genuinely concerned, one hand slightly raised as if to say, Don't, not if you're uncomfortable.

I look at Annie, who's looking back at me, head on one side, eyebrows furrowed, silently asking, What's going on? Instinctively, my lips part. I'll tell you what. Then, just as quickly, I close them.

I look back at him – still no smile, as if he's doing nothing wrong. Insinuating that I'm overthinking, overreacting. I swallow the saliva gathering in my mouth before undoing my robe. 'No problem.'

Twenty-two

A few days later I wake up crying and I can't stop. My head's beginning to ache and I'm worried the skin around my skull is tightening, pressing in on bone and brain. This must be what it feels like when you wear a corset. Ribs squeezing, organs shifting. Maybe that's why Suzon looks so dazed, because she's struggling to breathe. Constricted lungs. Everything inching upwards to that slender neck until her slowly beating heart is quite literally in her throat.

I don't know what I was dreaming about, but it must have been sad. Then again, I cry too easily, brimming with emotion like a Baroque painting, all frothy pinks and festering yellows. After Mum left there were many melt-downs – but I was five and upwards, and dealing with Dad, so that's not wholly surprising. After Grace? In private. I don't know why but I didn't want anyone to see me cry. Even at the funeral, as other friends who didn't know her half as well sniffled and sobbed, I didn't shed a tear – wouldn't let myself. When my eyes started to well up and I felt a pinching in my chest, I counted, sometimes up to a hundred, until it passed.

Now I make a conscious effort to settle my forehead, breathing in (one, two, three) and out (one, two, three), even massaging my temples – which I once read some people do on a regular basis, a form of self-care. Thankfully Max left early for work – something about setting up for a private event – so he won't have heard me gasping for air.

He said he'd call to let me know where to meet him later – which he does, just as I'm getting out of the shower. I reach over and brush my fingertips against a towel, then hold the phone an inch away from my wet face. 'What's the plan?'

'Soho. Seven o'clock?'

'Perfect, see you there.'

We haven't been out together much since I moved in – partly because he still has his job at the bar so works most nights – but yesterday he suggested dinner. It feels like a proper date. I scrunch my eyes shut and hug my arms to my chest, trying to keep hold of every ounce of happiness.

I make an effort. Black dress, tights, ankle boots. I paint my nails that deep burgundy (thanks to Annie) and draw Karina's lipstick across my lips, rubbing them together and defining my Cupid's bow with my little finger.

After tapping in at Kilburn Station – it takes two attempts because, in my eagerness, I come too close to the sensors – I step onto the escalator and for once I stand still. With no one in front of me, I watch the steps being swallowed whole by the gnashing mouth at the bottom. Give it your best shot, I think, leaping off the escalator before sliding into the pit myself.

It's quiet, left and right, but I'm not the only one on the platform. Standing too close to me considering the amount of sickly-sweet body spray she's wearing is a teenage girl who has yet to grow into her gangly frame. She's hunched, like she's trying to take up less space, and staring intently at her phone, scrolling through someone else's filtered photos – doesn't she know it's not real life? Further along the platform, two women are perched on a bench, one with her cheek on the other's shoulder even though it's pointy-looking. I catch the words 'rice', 'white wine' and 'mushrooms' amid the muffled conversation coming from their lips. Risotto for dinner.

The carriages of a tube come charging into the station, light replacing dark. On board, I look left and right as they snake around a never-ending bend. All I see are blank faces. They're catching up on the news (their own free paper or their neighbour's), reading books (actual or digital), or watching TV shows, playing games and listening to music on their phones. Tapping, scrolling, swiping. Phones, phones, phones.

I lock my eyes on the joined-up gap between my carriage and the next. Metal sheets slip and slide against one another, goading me to stand above them, arms wide for balance, just to see if I can. I resist the urge and, instead, turn my eyes to the speckled floor – light and dark grey, veined with Pollock-like blue, green and yellow flecks, and scattered with a constellation of Smarties. Caught in the crack between two seats is an open tube, plundered.

I close my eyes and cling onto that happy feeling, ignoring the unsettling rattle of the gap-toothed tracks beneath my feet.

By the time I emerge at the other end Max has sent me the location of the restaurant. I open Google Maps and weave my way through the streets of Soho, always chock-a-block but especially on a Friday night. When I round the final corner I see him before he sees me – standing outside the entrance, hands in his pockets. My Max. I resist running towards him.

When he does see me, he walks to meet me and we kiss hello.

'Hi there,' I say, throwing my arms around his neck. I nod towards the restaurant: 'This looks nice.'

'It is,' he says, moving to the door and holding it open. 'After you.'

The interior looks like it's been bathed in runny honey. Apart from the bright, open kitchen at the back, the only light is seeping out from dim lamps and candles in gilded sconces. Each table is topped with a glass vase filled with a single flower and some greenery. At the back is a big arched window overlooking a mini courtyard. I make a mental note to book us a table outside this summer – it could be a surprise – if the food's any good.

We're greeted by a girl with blue-painted nails and a tiny gold hoop pierced through the thin piece of cartilage between her nostrils. She shows us to a table for two that's nicely tucked away in a niche.

'Can I get you guys a drink?'

After asking what I want, Max orders a bottle of red.

'How was your day?' I ask, as he pours us both some water.

'Good, thanks. Alex got what he wanted.' He's spent the day suit shopping with a friend who's starting a shiny new job next week. 'And you?'

'Oh, you know, it was good.'

He smiles, though his eyebrows are dipped. A face like a faulty puppet's.

My stomach rumbles involuntarily. 'What are we having?'

We order a bunch of small plates, all of which are better than good – especially the *fritto misto*, with lashings of lemon and salt. When the bread arrives at the end of the meal, Max makes a comment about it being too late, but I grab a piece and mop up some garlicky butter from the prawns.

'I haven't seen you eat this much in months.'

'I haven't been this hungry in months,' I say, licking the butter from my lips. 'I'm also having the best time.'

He smiles, a proper smile. Then his eyebrows dip down again, like he's just remembered something.

'Why do you keep giving me that funny look?'

A pause, and then: 'Look, don't be mad.'

My fingertips start to prickle. 'What have you done?'

He puts down his knife and fork, picks them up again, pokes at some salad leaves – the kind used as a garnish rather than the stuff you're supposed to eat. 'I didn't just go suit shopping with Alex today.'

'OK,' I say, sitting up straight. 'Is this where you tell me you're seeing someone else?' I know he was on a couple of dating apps before.

He laughs, although his mouth is fixed in a straight line. 'No, Eve, of course I'm not seeing someone else.'

'What then?'

He looks up at the ceiling. Neck still craned, he says, 'I went to see your dad.'

My muscles strain and, for a few seconds, neither of us speaks. When my head starts to hurt, I realise I'm frowning and look down at my empty plate.

'I'm sorry, Eve, I was just talking to my parents and we decided someone should check on him.'

'Oh, because I'm such a lousy daughter?'

'I didn't say that.'

'You didn't have to.' The prickles are inching from my fingertips up my arms, into my chest, which is beginning to burn – no, not burn, but simmer on a low heat.

'Look, I'm not an idiot, Eve. I know how badly he screwed up.'

I guffaw. 'You don't know the half of it.'

'Then tell me.'

My eyes skip to the other diners, but of course everyone's oblivious, eating and drinking, smiling and laughing. 'I went to his before I came to yours that night.'

'You mean after Karina threw you out?'

I wince. 'Yes.'

'And?'

I start picking at a piece of skin hanging loose alongside one nail, pulling it up and away. 'And he didn't want me.'

'Eve, I'm sure that's not true.' He shakes his head. 'Did you tell him what happened?'

'I told him,' I say, trying to stop my voice from wavering, 'I told him I had nowhere to go. You know what he said?'

'What?'

'He said, "Oh dear."' I rip the piece of skin free. 'Then he asked for another drink.'

Max closes his eyes. 'Eve, I'm sorry.' As he reopens them, he reaches across the table to hold my hand. 'I wish you'd told me.'

'Telling you doesn't change anything.'

He waits a beat, then asks in a quiet voice: 'Are we still talking about your dad?'

I didn't tell anyone. Denial is automatic, a reflex. No different from the jolt your lower leg makes when someone strikes you just

266

below the kneecap. As soon as I say it, I want to take it back –
admit I did tell someone, explain – but I can't. I don't know why.
Maybe I'm afraid you won't forgive me. Though this is worse.
No one else knew, Eve.

'Eve?'

'What did you say?' I scoot my hand away. 'You mean Grace?'

'No, Eve, I meant Karina and Bill.'

'Oh, I'm sorry, it's a long list of friendships I've screwed up.' He puts his head in his hands.

I want to tell him that I understand, I'm overreacting. But it's too late. I've pulled out the pin and can't push it back in. 'You really want to know what happened there? Bill and I got drunk and kissed, a few months ago, and he decided to get it off his chest on Christmas Day.' I wait for him to react and, when he doesn't, I start folding my napkin. 'I have to go.'

'Come on, Eve, a drunken kiss doesn't bother me, especially one with Bill.' He tests a smile, trying to lighten the mood.

'Oh, so it's funny to you?' I ask, standing up and shrugging on my coat.

'Eve, come on, this is stupid.'

I know it is, I know it's stupid. But I can't stop myself. My cheeks are burning, I can feel it. Again, my eyes skip around the room. 'I'll see you later.'

Before he has time to reply, I walk away through the restaurant.

Outside the entrance, I lean up against the wall and catch my breath. I feel a lump form in my throat. I ball my hands into fists and press them against my eye sockets, ignoring what I'm sure are now the prying faces of a dozen strangers. What am I doing? Fucking up another friendship – more than a friendship.

I turn to go back in and, as I reach my hand towards the door, it swings open. Max has his coat on and is sliding his wallet into the back pocket of his jeans.

I don't know where to look so I look down at the ground as I say, 'I'm sorry, I've ruined our evening.'

The next thing I know, his arms are wrapped around me and tears are streaming down my face.

A silence springs up between us on the tube. We sit side by side, my hand in his. But as we're walking back to the flat at the other end, Max asks me – again – how I'm feeling. 'Honestly, Eve.'

'Honestly, I'm struggling.'

He breathes out, an audible breath, and puts his arm around me. 'I know you don't like to talk about it, but do you think it's to do with Grace?'

I clamp my lips together.

'You're not going to hurt my feelings, Eve.'

I try to keep my voice flat as I say, 'I think it's always been about Grace.'

I expect him to drop his arm, but he squeezes me tight. 'I know I've said it before, but I really think you need to go back.'

'You could be right – it's not like I haven't thought about it.' Thought about her. Every day. No, not every day, but most. For the past five years. 'I just don't know if I can.'

'What are you doing this weekend? Why don't we go together? Then you can start to move on, Eve.'

My mind drifts.

Coming to the library? I hover by the door, holding my books against my hip.

You shake your head, say you're tired, turn back to Gilmore Girls on your laptop. Besides, you say, my brain's chock-full by now – no use trying to squeeze in any extra names or dates.

Fair enough, we don't want bits of Grace brain exploding all over the art history section. I laugh at my own joke – an insecurity, I know.

You smile with your mouth but not your eyes. Your face is glowing, the brightness of the screen up too high.

I'll come and see you after, I say. I want to ask, You're sure everything's OK? I don't – I've learned not to push people after what happened with Dad. Yelling, bawling, sulking and then, worst of all, nothing. But you've been different the past couple of weeks. Quieter, more solitary. Looking down at the ground, up at the sky. Anywhere but my eyes.

Well, I won't be long, I say, I'll see you when I get back.

Max is saying something about closure. He sounds faraway, like he's speaking through a walkie-talkie. 'Eve,' he says, 'what do you think?'

'Molly,' I reply. 'I'm looking after Molly this weekend.'

I feel him tense up beside me. 'Are you sure you should be babysitting right now, while you're feeling the way you're feeling?'

I stop walking. 'You don't trust me?'

'Of course I do, I just wonder if you need to take some time to figure things out. Molly will still be here after.'

'No,' I say, my heart racing. 'I can't stop babysitting. Annie needs me. Molly needs me.'

'OK, Eve, it was just a suggestion.'

Twenty-three

Imagine if you stopped breathing. How horrible it would feel as blood ceased to pump around your body, cutting off oxygen from your brain. It happened to a thirteen-year-old boy yesterday – he dropped down dead on a football pitch in east London. I read about it in the *Evening Standard* just now, which has a big photo of him standing between his mum and dad. Imagine their terror when he didn't wake up.

Your parents arrive in silence, your brother and his wife walking in behind them. Your mum keeps her eyes firmly on the ground. Your dad doesn't make a sound, not even a sniff. After a while, he pulls out a neatly folded white handkerchief and dabs at his nose. It's running but he can't bring himself to blow it. Not now, not when he's trying to say goodbye to his daughter.

I don't know Mum so I shouldn't be sad that she's not here. I can't tell you what her favourite book is or what perfume she wears. I don't know whether she likes eggs or, like me, hates first the smell and then the taste, no matter whether they're boiled, poached, scrambled or fried. Does she hate milk too?

Is she a walker? Morning or evening person? Shower or bath? Red or white? Does she miss me?

It wasn't the milestones that mattered. It was the ordinary things she missed that made me miss her. I wanted her to cycle through London with me, to lead me safely along the busy roads to school so I didn't have to catch the bus – the way Suzie's mum did. To clink glasses with me at the dining room table before tucking into a Sunday roast and to insist that I finish my vegetables before helping myself to pudding. To tell me off for forgetting to fasten my seat belt and to reassure me, as I locked my lips together in front of a camera, that I looked pretty even though I was missing my two front teeth. To drop me off at a weekly piano lesson, perhaps even pick me up too. To help me with my homework and lend me her treasured childhood books. To say sweet dreams when I went to bed and, most importantly, to be there at the kitchen table when I came down for breakfast in the morning. I wanted her to be there for everything, anything. The big things. The everyday things.

And Dad? He could have done all that, but he chose not to. I'm his daughter. He's a grown man. He's the one who should be here for me. Me cleaning up after him isn't part of the deal. And yet, even after the way he treated me that night, I'm the one left feeling guilty. Maybe he was pissed and didn't know what he was saying. Maybe if I'd got there an hour earlier things would have been different. In a way, I'm doing to him exactly what she did to me. Abandoning him when he needs me.

It's early. The backs of parked cars have a clingfilm layer of silver dew stretched across them. The same with the odd patch of close-cut grass – silken quilts lie lightly on top.

South Kensington is quiet except for a teenage daughter and her too-blonde-to-be-natural mum. Funny how it happens to so many women that age – instead of going grey, their hair magically turns a brilliant shade of white gold. It looks quite convincing until you spot the heavily wrinkled forehead, or the Botox.

Anyway, I'm now the audience for a silly stand-off outside some flashy clothes shop. It's yet to open but apparently the window display is a source of great discomfort.

'Why do you always have to say that?' whines the girl.

'Say what?'

'That something isn't very me.'

'Because sometimes things aren't very you.'

'Ugh, this is why I hate shopping with you.'

I put my head down and leave them to it, imagining myself at sixteen, fists balled with injustice as I march huffily away from my own mum, the tone of her voice as she quietly tells me to buck up my ideas. Maybe that's why she went: she could foresee an unhappy ending and left to spare me from tragedy. She got out before the good got bad. Better to be strangers for life, she must have thought, than to pick each other apart, one long, slow day at a time.

'Eve, hi.' Annie opens the door, already wearing her coat. 'Come on in. How are you?'

I step forward and almost trip over Henry, splayed across the width of the hall like a welcome mat, grunty rubber pig between his front paws. 'All good, thanks. Where are you off to today?'

'Oh, just work, sadly.'

I relax in the knowledge that she isn't seeing Paul.

'No Molly? Is she OK?' I'm so used to her being the first to greet me.

'Eve!' The door to the downstairs loo flings open and she half walks, half skips towards me, hitching up her tights in the process. Hands unwashed, most likely.

'Hello there.' I bend down and she flings her arms around my neck, headbutting my shoulder in the process. A proper hug.

'Right, I'm going to have to whizz off, I'm afraid,' says Annie, jingling a set of keys at the end of her wrist. 'I won't be back until about eight. Is that OK?'

'Absolutely,' I reply. And turning to look at Molly: 'We'll find something to keep us busy, won't we?'

Nodding.

'Wonderful, thanks, Eve. My spare card is in the usual place if you end up going out for food or whatever.'

'Great, thanks.'

She bends down to kiss Molly goodbye. 'See you later, sweetie.' One final check in the mirror and she's out of the door.

I bundle Molly up into a coat and onto the bus.

'Where are we going, Eve?' she asks, once we're sitting at the front of the top deck.

We're going to the gallery. To see if Suzon's back.

'Eve?' she prods my side.

'Oh, sorry, Moll. I thought it might be fun to visit my favourite art gallery.'

'Where?'

'Near Covent Garden. Have you been there?'

She nods, hotches up onto her knees and presses her nose against the window. 'Why is it your favourite?'

'Because it's where my favourite painting lives,' I say, holding onto her arm with one hand. 'And I feel my most happy there.' I'm jolted by my honesty.

'Why?'

'Why what?'

'Why do you feel your most happy there?'

'Because when I'm there I feel close to my friend, I think.'

'Why?'

OK, I see where this is going. Instead of answering, I blow on the glass and write her name in big bubble letters.

'Let me!' She tries it herself but doesn't blow hard enough.

I show her again, inhaling deeply and creating a canvas of condensation. This time I draw a heart.

'What's your favourite painting, Eve?' She takes another whack at it and it works. Draws a smiley face.

'You'll soon see.' Hopefully.

Marjorie looks surprised to see me. And no wonder – it's been a while, the longest I've gone without visiting in four years. When I ask for two tickets, she must think I've lost my mind.

'Two?' she probes sceptically.

'Two,' I repeat, slowly and clearly. 'One for me and one for Molly.'

Molly stands on her tiptoes and slowly creeps her fingertips, spider-like, over the edge of the desk.

Marjorie almost falls off her chair. 'Goodness,' she says, standing up to get a better look. 'I didn't see you there.'

Molly giggles.

'Children under twelve go free?' It comes out as a question, rising note at the end. She irons out her skirt as she returns to her seat.

'Excellent.' Even so, I decide to use Annie's card, kept in a pot in the kitchen for expenses.

Marjorie looks equally bemused when I flash it at the machine and I can feel her ogling us as we climb the stairs. Like the woman in the park, maybe she assumes I'm a mum. With her daughter.

I try not to get my hopes up as we walk through the first few rooms. (Unsurprisingly, Molly loves Degas's ballerinas – stands in front of them and starts to replicate the poses.) Somehow, though, they elude me, swoop up and out of my control. By the time we reach room six, I'm sure she'll be there waiting for me. She isn't.

At least no one's tried to replace her. The long stretch of wall is still empty, except for the laminated notice. I find myself reading it again, searching for something – clues, maybe – among the words and white space in between.

It's like waiting for a missing person to be found. For your mum to decide she's made a horrible mistake, that she misses you and wants to be in your life after all. For your dad to snap out of it, to call you and tell you he cares, that of course he'll always be here to support you when you need him. For it all to be a weird joke, like saying you're allergic to blueberries – your friend was messing around, she's fine. Have you heard anything? No. Any news? No change, I'm afraid. We'll tell you as soon as we have any updates.

No audible breath, your chest horribly still, though you've always been a heavy breather.

'Eve?'

In fact, there is an update: Badger must have got it wrong. The notice has changed. It says Suzon is in Paris until April. Fucking April. I feel a sharp pain in my chest.

'Eve, what are you reading?'

Molly.

'A notice about my favourite painting. This is where it hangs, but it's away at the moment.'

'On holiday?'

The pain morphs into a mild ache.

'Yes, she's on holiday.'

Molly smiles, slips her hand into mine. 'I'm sure she'll be back soon then.'

Like a tablet, the mild ache briefly effervesces before dissolving.

To my surprise, I smile back. My heart beats hard against my chest, an idea percolating.

By the time we're back outside my mind's made up. Max is right. I've been putting it off for too long. Getting out of London. Going back. It'll help. And if Molly made going to the empty gallery more bearable, maybe she'll make this easier too. I look at her and ask, 'What do you want to do next?'

Shoulders shrug.

'Well, I have an idea.' A good idea, I think. I bend down and she starts to swizzle her fingers through my hair. 'Do you want to hear it?'

'Yes.' Fingers begin imaginary snipping.

'How about we go for a train ride?'

'Yes!' Louder this time.

'Perfect. Here, get your hat and gloves on and we can go.'

'Where are we going on the train ride?' She laughs as I help with her hat, pulling it down over her eyes. 'Hey!'

I breathe in and out and say four words I never thought would leave my mouth again: 'We're going to Oxford.'

'Where's Oxford?'

Not far, I tell her, checking the route on my phone. I contemplate stopping off at Annie's on the way and taking Henry out for a quick walk but decide against it. No time. I mustn't change my mind; it would be as easy as flicking a switch.

Paddington Station is teeming with travellers. Suited businessmen and women are striding with purpose, their shiny black cases slipping and sliding along on either two or four spinning wheels. Tired-looking parents laden with luggage are trying not to lose their overexcited children in the crowd – there's a little one with corkscrew curls, peeking out from behind a red post box. Loved-up couples, supremely unaware of the chaos around them, are setting out for a romantic weekend. A gruff voice is sounding through the speakers, warning passengers that the platforms might be slippery. Is it raining outside? I look around: everyone but me is carrying either a little or large sopping umbrella. I look at Molly and catch a drip falling from the front of her hat onto the tip of her nose. We zigzag through the mob.

I scan the electronic board of departures. Bingo. A train leaves in ten minutes. 'Come on, Moll.' I cling on tight as we weave our way to the ticket machines, letting go for just a moment when I have to fish Annie's card out of my purse. Two return tickets to Oxford. Card in and out.

We follow a boy and girl about my and Max's age onto the train, stationary on platform one. He whispers something in her ear, and she flashes him a smile. I look away like I've been blinded.

'Eve, can you plait my hair on the train?'

Chestnut hair pulled back off your freckled face, woven in a single loose plait. The wispy tips kiss your collarbone.

'Eve?'

I haven't plaited any hair since yours. 'I can try.'

As the girl climbs the steps she reaches back with one finger, which the boy hooks with his.

We find two seats in Coach D, both forward-facing. Five minutes later we're gliding through the grim industrial outskirts of London. Everything has been covered in a cool grey-blue glaze: tiled roofs, the chimneys of which are belching smoke; grubby brickwork; old and new factories, blazoned with the names of companies. Graffiti that says, in capital letters, EAT DA RICH. The window has a filter switched to dreary. I blink, just to see if I can change it to a warming sepia. It doesn't work, but soon we're in the rolling countryside, all fields and trees, branches swaying in the breeze.

Opposite is a woman with caramel-coloured hair who could be Annie's doppelganger. I glance at her left hand, home to a twinkly diamond ring. She licks her index finger and thumb as she flicks through the pages of a glossy magazine while half looking at her phone resting on the table between us. She doesn't notice that she skips a spread and I don't bother telling her. It's probably an advert anyway.

I seem to be getting somewhere with Molly's plaits when a big-bellied ticket inspector appears in our carriage.

'Tickets, please.'

I quickly wind a hair tie around the plait-in-progress and retrieve ours from my purse.

'You know you don't need to pay the full adult fare for her?'

'Excuse me?'

'Is this your daughter?'

I look at Molly.

'Well, miss?'

'I—'

'She's my nanny.' Molly gestures with her hands as if presenting me as a priceless gift to a king.

He rolls his eyes – just the hired help of another middle-class family – and hands back our tickets. 'Children under fifteen get a discount.'

I should have guessed.

'Tickets, please.' He continues waddling down the carriage.

People are staring, enquiring, questioning, judging. I can feel their eyes on the scratchy surface of my skin. I can practically see the ears of the man with the newspaper across the aisle prick up. The Annie lookalike sighs, though I'm sure it sounds more like a tut. I had a terrible mother and I was a terrible best friend. Maybe I'm a terrible daughter too. I'm sure Dad would say so. They're waiting for me to mess up again. Maybe this was a bad decision.

'My plaits, Eve.'

One half of Molly's hair is hanging loose while the other half is an incomplete plait, dangling from her head.

'Here, let me start again,' I say, unwinding the hair tie. 'I'll get it right this time, I promise.'

*

We arrive at the station and walk up the steps, which are labelled with long yellow stickers: PLEASE TAKE CARE ON THE STAIRS. As we cross over the tracks and walk down the other side, a voiceover plays: 'When on the stairs, please use the handrail and take care.'

Molly in hand, I ignore the taxis lined up outside the exit, and the graveyard of identical bicycles, and follow the straight road leading into the city centre. It's a fifteen-minute walk that takes us over the river and past some scrappy Chinese takeaways. Then on to some nicer-looking buildings. Oxford stone. I may not have been back in five years, but I remember the way.

A whimper.

'What's wrong, Molly?'

'I'm hungry.'

Damn, I should have picked something up at Paddington. 'I know, we can go to my favourite café.'

'How far away is it?'

'Just a little bit further, up here and round to the right.'

She puckers her lips.

'Really, Moll, it's a good one.'

The one where we used to go once a week, where you'd order a bagel with smoked salmon and cream cheese.

Molly and I arrive and nothing has changed, except for the addition of some raw cacao energy balls in a ceramic bowl by the till. Laid out before us is a glass counter filled with cakes ready to cut and pre-made sandwiches waiting to be toasted. Behind it is a row of bagels and a fridge full of cold drinks, mostly in cans.

To the right, a shiny coffee machine. A waft of freshly ground beans.

I notice there are only three spare tables. Make that two: a university type with a shiny MacBook slides behind one, scanning an email as he settles his things on the tabletop.

'Do you want a grilled cheese, Moll?'

'Yes, please.'

'OK, you go and sit.'

Another pucker.

'I'll be there in a second.'

'And for yourself?'

I didn't notice the boy behind the counter jotting down our order. He's wearing a vest and has tattoos for sleeves. 'A bagel with smoked salmon and cream cheese, please. No capers.'

'Plain or wholemeal?'

'Plain.'

'Oh, or we do have sesame.'

'Plain.'

'OK then. That's eight pounds ninety.'

I tap Annie's card on the reader, then pretend to scan the room, holding my right hand above my eyes – I'm the captain of a white-sailed ship surveying the horizon on a sunny day. 'Ahoy!' I call, searching the crowd.

'Ahoy!' Molly slowly waves her arm from side to side, less like a sailor and more like a fan at a concert.

I swim over to her, my arms doing breaststroke. 'Phew, made it.' I stuff my bag under the table and hope it doesn't float away or, worse, sink.

Five minutes later our lunch arrives. As she eats, Molly moves to the trippy music sounding through the speakers.

When I ask her a question she points at her cheek, as polite people – and apparently children – do when they want to swallow a mouthful before responding. Max does it. I normally try to talk through my mouthfuls and end up spluttering.

Now she needs a wee and there's no loo in the café – at least not that we can see. Surely there's one for staff tucked away at the back. I send her up to the counter to ask by herself, hoping someone will take pity, but the boy shakes his head and sends her away. Heartless, I tell him, bundling her out of the door. How would you like it if your bladder was about to burst?

Out on the pavement, I look down at Molly. She's clutching her tummy, perhaps because she really is bursting, but more likely because she's gobbled too much cheese. 'I know a museum you'll like, Moll. Shall we go to the loo there?'

'We always have to go to museums.'

I crouch down in front of her. 'What's wrong?'

'I need a wee.'

'I know, that's why we need to find a loo. We don't have to go to the museum, but I do think you'll like it. It's kind of like the Natural History Museum – you've been there, haven't you?'

'Yes.'

She seems quieter today. Pensive, perhaps sad. I wonder if she realises something's up with her dad spending so much time away. Maybe she's cross with him, blames Annie. I want to tell her it's OK to be angry, just like it's OK to be sad. I want to tell her that she must say how she feels rather than bottle up her emotions, always. I squeeze her hand.

We walk past our old college – or at least its façade, a sandy stone. My heart thumps. I want to go inside but

Molly really is desperate now, holding her hand between her legs. We continue to the Pitt Rivers Museum and head to the reception desk. A woman with an owl-like face and wiry black hair spun with white threads kindly directs us to the loos.

We make a speedy tour of the displays. Molly perks up at the sight of a stuffed ostrich and yelps at the live cockroaches crawling behind the glass. In the lower gallery she finds an ivory dog team with a sledge of kayaks.

'Please can I take it home for my doll's house, Eve?'

I lean forward for a closer look, then tell her I'm not sure it would go and buy her a pencil topped with a wooden elephant head instead. I pay while Molly gawps at the taxidermy fox perched beside the till.

Our hearts aren't in it, not really. Besides, we should head back to the station soon. I find myself wondering if this is even helping because I don't feel any different. These are places that meant something to us, places full of happy memories. But then, maybe it's not the happy memories I need to revisit.

'This way, Moll.'

It's getting dark, the brightly lit shopfronts beacons in the almost-black, the streets starred with the gentle glow of lamp posts. We take a left and that's when I see it. The bar. *Our* bar. The bar where Grace and I used to work, where the second screw came loose. The bar where one night, after closing, I went home without her.

My phone vibrates in my pocket. Voicemail, though I didn't notice it ring. I hit the button and hold it to my ear.

'Hi, Eve, where are you? I'm back early and Henry's peed

all over the floor! I'm guessing you've taken Molly to yours, so just head on home when you get this.'

A puddle of piss beneath your feet.

I fire off a quick message – *sorry, lost track of time. back soon –* and tighten my grip on Molly's hand.

It looks just the same. The stone façade, punctured with windows, an unlocked bicycle leaning up against it. A swinging sign stamped with white font, ivy creeping up and around the crusty drainpipe. I cross the road to get a better look, even peek through the glass at the downstairs bar. And there, beside the fire on the right-hand side, a man. Surely not. But that dark hair, those rounded shoulders, always a little hunched over.

I start to feel faint and realise it's because I'm holding my breath.

He's sitting in one of two brown leather armchairs, his arse slid halfway forward along the seat. His legs are spread-eagled like they're funnelling a lone ship into the safety of a harbour after a dark and stormy journey at sea. For a moment, I imagine his trousers are stitched with cat's eyes along their inner seams.

His dark stubble has grown out, a shadow across his chiselled jaw. His hair is slicked back, like he's just got out of the shower. He yawns at the newspapers spread out on the small wooden table in front of him and raises a pint glass to his lips. I can tell his eyes are bloodshot from here. He wipes his mouth with the back of his sleeve and turns towards the window.

I hold tight onto Molly's hand and walk away, fast.

Twenty-four

Do you remember, Eve, a few weeks ago, when you went back to your room without me?

No. Why?

Something happened.

What happened?

Something bad.

Tell me.

He told me not to say anything but I—

Who told you?

Who do you think?

What did he do? Grace?

'Hi, Eve.'

I freeze and slowly turn around. Behind me is a woman I don't recognise. 'Do I know you?'

Between her fingers she twirls two skinny black wires, dangling down from her ears. She continues talking, shooting me a look. Headphones, of course.

'Sorry, Eve, you're breaking up.'

Up . . . or down?

'What did you say?'

He forced himself on me.

Grace, no.

We were fighting. I told him I didn't want to. But he wouldn't stop.

Why didn't you tell me before?

He's my boyfriend.

It still counts, Grace.

'I want my mummy.'

Molly. I squeeze her hand.

'I want to go home now.'

'It's OK, Moll,' I say, trying to get my bearings while avoiding eye contact with the stony features of strangers and unfamiliar buildings staring back at me. 'I just need to figure out where we are.' I must have taken a wrong turn. It's like someone's turned out all the lights and I'm feeling my way in the dark.

Eve, I need your help.

Anything.

I need to get rid of it.

Oh God.

You have to promise me you won't tell anyone.

Grace, it's me, who would I tell?

We walk on, or maybe in circles. I can't concentrate, my mind catching every conversation we had towards the end. The air's thick with mist – a constant drizzle falling onto my face, making it feel damp.

286

Someone bumps into me with an umbrella in full bloom. Not damp enough for that, for fuck's sake.

A whimper.

'Come on, Moll, just a tiny bit further.' I look down at her – Grace's baby would have been just a year or so younger.

The clinic is a little way out of town, a ten-minute bus ride. You don't talk, just stare out of the window, your eyes flashing left and right as men, women and children cross your field of vision. I notice you pull back when we pass a pregnant woman, her belly button jabbing against her strained T-shirt.

Molly's dragging her heels.

I stop at the next corner. 'Do you want me to carry you?'

She nods, starts to sob. 'Because my legs ache.'

'OK, here we go.' I lift her up and she clings on like a barnacle, fingers clasped around my bare neck.

'Not so tight, Moll.'

She loosens her grip, pulls my hair in the process.

It's a sad-looking brick building like those on the council estate near Dad's. Small white windows letting in minimal light. A matching door.

Don't look, Grace. Stuck to the wall is a photo of an unborn child – a protest – prawn-like but fully formed.

An arrow points us towards the main reception. I take your hand.

I hitch Molly up onto my hip and keep walking, careful not to slip on the pavement – slick as a seal from all the spotting. A rumble of thunder and the spots start to fall faster, bigger, one after another. Soon it's hammering. The sound of footsteps, running.

We're getting soaked. Molly's crying – as if there isn't enough wetness. My chest feels tight, pinned with fear as the water pulls me under. I have to look after Molly. I squint through my eyelashes, weighed down with raindrops. Bust windscreen wipers. Deeper and deeper.

The nurse tells me I have to wait outside. Says it in a raspy voice from deep within the kind of throat that needs to be cleared.

I want to go in with her, I say, still holding your hand. She needs me.

I'm afraid that's not possible.

You nod, I'll be OK.

I'll be right here, waiting for you. I let go.

You follow the nurse through the swing doors, disappear for the first time.

Up ahead, the cobalt-blue sign of a cheap hotel glows in the dark. Should we stay? We can't, I told Annie we'd be back soon. Then again, it's late. And Molly's tired. I don't know where I'm going. I bite down on my lower lip. It's the sensible thing to do.

'Moll, shall we have a sleepover?'

She buries her face in my chest.

'It'll be fun.'

Will it?

'What if we have a midnight feast like big girls do?'

'OK.'

After, you don't want to talk about it. And that's fine.

The woman behind reception gives you a cup of sweetened tea and a piece of toast, except she doesn't toast the bread for long enough so the butter won't melt.

You sip, chew, sip, swallow. All the while clutching at your empty womb.

The nurse says, Once you're finished, you can go.

I give her the finger when she turns around, look to you and smile.

No smile from you.

I lower Molly to the floor as soon as we're inside, sheltered from the rain, and run my hand over my sopping hair, lying flat against my skull. To ease the pain in my back, I fold forward over my knees, reaching for my toes. She's not exactly heavy but I'm not used to carrying her around. What would Youla think if she saw me now? What about Karina and Bill? Max?

Behind the desk is a balding man with a worrying number of coffee-coloured moles on his scalp. Three red lines from where he's been scratching at an angry-looking scab. He catches my eye and nods his head, either in silent greeting or acknowledgement of my presence: I'll be right with you. He's talking on the phone too.

I pull out my own phone and find three more voicemails. All from Max.

'Eve, where are you? Annie just called, assuming you and Molly were here. I only got back five minutes ago so I told her I'd probably missed you and that you'd be on your way. Is that true?'

He sounds nervous, a crackle to his voice.

'Eve, she just called again. I'm starting to worry. Has something happened? You have to call me right away.'

I feel a prickle of frustration. We're fine.

'Eve—'

Molly starts to sniffle again.

I stop listening. 'Not long, Moll.'

'Can I help, miss?' asks the receptionist, returning his phone to its cradle.

'Do you have a room available?'

'We do indeed. Would you prefer a twin or a double?'

'Either will do.'

He tells me the price, I insert Annie's card, punch in the numbers, and he hands over the key. He has big, puffy hands, fingers like uncooked sausages. 'Up to the first floor in the lift, turn right and keep going to the end.'

'Is there anything to eat?'

'You'll find a vending machine opposite when you get out of the lift.'

'Thanks. Moll, do you want to press that silver button to call it?'

We take the bus back, another voiceless journey. This time you slink down in your seat and close your eyes.

When we reach the college you say you're tired, that you need to sleep.

Of course, I'll come back in the morning.

That evening I go out and drink too much. I sit down, sipping clear liquid, thinking about how I can step up, repay everything you've done for me. That's when I run into her – the chatty girl who lives in a room a few doors down. She takes a seat beside me, asks me how I am, what I've been up to. I can't think of anything to say. She asks about you, since we're usually together: How's Grace?

It's out before I can gulp back the words. I need help. You need help. I don't know how to make it better.

Her mouth gapes for a while, then she starts nibbling her nails. Oh shit. Poor Grace. This is fucking awful.

I swallow the rest of my drink. I'm sorry, I say, I shouldn't have said anything. I promised. Please forget it.

Don't be silly, this is way too much for her to handle by herself.

She's not by herself, I say. She has me.

Of course, but still . . . We'll help her, don't worry. She holds my hand as she says it.

I feel sick, probably from the alcohol, but maybe with guilt. I excuse myself and go to the loo.

I don't know that she means she'll talk to her tutor, tell people. Your knotty secret unravelled and examined by strangers. Reduced to dirty gossip. A loose thread of Chinese whispers.

She what? What did you say?

In the lift, I quickly type out a message to Max: *all fine, sorry, too late to come back so going to stay*

He replies within seconds: *Are you in Oxford?*

yes

Eve. You have to bring Molly back now.

it's too late

The lift dings as we reach the first floor. The doors open but my feet are frozen, rooted to the spot. A sensor in front of a canvas, keeping you from coming too close. His sense of urgency is bleeding into mine.

My thumbs move quickly: *she's exhausted, needs to sleep. i've got us a room. please tell annie everything's fine. back in the morning*

'Our midnight feast.' Molly yanks on my sleeve.

'Of course.' I put on a smile, holding down the power button of my phone, a superficial warmth spreading through me as the screen turns black. 'What would you like?'

She crouches in front of the vending machine, nose pressed against the glass and eyes as wide as bicycle wheels. 'Can I have chocolate?'

'You can have anything you want.'

She traces a snaking route with her fingertip, then stops. 'Smarties, please.'

Her finger slides south. 'No, Buttons.' Her bottom lip begins to wobble. 'I can't choose.'

'We can get both if you don't cry.'

It's not long before you hear those whispers, first from your own tutor and then from other students. Some are embellished with shiny details.

Did you say something? You ask me while we're walking through the front quad, your eyes fixed on the grass, freshly mown that morning – sweet-smelling and striped from certain angles. Not that it even matters, you add.

No, I promise. I lie, looking away. I'm sorry, I think, my legs suddenly sluggish, laden with guilt.

I unlock the door and switch on the two bedside lamps, one on either side of the pushed-together twin beds. The carpet is the same shade of blue as the sign in front of the building and spattered with splodges that look like spilt milk. White bedding plus a stripy blanket in red, white and grey. A crab-apple-red foamy chair with spiky metal legs. I tug at the curtains, which are heavier than they look, before realising there's a drawstring.

What now? I look at Molly, wet through from the rain. 'Do you want a bath, Moll?'

'Can I eat my chocolate in the bath?'

'Why not?'

Exam season. We're revising in my room. You're quieter than before, say you're happy to sit together but prefer to work by yourself, if that's OK.

Do you want to test each other?

I'd rather reread my notes.

I try to reread mine, which is difficult when my eyes stray to your face every five seconds.

The next day I ask if you want to come for a final cramming session in the library. You say no.

OK, I say, I'll come and find you after.

You nod, smile and say goodbye.

'Are Mummy and Daddy coming to stay in the hotel too?'

I twist off the hot tap but leave the cold running, swooshing the icy torrent around the bath with my reddening hands until the water has cooled down enough for Molly to climb in. 'No, Mummy and Daddy are busy tonight,' I say, helping her out of her soggy clothes and day-of-the-week pants, and hanging them on the toasty-warm towel rail – a small source of comfort. 'But we're having fun, aren't we?' I lift her up and over the side of the bath, then transfer the open tube of Smarties to her wriggling fingers.

'Yes,' she says, balancing a green on the tip of her tongue. I watch as she flicks it back and crunches it between her little teeth. She peers inside the tube.

'Are you feeling all right, Moll? You can tell me.'

She slides a blue along the inside of the tube with her finger, leans forward and hooks it straight onto her tongue.

'What's your favourite colour, Moll?'

More crunching. 'Brown because it's extra-chocolatey.'

A-ha, selective hearing.

'What's your favourite colour, Eve?'

'I'm not sure. Is there an orange?'

She peers inside, then tips an assortment into her hand. Two spill overboard and into the bath. *Plop. Plop.* She fishes them out and pops them in her mouth before I can tell her not to. 'There you go.' She passes me an orange, the food colouring runny between her wet fingers.

The weight of your door, heavier than normal, like it's been gorging on junk and gained a few pounds since I pulled it to. It opens, but not fully. I call your name – Grace? – and try it again. I press my shoulder against the wood and I push.

'Time to get out, Molly.'

'But I'm cosy.' She flops onto her tummy, pink bottom cheeks bobbing above the water like baby buoys.

'You're going to turn into a prune.' I yank one of two white towels off the rail. 'Come on, bedtime.'

She stands up too quickly and slips, tumbling backwards.

'Molly!' I reach out my hand and catch her by the arm, heave her out of the bath. 'You have to be careful!' I wrap the towel around her – it's big enough to cover her entire body – and hold her close. Once my breath has slowed, I sit her on the loo so I can dry between her toes.

'I'm sorry, Eve. Don't be sad.'

'I'm all right, Moll.'

'You're crying again.'

'Am I?' I stand up and wipe a circle in the misty mirror. The whites of my eyes are streaked with crimson and my cheeks are puffy. The rest of the bathroom is a blur. All I can see is my blank face staring back at me – drained, sapped of life. When I blink, I half expect myself to disappear.

You're slumped against the back of the door. No, not slumped – suspended. Hanging from the hook where your towel usually lives. Grace? I reach forward – I'm on the floor, I don't know why I'm on the floor – and touch your feet, still, bare, just a few centimetres above the worn carpet. For a split second, I think you're levitating.

Your skin looks different, a purplish-grey. Slippers. You're wearing your pyjamas but not your slippers. You always wear slippers. Where are they? I look to the left. Your desk chair, on its side instead of its legs. Back to you, but not you, not yet. Toes with nails painted that poppy red. The polish looks spongy, like you've applied more than one layer so it'll last. Last for what?

Grace, can you hear me? I'm kneeling now, I think, or standing, trying to lift you. Failing.

Does someone hear me scream? Do I imagine the siren swelling? I try to cling on, but they unpeel my arms from around you, tell me to get out of the way.

By the time I get Molly into bed it's past ten. Her eyes are closing and so are mine. I wrap her up in one of two dressing gowns and slide her beneath the crisp duvet cover and sheet.

'Goodnight, sweet girl.' I tuck a loose strand of hair behind her ear and kiss her on the forehead.

The wooden floorboards. A rolling of wheels.

Two or three paramedics.

It takes two of them to lift you up and off the hook. Your neck is berry-red when they unfasten the belt.

A policeman points out two envelopes – there, on your desk, backs stuck down with spit. One addressed to your parents and a second addressed to me. Mum and Dad. Eve. He promises to return them. Keep them, I think. I can't bring myself to read it, Grace. I don't want to hear it.

The same policeman – or maybe another – asks questions. He asks if you've been acting out of character. If you'd been putting extra pressure on yourself. If there's anything I'm aware of that might have prompted you to end your life.

He sends me spiralling, drowning in liquid glass as it gurgles down the drain, shards scraping against the pipes, a thousand sharp knives. I am the liquid, I am the drain, I am the pipes. And I am to blame. You trusted me.

Back in the bathroom I peel off my own clothes, still damp from the rain. I fold them over the towel rail together with Molly's and try to rub warm my arms and legs. I leave the bathroom light on and the door ajar, a night light of sorts. I tiptoe towards the second bed and quietly let loose the tightly tucked sheet, wondering if any adults enjoy being swaddled.

'Eve?' Molly cracks open an eye like you might a window, just to check I'm still here.

'Yes?'

'Please can you snuggle me up?'

'You want me to sleep in your bed?'

She shuffles to one side. 'Yes, please.'

'OK then.'

296

She's had a lot on her mind, I say. It's been hard recently. I look down at his big feet.

Your tutor whispers in his ear.

The policeman turns to me. Was she struggling to cope after the incident?

Twenty-five

I wake up with a dead arm. When I slide it out from beneath the pillow, it feels like the bones have disintegrated and all that's left is wobbly flesh. My body's heavy, thick with exhaustion after a nearly sleepless night, hazy mind, foggy thoughts. Molly's breathing softly through her button nose, her chest gently rising and falling, eyelashes fluttering as she dreams. Happy dreams, I hope. I slip out of bed and pull on the second dressing gown, my arm tingling as it comes back to life. I give it a shake. Not dead yet.

A gap in the curtains. Yellow-pink rays of sun are beginning to break through billowy white clouds, caressing the tops of trees and buildings. Down below, people are going about their business as usual. A tatty-looking man with a beaten-up black suitcase and a bunch of orange plastic bags is feeding a flight of dirty pigeons – Dad calls them rats with wings. Passers-by shake their heads. I can almost hear them tut as the pigeons coo. Five or six of them are texting as they walk (the passers-by, that is). Which reminds me, I should check my messages.

I reach for my phone and hold down the power button, my eyes narrowing as I wait for it to wake up. To begin with, nothing. Then, as the signal kicks in, tiny white bars sprouting like weeds, dozens of voicemails. One by one, I start to play them.

Annie: 'Eve, please. Where *exactly* are you? Where's Molly? Tell me and I'll come and get you.'

Max: 'Eve, it's me—'

I press the phone hard against my ear. Max. For a moment I wish he was here so badly it hurts.

'I've told Annie you're in Oxford. We're on our way.'

The crackle in his voice has been replaced with a certain clarity, each word highly articulated. He sounds less nervous. More practical, resolute.

Annie: 'Is she OK? Look, Eve, I'm not angry. Please just call me and let me know that she's OK.'

What does she mean, is she OK? Of course she is. Annie knows me better than that. She knows I'd never let anything bad happen to Molly.

My phone vibrates against the side of my face. I close and reopen my eyes, take a breath and answer.

Annie's voice is saying, 'Eve?'

'Yes, it's me.'

'Oh, thank God. Is Molly OK? Can I talk to her? Are *you* OK, Eve?'

When I try to reply, I start to cry and I can't stop. I can't speak.

At the funeral I quickly realise it's best to remain quiet, to keep my eyes and mouth closed at all times. If I open them, the tears will spill out and nothing, no one will soak them up. Whatever you do, don't try to sing the hymns.

'Eve, it's fine. I'm not angry.' Her voice breaks. 'Please can I just have a quick word with Molly?'

She thinks Molly's in danger, that I'm not safe to be with. A mistrustful voice creeps into my head. Again, I try to speak and my own voice catches. She won't have me in her house after this. She won't let me see Molly again.

'Eve?'

'We're in Oxford. We weren't supposed to stay, but it was getting late and Molly was tired.'

'I know that, Eve. You did the right thing. Where are you exactly?'

I pick a point across the road – the blue 'Plastics Only' sign on a round recycling bin – and stare at it. Another tactic. Focus. Balance. Just like in the studio when I'm posing and I don't want to tremble or, worse, fall flat on my face. Pick a spot and stare at it, Eve.

'OK, Eve, what I want you to do is go and find a nice café, have some breakfast and text me where you are. OK? I'm with Max and we're coming to get you, both of you. Can you hear me, Eve? I know you didn't mean for this to happen.'

Someone pauses to stub a cigarette butt on the lid of the bin, obscures my view. I lose my footing. It was an accident. An unfortunate incident.

'The train, we'll get the train. I'm so sorry, Annie. I'll bring her home.'

'No, Eve—'

I end the call. I need to fix this.

I wonder if Mum ever worries about me. If her heart cracks with concern every time she sees a girl my age doing something she shouldn't, or with someone she shouldn't be dating.

I wonder if she ever talks about me. If she remembers the colour of my eyes and hair, that I have freckles. Maybe she has them too, especially on her shoulders. I'm not sure I'd be able to pick her out in a crowd – I've seen photos of her when she was younger, in her bohemian clothes, but I don't know what she looks like now, not really. We'd probably walk straight past each other, oblivious, if we crossed paths on the street.

It's also possible that she's blocked me from her memory like I did those one-night stands after university: fifteen faceless men in the first three months, each one a walking placebo. It would make sense if something bad happened, something that made her panic and feel she wasn't fit to be a mother. If she dropped me. Forgot about me for an hour, all alone, strapped into a booster seat in the back of a car. Lowered me into bathwater hot enough to make me scream. She probably thought I was better off without her. I could have been a mistake – another accident. An unwanted and unwelcome surprise. Maybe she couldn't bond with me in the beginning and, when nothing changed, decided it just wasn't right.

I glance at Molly, peaceful beneath the duvet. She's lying on her front, a little way down from the pillow now, her arms stretched above her shoulders. Eyelids closed, eyelashes flat. Mouth open. Blonde hair wavy from being in plaits. I was younger than she is when Mum left.

Trauma. Depression. Suicide. You would think there's a bigger gap between each. That you can mind that gap, stand back from it. But Grace crossed from one to the other to the next without me realising.

She didn't explain it, either, not in the letter she wrote to me. There were just a few scribbled lines telling me she loved me and that she hoped I'd be happy. Wishing me good luck in my exams. Really, Grace?

Did you know, Grace, when I told you I'd come back, that I'd find you like this?

I knew what had happened. I promised to keep it a secret. And I let her down.

I look over at the bed, my mind starting to race like it does when I'm reading a book and trying to figure out how it ends. I need to get Molly home, now.

'Moll?'

She sighs and rubs her eyes, slowly blinking them open, then quickly squeezing them shut. The overhead light's too bright.

'It's time to go home.'

She squirms into a cross-legged position and opens her eyes again, this time looking at me expectantly. 'Is there Weetabix?' She licks her lips.

No time. 'Can you wait until we're home?'

She scrunches her face. 'I'm hungry.'

'Fine, I'm sure we'll be able to find some. But we have to be quick. Come on, let's get dressed.'

She doesn't move.

'Now, Molly!'

Her eyes slowly fill with tears.

'I'm sorry, Moll,' I say, holding out my hand. 'Here, I'll help you.'

Our clothes are warm from spending the night on the towel rail, so warm that I have to shake her tights out to cool them down before she puts them on. She asks me if it matters that she's wearing the same pants two days in a row.

As she brushes her teeth with her index finger, like I taught her last night, I look again at myself in the mirror. My unwashed mousey hair is scrunched into a knot on the top of my head. Purply pink bags beneath my brown eyes, with irises so dark I can barely distinguish my pupils. Unruly eyebrows of a slightly more tawny shade. Middling height, weightless build. Nothing recognisable. Nothing distinctive. I let my forehead rest against the mirror.

'Eve?'

Grace?

'I'm ready.'

We find a table at the café downstairs and, to Molly's delight, a woven basket filled with mini packets of cereal.

She reaches for the Weetabix and then looks at me, nose and mouth crinkled as she tries not to smile. 'Am I allowed Coco Pops instead?'

'I don't see why not.' I pull a packet of Bran Flakes out of the basket for myself, then tip hers into a bowl and add some milk.

'What about yours?'

'I don't like milk.'

Her mouth gapes open. She's appalled.

'Scoot in there, Moll.'

I follow, slipping through the narrow gap between our table and that of a man and woman who must be a couple (interlaced legs) but look like brother and sister.

Molly chatters mid-chomping, her metal spoon clattering around the china cereal bowl, about Mummy, Daddy, Henry and some other names I fail to catch – presumably friends. Cradling a big mug of black coffee in both hands, I ask her when she last saw her dad and she says yesterday. So I'm not the only one in denial then.

In return, she asks if I'm going to stay the night at their house – we can sleep in her bed – and I tell her no, I don't think so, not tonight. The corners of her mouth fold down, her eyes drooped, until the waitress brings her a couple of sheets of colour-by-numbers and some crayons. A moment later, she's all giggles, chocolate milk drying around her lips. She sounds both excited and disappointed, a high and low lilt to her chirpy voice, as she continues to jabber. Like mother, like daughter. She has the on–off switch for her emotions too.

We walk to the train station hand in hand, Molly skipping to keep up as I pick up the pace. The streets are quiet, too quiet. I feel hot, feverish, even though it's cold out. I reach my hand around to touch my lower back and find it wet with sweat.

When we arrive at the station I check the board: a train to Paddington leaves in nine minutes. The barriers are open, so we show the burly man standing beside them our tickets – I nod and grimace when he says Molly can travel using a child's ticket – and walk through to the other side.

The platform is pockmarked with puddles. Molly slips her hand out of mine and starts testing those nearest to us with her toes, seeing whether she can rest the tip of her shoe on top of the muddy water. People are disembarking from a train onto the platform opposite.

I close my eyes and rub the inner corners, dislodging crusty bits of sleep. God, I'm exhausted. I wonder if there's an alternate universe where all the people who have stepped out of my life are together. Mum. Grace. Suzon. I wonder if Annie and Molly will end up there too. If everyone will get along.

'The next train will not stop here. Please stand back from the platform edge.'

In my head, I see Suzon staring back at me, wearing that same blank, bleak expression. Cheeks flushed, this time from the cold air. Head tilted to the side, eyeing something up ahead. Leaning forward, like she does in the reflection.

Go on, I dare you.

Twenty-six

Grace?

I take a step towards the tracks, eyes still closed. Clamped shut. I take a deep breath and splay my fingers, then press them together, squeezing out the pain.

It wasn't a mistake. She meant it. She was unhappy and she wanted to die. And I should have known.

I should have recognised how she was feeling and helped her get better. Been there when she needed me.

I look down at the platform. A yellow line. Beyond it, a nubby bit. Some grooves. A faded white stripe that marks the edge.

I wonder how it felt. Stepping onto the chair. Buckling the belt. Like shouting out in a hushed classroom while everyone else is quietly reading. Pulling the red passenger alarm on a tube mid-tunnel. Poking a painting, hard, just to see if the pad of your finger can pierce the canvas. Telling someone a secret that isn't yours to share. Taking something that doesn't belong to you to see if you can get away with it, to feel less alone, if only for a moment. Standing naked in front of a room full of strangers.

I open my eyes, glance to the right. Almost here. And on the platform opposite: Annie and Max. Or am I imagining it? The parked train has pulled away, the passengers have exited the station. Max is running for the stairs. But not her. There she is, her entire body visibly tense, arms glued stiffly to her side, each of her elegant fingers extended towards the pitted concrete, straight like the pencils she uses to sketch me in the studio. She raises one arm level with her shoulders, points one of those fingers towards me. Shouts, or at least opens her mouth. There's no sound, not from her. Just Molly splashing a puddle.

I close my eyes. Rock lightly back and forth on the balls of my feet.

The greeting of a whistle.

What does it feel like, Grace, when you escape the haze? When you disappear? I imagine floating away like a piece of paper, a lone feather, the seed head of a dandelion.

Take a breath.

Take a step.

I'd evaporate, or dissolve.

The rumbling of the track.

Grace, I'm so sorry.

Big hands, firm hands, locked around my arms.

A wall of air hits me, making my body shake.

'We've got you.'

After

I dunk the brush into the pot of white paint, glossy and wet, then drag it up and down the wall. Broad strokes, side by side. I'm working more slowly today, to try to make it last. This is the final room. Then we're done, the flat ready to sell.

I got the phone call about Dad a few weeks after Oxford. Liver failure. He'd been dead for two days before someone found him, slumped in his favourite armchair with a bottle of whisky tucked between his toes. The news made me retch. I felt a slow pooling of regret in my stomach, knowing there would never be a new version of us, that we'd never have a chance to make amends.

Thankfully, by then Max had already persuaded me to go back to the doctor – this time I'm actually taking the pills – and Annie had introduced me to her therapist. She's paying for it too, which after a lot of back and forth I agreed to on the condition that she lets me repay her with interest. For the first time in my life, that's something I might be able to do. Our old flat may be small and in need of a lot of love, but it's still in north London.

'I better get going,' says Max, wandering into the living room in an old hoodie and blue jeans flecked with white. 'Not sure Nina would be very impressed with my new work attire.'

'She doesn't know what she's missing,' I say, laying the paintbrush on the pot and going to kiss him goodbye.

He wraps his arms around me and I cling on tight. He whispers in my ear: 'Don't forget.'

He means therapy. 'I won't,' I say, hooking my little finger around his.

'I'll see you at home then?'

Home. After what happened with Molly, I thought he'd want me gone. I tried to ready myself for a conversation about me moving out, but I couldn't even do that. Instead, he held me close against him and told me we were going to get through it together. He must not have noticed the relief flood through me, an instant hit, because he quickly added that there was zero pressure in terms of us. He picked up the rest of my things from Karina and Bill's and bought a second chest of drawers. While I put my clothes away, he lined his shelves with my books – in alphabetical order, which made me laugh. The first time in a while.

'Eve, everything OK?'

'More than.' I give his finger a squeeze. 'See you at home.'

He made his place ours.

There's plenty of time so I decide to walk. The temperature's rising and soon I won't need my coat. Tufts of pinky-white blossom are daubed on branches and everywhere I look the grass, trees, hedges are greener. The sky is a pale blue, the gaps patched with gauze-like clouds.

I took Molly to the zoo last weekend. Max came too. I was terrified Annie wouldn't let me see her again, but she told me – holding my hands in hers – that she trusted me. Plus, she said, Molly misses you. Max suggested he join us for the time being and that seemed to make Annie happy. Molly too. After getting overexcited about the penguins shooting like bullets through the water, her limbs were suddenly sluggish. For the rest of the afternoon, Max carried her around on his shoulders. When he dawdled, she clicked her tongue and told him to walk on, horsey.

I turn onto the crescent, lined with tall terraced houses, and stop outside number seven. To the left of the front door is a bay window that looks onto a soft-hued kitchen; the back door to the garden lets in lots of natural light and there's always a vase of freshly cut flowers on the table. It's a home practice, Annie told me, which makes it less intimidating, more intimate. It's strange to think that this is where she came during the divorce when she needed to talk to someone who wasn't her lawyer. As I ring the bell, I picture her standing on the doorstep, smoothing down her shirt, coaxing her lips into a smile, which, when she's asked how she is, doesn't last long. Neither, much to my relief, did her relationship with Paul. She found out he was seeing someone else and, like me, has since stopped going to the studio.

A few seconds later, the door opens. 'Lovely to see you, Eve.'

'You too.'

'Come on in,' she says, holding the door ajar with one hand and gesturing for me to go ahead with the other.

'Thanks.' I walk past her and into the study on the right, untoggling my coat and hanging it on the armchair.

The first time I came she said I could use the hook on the back of the door. I cried. I apologised for crying. I still cry, but I no longer say I'm sorry.

'It looks like a nice day out there,' she says, closing the door behind her as I greet the inhabitants of her fish tank with a gentle tap on the glass. I'd heard of therapy dogs before but not goldfish and, really, I'm not sure how much comfort and support they provide.

'It is.'

She pulls her black mesh ergonomic chair out from behind her desk and swivels it into position opposite me. Only then does the session begin. It's the same routine every time, every week. There are two clocks, one facing her and one for me. Tissues. Water. It's always on the warm side and I often end up opening a window. I no longer bother to prepare talking points – mostly because, even if I do, as soon as I arrive they pour out like cream.

'So, how are you, Eve?'

'I'm good, thanks.'

'You sound surprised.'

'I am,' I say, running the palms of my hands up and down the armrests. 'I'd almost forgotten what it's like.'

Her lips curl up at the corners. She has an angular face and hair like a magpie, which she occasionally tucks behind her ears. There, just now. Beady eyes behind big glasses. Dainty hands and ringless fingers – not always, but today. On again, off again. 'One day I'll lose them,' she told me when I pointed it out. One hand picks up a pen and starts scribbling. I no longer strain to see the pad.

It made sense that the first thing we talked about was Grace. I explained what happened, how I found her, the vice-grip guilt that's squeezed me ever since. How I worried that forgiving myself would mean forgetting her. That our shared memories were tangled up with my regrets. But I remember all of it. I don't talk to her anymore – nor to Suzon – but I do talk about her. Instead of going to the gallery, I come here.

'Have you been painting again?' She points to the dried hunks of bright white in my hair.

'Yes, nearly done redecorating.'

'Oh well done, you. And then you're selling?'

'That's the plan.'

'What a good idea – a fresh start.'

'Something like that.'

She's still a part of me, always will be. But she takes up less space than she did. There's room now for both of us.

Acknowledgements

First, thanks to Emma Finn, for believing in this story from the start and helping me shuffle it into the shape it needed to have. Also to Rachel Neely for her enthusiasm and her edits, and to Zoe Yang and the entire team at Trapeze for taking my manuscript and turning it into a book that people might just pick up and read.

To all at C&W, and to international publishers and translators.

To the galleries and museums, and the artists whose works fill them, for endlessly inspiring me.

To my teachers and those who have studied alongside me.

Thanks to Daisy Watt, for her encouragement and guidance.

I'm grateful to everyone who read earlier drafts, especially Steph Siddall. May this book be in loving memory of our brilliant friend, Rose Acton. I wonder where Eve would have lived if we three hadn't shared our flat in Vauxhall.

To the whole extended Ashby/Cotton/Begley family, in particular my stepdad Adam, for always being my in-house editor, and my mum Anne, for, well, everything. Thank you both for reading and rereading (and rereading). To my dad

Charlie, for his generosity, and to Tristan and Fran and GJ and P for their tireless support.

And, of course, to Ollie, for making my novel an exception to his rule, and for never getting tired of me turning to him as we're walking or cooking or watching TV – doing anything, really – and asking, *What do you think of this?*

Credits

Trapeze would like to thank everyone at Orion who worked on the publication of *Wet Paint*.

Agent
Emma Finn

Editors
Rachel Neely
Zoe Yang

Copy-editor
Holly Kyte

Proofreader
Jenny Page

Audio
Paul Stark
Jake Alderson
Georgina Cutler

Editorial Management
Clarissa Sutherland
Charlie Panayiotou
Jane Hughes
Tamara Morriss
Claire Boyle

Contracts
Anne Goddard
Ellie Bowker
Humayra Ahmed

Design
Nick Shah
Joanna Ridley
Tomas Almeida
Helen Ewing
Natalie Dawkins

Finance
Nick Gibson
Jasdip Nandra
Elizabeth Beaumont
Ibukun Ademefun
Afeera Ahmed
Sue Baker
Tom Costello

Inventory
Jo Jacobs
Dan Stevens

Marketing
Helena Fouracre

Production
Claire Keep
Fiona McIntosh

Publicity
Alex Layt

Sales
Jen Wilson
Victoria Laws
Esther Waters
Frances Doyle
Ben Goddard
Jack Hallam
Anna Egelstaff

Inês Figuiera
Barbara Ronan
Andrew Hally
Dominic Smith
Deborah Deyong
Lauren Buck
Maggy Park
Linda McGregor
Sinead White
Jemimah James
Rachael Jones
Jack Dennison
Nigel Andrews
Ian Williamson
Julia Benson
Declan Kyle
Robert Mackenzie
Megan Smith
Charlotte Clay
Rebecca Cobbold

Operations
Sharon Willis

Rights
Susan Howe
Krystyna Kujawinska
Jessica Purdue
Ayesha Kinley
Louise Henderson

About the Author

Chloë Ashby is an author and arts journalist. Since graduating from the Courtauld Institute of Art, she has written for publications such as the *TLS*, *Guardian*, *FT Life & Arts*, *Spectator* and *frieze*.

Wet Paint is her debut novel.